CROWDED
HOUSE

CROWDED HOUSE

THREESOME AND
GROUP SEX EROTICA

EDITED BY
RACHEL KRAMER BUSSEL

CLEiS
PRESS

Published in the United States by Cleis Press, an imprint of Start Midnight, LLC, 221 River Street, 9th Floor, Hoboken, New Jersey 07030.

Printed in the United States.
Cover design: Jennifer Do
Cover photograph: Shutterstock
Text design: Frank Wiedemann

First Edition.
10 9 8 7 6 5 4 3 2 1

Trade paper ISBN: 978-1-62778-316-3
E-book ISBN: 978-1-62778-529-7

Contents

INTRODUCTION: THE MORE, THE MERRIER

When it comes to sex, sometimes three—or four or five or even more—is the best kind of crowd. In these erotic stories all about threesomes and group sex, you'll read about characters who can't get enough of couplings that go beyond the number two. In some cases, they're couples who want to get it on with other couples; in others, they're individuals coming together to each fulfill a sexual fantasy or simply savor each other's bodies. In all of them, the sexual tension is heightened with a sense that, moving beyond sex for two, anything can happen.

Some stories involve passionate relationships, where the participants know and care for their partners in ongoing ways, nurturing their desire with each further encounter. In others, sex with more than one other person is something new, an erotic adventure that a character has dreamt of and is finally ready to make sexual fantasy into reality.

There is no typical tale in this book, with multiple partners including mermaids and otherworldly creatures. Sometimes the action starts in a nightclub, sometimes a party, sometimes at home. You'll find everything from a very dirty sex game to a swingers retreat to sex in the woods and so much more within these pages.

Wherever these erotic encounters start or end, they're all full of the kind of passion that can't be sated by a single partner. In "PTO," Katrina Jackson puts a very sexy spin on personal time with this sensual story about a woman who visits her lovers every summer and surrenders to their commands. In "Able Bodies," Michelle Cristiani explores what happens when Kira, who is blind after a car accident, seeks to "live well" and pursue the pleasure on her terms. Relationship dynamics take an unusual turn in "Forget about Me" by Nikki Ali, in which narrator Ashlee brings her wife and ex-boyfriend together for a sensual threesome that shows her a new side of each of them.

There is a lot of sexual discovery here, as new sexual partners heighten the intimacy of longtime lovers and characters find new ways of exploring themselves—and being explored in every possible way.

I hope you enjoy these sexy stories as much as the characters in them enjoy saying yes to more pleasure, more partners, and more intimacy.

Rachel Kramer Bussel

PLAYS WELL WITH OTHERS

Angora Shade

"Hey, June."

I almost dropped the phone hearing the voice on the other end. I liked Caylen a lot—likely more than any other singles in my forty-plus playgroup. I felt a rush of heat enter my face. It was always like this when talking to, or even thinking about, this man. Suddenly I became a drooling teenager. Perhaps it was knowing what he could do to me—or make my body do—that made me respond so hard. I was an instant puddle of lust, melting into the phone, catching myself on a chair before I hit the floor.

"Caylen . . . " A lump stuck in my throat. Even with a regular lover in my bed, it hadn't been often enough to fill my endless sexual cravings. I always have, and think I always will, want more. I found myself visualizing Caylen's tall muscular form, his smooth, dark skin, and his thick, meaty cock. The heat in my face traveled downward, growing in my belly, and warmed me straight to my toes.

"I've got this naked new apartment. It's stark white and ugly. I need you to come over and help me paint."

Busy street noises filled my ear. I visualized Caylen on the city sidewalk, walking his commute, as I understood he liked to do. A car horn honked impatiently and Caylen's voice became difficult to hear. The timing was brilliantly convenient because naked was the one word imprinted in my brain.

I mentally slapped myself. "I'm sorry, what?"

"My apartment," he said. "It'll be all of us: Jayne's an artist, Sue's crazy, Justin is a goof, and you're . . . stylish and fun."

Having already been intimate with this man didn't seem to matter. I had to hold back excited giggles and try not to completely lose my head. Thoughts of Caylen's mouth working my clit, his fingers inside me, his full weight on top of me— they'd found their way into my thoughts numerous times. I couldn't forget his eyes: dark magnetic orbs, long lashes, penetrating me as strong as every thrust of his—and OMG: all of us hadn't been together in a while . . .

I licked my lips and had to clear my throat in order to speak. "You're sweet. I'd love to help." I didn't add, and get back into your pants, but it was exactly what I was thinking.

"Great. Saturday at three," he said. "Wear old clothes and bring some bath towels."

"Bath towels?"

I heard Caylen hum into the receiver. "Yeah," he said. "You're gonna want to shower after I paint your naked body and use it as a stamp. Your glorious form will be immortalized for me to see every time I look at my walls."

I almost dropped the phone again. I wasn't sure what was better: Caylen suggesting he paint me naked or admitting he thought me glorious. People just didn't say that kind of thing. At least, not out loud. But as the seconds ticked by, and thoughts of Caylen's hands smearing me with paint, and pressing me tightly against a bare wall from behind, perhaps his cock slipping between my legs, filled my mind . . .

Yeah. Sign me up for fantasy class.

"Um . . . Okay."

I heard him chuckle and visualized his face making that seductive grin like the first time we'd said hello. If only I'd been able to articulate more words then, I might not have felt so stupid, but I found it hard to form complete sentences with my vagina secretly clenching. She's a greedy, greedy girl.

"Good. I'll see you then."

I didn't manage to say goodbye. I think I sat on the chair in my kitchen for several minutes before hanging up. Excitement is sometimes paralyzing.

Paint. Naked. Caylen.

"Hey, you."

There was always a magnetic pull between us. It was like my gut was connected to a fishing rod, and every small movement of Caylen's eyes looking me up and down reeled me physically closer. His eyes never broke their hold, not even when Jayne's lithe form in her yummy yoga pants stepped up to the apartment door behind me. He greeted her with a tender kiss to the cheek, but he was absolutely focused on me. I was mesmerized, standing like a moron, unable to step inside his door. Perhaps it was the gap between our playing activities, and I was only extra nervous, but I think it more likely I was caught like the proverbial deer in headlights, except I wasn't filled with fear.

It was lust.

Caylen came to me instead, standing intimately, almost pelvis-to-pelvis, in the hallway. His tall, bulky frame seemed to look down into my soul while his hands wrapped themselves around my waist.

"You all right there, June?"

Caylen's voice had been a whisper, but his presence was loud and clear. The proximity to his smooth flesh and the scent of his fresh masculine cologne had me swooning. I liked how he allowed my fingers to trace the outline of his fit abs through his T-shirt. I liked how I felt his heat through the fabric. I liked how stable I felt in his arms. My body responded to his, sending my desire quickening in my chest and a hot tingle over every inch of my skin. But what made the sensations even more intense was knowing he wanted me too.

Caylen grinned and turned, pulling me along behind him. We stumbled into the apartment, the furniture pushed into the middle of the room and everything covered with either plastic tarps or old bed sheets. The edges had been taped down to the hardwood floors, and an old coffee can filled with brushes sat atop an upside-down box. An opened box of condoms stood next to this with a hefty bottle of lube. There was no sex without safe sex.

"I got a bucket of green off the Internet!" Sue shimmied into the living room, her breasts bouncing with her enthusiasm. "It'll be perfect with yellow and pink. And they're apparently not only wall-worthy, but actual, nontoxic, edible body paints."

"What do they taste like?" Jayne asked.

"Like blah. But anyway . . . " She smiled wide as she set a third bucket down on a tarp. "We'll mix colors to make orange and brown, and then hopefully Caylen will be able to live with it."

Live with it? I doubted I'd be able to walk past any wall where a group of sexy people threw their naked bodies against it without squirting in my panties. And there were a lot of walls. The living room was a large space with two windows and an air conditioner, and enough room to house a three-seater sofa and two cozy armchairs. An adjacent kitchen was at least twice the size of my place, and a short hallway held three more doors. "Hey look! It's June!" Justin was suddenly in front of me. He'd grown a scruffy brown goatee since I'd last seen him, and he'd styled his long hair in an almost lazy way. His look made me think dad-bod-rock-star. "I'm stoked you're here!" He hefted me into the air by my waist. I held my breath as he spun me in a circle. Grasping his arms for support, I admired the beautiful tattoos that covered his arms and neck. His mouth pressed against mine and his hand grasped my ass while he lowered my feet to the floor. I'm sure my eyes closed. The kiss lingered several moments on my lips despite being only a few seconds long. I remained in a daze, my pulse racing, as Justin pulled away.

Jayne's voice broke the spell, her tone a tease. "If you start playing without us, you'll both be due for a spanking!" She made the punishment motions with her hand in the air, her long hair swishing free against her waist.

I collected myself with a deep breath and felt my pulse return to something more normal.

Suddenly Sue was in front of me, tracing her finger down between my eyes and over my nose. "I love looking at your face," she told me, "but . . ." She dragged her arms down both of mine on either side to my wrists, skipped an inch to my waist, and tapped her fingers above the hemline of my jeans. "I like your body even more." Her smile was easy to match. Of course, just then, we were both likely remembering eating each other out like insatiable teens the last time we'd met.

One of the best things about being single and with people like these: there is no judgment. The motto is: Play well with others. We're in it for the pleasure and the company, comfortable with a lack of commitment. We're committed only to ourselves, honesty, exploration, and our physical, sexual appetites, unlimited in how, when, or with whom. Male, female, or wherever on the spectrum—my appetite is never sated.

Justin shouted, "Let's get this thing started!"

We gathered in the middle of the room, responding with electrified cheers of agreement.

"I can't wait to see what kind of pattern I can make with my tits," Sue squealed.

I almost burst into laughter, but I was cut short as Sue pulled her '80s rock band T-shirt over her head and began wiggling out of her jeans. She was a thick, short woman, who wore her back rolls with all the pep of a twenty-something supermodel. But like the rest of us, she was middle-aged, had a healthy bit of gray, and was one hundred percent proud.

"We should make a collage of everyone's magnificent tits and Justin's tasty ass," Caylen suggested.

Justin blushed and stood patiently while Sue took charge of popping his waistband.

Jayne stepped in to protest. "No-no-no, Sue. Can't have him all to yourself." She swatted Justin through his jeans with a playful gesture, and then tugged forcefully at his fly. Together with Sue, they pulled his pants to the floor, exposing Justin's happy erection that matched the ecstatic, wide-eyed look on his face.

All around me, bodies began to strip while I watched. And watching is something I love to do. Arms were lifted, shirts and pants were discarded, blinds on the windows were drawn, and someone had turned on the stereo. Techno music thrummed in my head, matching the contracting muscles of my eager pussy.

"Get over here, June."

It was easy to go after whom I wanted most just then. I chose to close the gap between our faces and push our lips together.

The hair on my neck stood on end as my body leaned into Caylen. For a moment there was no apartment, no other people, and no task ahead of us; there was only my longing to fuck— and be fucked by—this man.

Caylen's lips consumed mine, but teased me too. The moment wasn't as long as I would've liked. His lips became thinner as he smiled wide, and his hands spun me around, briskly lifted my shirt, and dragged it off from over my head before I could utter a word. Sue's lips replaced Caylen's on my mouth, while she drew a pink squiggle of paint over my collarbone with her finger. Before I knew it, the others had stepped up and stripped me as naked as the rest.

I'm no artist. I can't draw convincing, simple stick figures. And no, I had never body painted before. I needed some guidance, some direction. But once given, it by no means meant I needed someone to hold my hand.

I reached over to the bundle of paintbrushes and grabbed a long handle with a thick, round brush, slopped it into the green, and let my eyes capture the first bit of exposed flesh I saw. A limb bumped into me while my hand dotted a shoulder with thick globs, and a cool caress fell down my back that transformed into goosebumps. Spontaneous motion took over me, where my globs became zigzags and lines of both thick and thin. Others joined my paintbrush, and soon the body before me was a living work of art. I was so enamored by the flourishing of movement and naked flesh, I'd lost track of things. It was only when my brush ran out of paint on a small, pale ass cheek where I was painting a solid shape, that I realized I had been painting Jayne. Looking up, taking in her whole form, I saw palm prints of yellow, pink dots, and green swirls covered her back, while smears of a muddy mix had dribbled down over her upper calves like molten candle wax. She was a goddess of color.

I paused in my work to watch as Sue's hungry mouth found Jayne's. Her tongue slid between Jayne's lips as it sought to make contact, and she held up Jayne's hands over her head as she forced her back gently against the largest wall. Justin kissed the back of Sue's neck then, nibbling down over her spine while Sue printed Jayne's body hard against the stark white. She pressed with firm pressure over every limb, working in complete concentration, despite Justin playing with Sue's breast and Jayne's landscaped landing strip. Pleasant moans joined in harmonious song with the active techno, and I felt my body respond.

Sue and Jayne became locked in a lip war. Hands ran everywhere. Wild, untamed, chaotic, but more importantly—human. This was exploration at its most basic level. And it was hot. Although naked, my body felt flush as I watched Jayne drag her hands down Sue's ample midsection, flicking her tongue, while Justin turned away and reached for me.

Justin's hot cock bumped my sticky, paint-smeared stomach. Color covered him everywhere I could see, except perhaps the top of his head, above my eye level. He guided my hand to his green and pink cock, slathering it well, and stamped my hand upon the wall until clean.

My body was turned once again and I came face-to-face with Caylen. He painted his lips with a fine line of pink. Smiling mischievously, he bent down, cupped my small right breast, and planted his imprint slightly above my nipple. The contact against my skin almost burned despite the cool, gooey texture of the paint, encouraging my nipple to stand on end. How I wanted more of his mouth, concentrated and specifically targeting me, suckling and nibbling, but instead his face dragged downward, smearing the remainder of paint on his lips down between my cleavage in a broken line.

Hands were on me everywhere. I couldn't discern one from

another. Brushes and mouths and fingertips trailed over me, tickling my flesh and arousing me further. My flush spread evenly over me, and I felt my pussy contract. I enjoyed the shock of a brisk slap across my backside and the way the hand there kneaded paint into me, the warm breath against my neck that followed, as Sue's heavenly tits—covered in bright yellow—smeared up and down my left side. I couldn't help but close my eyes, victim to it all. Briefly, I smelled the fruity scent of feminine soap, mixed with aftershave and something lighter like a sweet white wine. Someone nibbled on my ear as I stood there, enjoying the sensations, but it ended abruptly as other hands guided me to the wall, rolled me like a spindle, and pressed me from back to front.

"We have lots of color on this wall," Caylen remarked. "Now I want my cock in a tight hole."

Hungry lips met mine. The press of Caylen's body against me was warm and intoxicating, and the slip of the paint between us made for a strange sensation as I wrapped my arms around his neck. He spun me and pressed me to the wall again, chest first, exploring the curves of my body. The room disappeared as it had earlier. My eyes closed as his hands trailed down my flanks and spread my thighs. His firm fingers pushed eagerly into the depths of my swelling arousal.

I was going to have him again, feel him everywhere again. His fingers pushed and stretched my pussy wide. I couldn't help but moan as I felt a tightening in my abdomen. I knew an orgasm wouldn't be long with attention like this. I was already so aroused, and he was just too good of a lover—perhaps even the best I'd ever had.

"My cock needs a tight hole too," Justin remarked.

Justin stood behind Caylen, kissing and caressing. All the time I could hear Sue and Jayne, who'd slid to the floor, their bodies bunching up against an old sheet. Sue was between Jayne's legs, Jayne's legs wrapped around Sue's head, while Sue simultaneously plunged her fingers into Jayne's cunt and lapped at her clit. Their verbal melody matched the rhythm of the techno, cutting the air like a lightning storm.

"Grab the condoms, buddy," Caylen instructed. Then he turned back to me, whispering in my ear as I patiently waited, "I want to fuck you against the wall, while Justin's fucking me."

My head swam. This was better than the fantasy I'd had when he'd called with my invite.

"You cool with that?"

I turned around to face him and nodded to show my consent. I had total trust with these people. I knew I only had to say the word and our play would stop or change to accommodate. Reaching for Caylen's cock, I gave him a hardy squeeze as Justin handed me a condom. I ripped the packet impatiently and kissed him like a feral creature, rolling the shield over his thick girth. I couldn't wait to feel him inside me, knowing he'd pump me harder and faster than the way I could pump him with my hand.

Justin interrupted, joining our kiss in a strange, multi-lip assembly. Kisses like these are sloppy in nature, but wonderful in arousing the sensitive skin of one's mouth. A tongue tracing here, a nibble there—the wonderful smacking of contact and retreat. Lovely.

Jayne was verbalizing her loud release when Caylen had me pressed against the wall. He lifted my right leg onto a paint can while he played with my right breast, and then between my legs. It was hard to say what was my arousal and what was paint, but I didn't care. He probed me with his cock at my ass, and sucked the skin on the side of my neck into his mouth. I closed my eyes, hearing Jayne continue to sing-shout her pleasure. There was a splurt of lube shooting from a tube nearby, and I tasted the tacky, neutral flavor of the paint as I licked my own lips.

The techno boomed when Caylen entered me with a hard upward thrust that took the breath out of me. I gasped at the feel of his wonderful cock stretching my pussy wide. He placed one hand against the wall to brace himself, sandwiching me tight between. His other hand massaged my bottom, then wiggled in front of me to reach my clit. Each hard thrust of his hips and brush of his forefinger on my sensitive bud was bliss.

Or I thought so, until I felt the extra push of Justin thrusting into Caylen.

Caylen grunted. I couldn't see their position, but every exhale in my ear was heavy, every grip on my body, intense. With my head to the left, I saw Caylen's fingernails dig into the wall, dragging marks through wet paint. Justin placed his hand on top of Caylen's and held fast. In almost unison, the men pulled in and out: Justin-pumping-Caylen-pumping-me. Every motion hit harder and deeper than the roughest sex I've ever had, reaching parts of me I hadn't know were still virgin. I was hot, almost overheating, but not uncomfortable. I just didn't know what to do with myself. Pinned and taking it all in total submission was something I hadn't explored before.

I loved every moment.

Just when you thought you'd lived and done all the wild stuff, you discover something new and memorable. Another exploration to daydream over later. Another appetite demanding satisfaction again on another day.

Sue and Jayne had changed places, Sue well on her way to her happy place, sitting on Jayne's face, arms on the floor, squeaking a crescendo of satisfied noises. But I couldn't focus for long. Caylen's long moans and Justin's grunts triggered something primal. I bucked my hips backward into Caylen as he thrust into me. Moving in trio, my core ignited and my pussy pulsed around Caylen's cock. I was gasping at the buildup inside, like a shaken champagne bottle. The sensation was claustrophobic. I was under pressure inside and out. It was almost too much, and I teetered for balance with my foot on the paint can. He kept fucking me, as Justin whispered inaudible things behind him, communicating something only between them. A moment later both were vocalizing, and still fucking me. My pussy suddenly spiraled into orgasm as the condom filled with the physical evidence of Caylen's pleasure.

We were not really standing then. We were a heap of limbs held upright only by one another. I felt that even the wall was no help. I was flying in some other plane of existence only reachable by the mystical Fuck Supreme: all limbs, slow rocking, labored breaths. My pussy continued to pulsate with Caylen still inside me, my whole body quaking under his.

There was only the techno music playing for long moments until Caylen's voice broke the spell. "You alright there, June? You crushed?"

I wasn't sure my mouth had worked—"So long you fuck me like this till I die . . ."—but apparently it did, because the whole room laughed. The air smelled heavily of sex and exertion. Tasted of sexual freedom. What an amazing group of people I had in my life. How lucky I was to be a part of them.

But then again, I play well with others.

HOW TO SEDUCE A MERMAID

C.C. Bridges

Shea crawled out of the ocean before she tried to stand. She'd done this before: drag herself onto land before sunning herself on the rocks, or—even better—wait in the shadows to watch the humans frolic on the beach.

Now things were different. She had two extra appendages—legs, they called them legs. But they hadn't come with instructions, so it took a moment for her to figure out how they folded and which way they couldn't go—ow, not side to side at the . . . knee?

"You'll learn quickly," the sea witch had told her. "It's part of the spell."

There was nothing for it then but to rock up onto her knees, and then to stand. She gasped at the sensations on the bottoms of her feet. She'd felt sand before, but now it seemed like every grain cut into her skin. Dare she try to take a step?

It took longer than she expected. Shea swayed and fought for balance. How did this work? When she swam the ocean depths she didn't think about the way her tail needed to move. She narrowed her eyes and concentrated.

There, one foot up in the air, oh, she needed to put it down before she lifted the next. Shea felt heavy, her body thick and slow as she took her first step, then another. It almost wasn't worth it fighting against the sand as she made her way up the empty beach, lit only by the half-moon in the black sky. But she was walking. The thrill of doing what no mermaid had done in centuries made a little giggle burst out of her mouth.

She gave into the laughter as she started to speed up, until she broke out into a run, the sand flying behind her feet. Oh, now this was fun.

As she came to the entrance to the boardwalk she slowed down. Humans didn't typically walk around without clothes, so she'd come ashore on this end, where there were mostly houses. To the left she could see the bright lights of the amusements— the rides and arcades, the bars and restaurants. Here few people walked in small groups, but if she waited, crouching down by the entrance, she could dart out without anyone seeing her.

The house directly across from her had a little deck, and across that deck someone had strung a rope, with clothes swinging from it.

Shea held her breath and stepped onto the boardwalk. The wood didn't feel nearly as nice as the sand, and caused her to limp. The house had a painted fence protecting it from the boardwalk, with its deck and tiny yard like the houses all down this stretch. She'd figured out walking, but now she had to try climbing. Shea could use her arms, and she had to trust her legs would follow.

The sea witch had been right. The more she used them, the more comfortable Shea grew with her new appendages. With a grunt, she made it over the fence. Before she could reach for the clothes, she caught sight of her reflection in the tall glass doors that led inside. There was her familiar face, the seaweed-green locks of her hair trailing down to cover her breasts, but below that, in between the V of her legs was that shadow, the place where she now had hair instead of scales. One hand crept forward, almost of its own accord, to stroke the sensitive skin.

This had been the point, after all, the whole reason she'd gone looking for the sea witch.

She'd spied the couple from the rocks at dusk. They had found the area of the cove where you couldn't be spotted from the boardwalk, and where humans seldom walked when the sun went down. Too dangerous near the sharp stone jetting off into the sea. Shea had watched the male strip his mate, his hands stroking in a slow caress, along her pink nipples, to that shadow between her legs. The female had thrown her head back and gasped, a slight sound that somehow seemed to carry across the beach.

And oh how Shea had wanted. She didn't understand desire, not like this. But how she wanted to.

The couple had come again, the next night, laying out a blanket on the sand before stripping down. This time the male spread her legs wide, and her feet clutched his hips as he mounted her. What did that feel like? To be penetrated in that way? Shea may have gotten too close, too enraptured by the high-pitched sounds coming from the woman's mouth. They were cries of pleasure, but what kind of pleasure?

That's when the woman had turned her head and looked right at Shea, floating in the water a few feet away. She'd smiled and winked, with one hand held out toward the sea. It startled Shea, who dived beneath the waters to hide.

Shea had watched humanity for decades, and had indeed seen this kind of thing before. But something inside her had changed.

It had to have something to do with this couple. They ensor-celled her in some way. She hadn't been able to stop thinking about them, about what would have happened if she'd swam up to them and taken that offered hand. But Shea didn't have the right parts to participate, so she'd gone to the sea witch.

Now, she snatched her fingers away from her body, to clutch the shell tied around her neck with a piece of twine. That shell kept her human, but only for a few days. Shea didn't have time to waste.

She pulled a pink bikini top from the clothesline and put it on, following with a long black wrap skirt. Next she needed shoes of some sort, because she hadn't liked how that wooden boardwalk felt beneath her feet. That must be why humans put such things on. There was a selection of sandals propped up against the side of the deck, and after a moment, she tucked her feet into black slides that were just a tiny bit too big.

She's overheard the couple talking the night before, as they lay together. The male had mentioned his plans for tonight, Shea remembered, and if she hurried, she'd find him at the bar called Martin's with some friends he hadn't seen in a while. As she strode down the length of the boardwalk, the lights got brighter, and the narrow homes were replaced with the arcades, food stands, and rides that dotted this half of the town. She rarely got close enough to this section to see all of this—too risky. But what she did see wasn't that impressive. There were too many people pressed together, and it took her a moment to figure out the currents of movement.

Much of this was senseless noise—bells going off, people screaming, the whine of the rides as the cars whooshed past on the rollercoaster. It was a relief when she saw the word "Martin's" in blazing gold letters, letters she'd learned after years of reading what the humans had left behind on the beach.

Inside, they kept the place dark, and the glass doors blocked off much of the noise of outside. Soft music played, and the hum of conversation flowed like the ocean waves. She walked past the tables, staring at each young man with sandy hair.

Past the long wooden bar in the center of the room, the walls dropped away, open to the beach with an area sectioned off with lines of rope. Nobody was sitting at the wooden tables and chairs back here. A crowd had gathered to watch the ocean, loud here in this little alcove. Shea crept closer, because she recognized the back of a head, those golden curls, the curve of his neck and shoulders. The tight tan pants he wore couldn't conceal the recognizable shape of his ass.

She walked over, ignoring all of the other humans as she pushed into place next to him. "Buy me a drink?" she said. She knew that was a thing, that human women asked that of their conquests all the time.

He turned to face her, and the confused look on his face changed. His eyes widened, and somehow, he knew her. But he didn't say anything other than, "All right. What would you like?"

She didn't know how to respond. "Surprise me?"

He smiled and left her side. Should she follow? Shea stared at the sea and tugged at the shell on her neck. She didn't have much time. Shea had to make the most of every second, and now she was conscious of each of those seconds dripping away, like grains of sand.

"Here." He had come out of nowhere, holding a clear glass with bubbling liquid and a straw. Two bright red cherries floated on top.

Shea took it and regarded it carefully. "What is it?"

"It's just water with a sprinkle of fruit juice. Sparkling water," he clarified when she looked at him like he was mad.

She took a sip, and nearly spit it out. The bubbles burst over her tongue, making her entire mouth feel all tingly. This tasted nothing like water should. However, it was a little sweet, and she liked the way it felt going down her throat. Shea nodded. "This is acceptable."

He smiled, and what a smile! It lit up his entire face, somehow brightening those pale blue eyes. Shea took a moment to appreciate his face, the careful cut of his jaw, sprinkled with golden stubble a shade lighter than his hair, and the slight bump in his nose. When his cheeks grew pink beneath his tan, she realized she might be staring a bit too intensely. Humans could be bashful.

"She was right. I don't believe it." He shook his head.

"Who?"

"My girlfriend Julia. She said you'd come. I honestly wasn't sure what I even saw at the rocks, but . . ."

She grabbed his arm. They had noticed her at the rocks. Shea hadn't imagined any of it. "Julia. Where is she?"

"Back at the rental." He looked down where she still held onto his bare skin. "My name is Eric by the way."

"Shea," she said. "Now can we go to Julia?"

Something changed in his eyes. They tightened at the corners, but she didn't understand humans enough to even guess what that was about. "All right. Come on."

He led her back out to the boardwalk—after leaving her empty glass on the bar. She waved goodbye to the man behind it who stared at her before scooping it up. "Do I not look human enough?" She glanced down at her legs, kicking up the edges of the black skirt she'd borrowed.

Eric laughed. "Your legs are fine. Gorgeous, actually. Most people don't have dark green hair naturally, and the way you look at people, well, it's kinda intense."

How strange.

* * *

The "rental" that Eric referred to was a house tucked away from the beach. Close enough to hear the waves, but far enough away from the boardwalk chaos. Shea could still see the lights, but the streets were quieter, and nobody saw him open the door and gesture her inside.

"Julia?" he called. "We have a guest."

"I told you so."

Shea turned at the sound of that voice; it was deeper than she had expected, a sultry rasping tone. It made her shiver, although Shea didn't quite understand why. Julia appeared in the doorway of another room, wearing a blue robe cinched tight around her waist. The fabric looked so soft that Shea wanted to catch her fingers up in it to see how it felt. It looked so different from the fabric humans wore near the sea. The robe gaped at her chest, baring a bit of curved breast, making Shea's fingers twitch for another reason.

She stalked across the room, having eyes only for Julia, who smiled that familiar crooked grin and narrowed her dark eyes. But Julia didn't move when Shea seized the belt of her robe and fumbled with it. "Easy, sweetheart, we have all night for that." She took Shea's wrists in her hands and held them still. "That is what you're here for, isn't it?"

"It was an invitation, wasn't it?" Shea asked, suddenly unsure. "When you reached out to me on the beach."

Eric came over and put his arm around her waist. "Of course it was. But we didn't realize what you were until you splashed away."

"You thought I was human."

"To be fair, I've never met a mermaid before." Julia let go of Shea's wrists and slid her hands up to her shoulders, which she massaged in slow soothing motions.

"I couldn't join you. I didn't have . . . that . . ." She pointed to the area beneath Julia's robe and inexplicably, her cheeks heated.

Julia stepped away, and the loss of her warmth almost hurt. But she made up for it when she untied the knot on her belt. "There are so many more words better suited to it than . . . that." She laughed as she bared herself, revealing a thatch of dark curls between her legs. "Vagina. Pussy. Cunt."

"Folds of pleasure," Eric said.

"Eric's the romantic. Trust him to come up with the purple prose." Julia rolled her eyes. "You want to see how it works?"

Shea swallowed as she soaked in the sight of Julia's nude body. She'd seen it all before on the beach, of course, but now, here in the intimacy of their home, it felt different. Her fingers twitched again, eager to touch, but where? The soft curve of her breast? The tip of her nipple? Or did she dare slide down into the shadows, to see what that place felt like? She wanted, desperate for something she didn't know how to ask for.

"Please," she whispered.

"Easy," Eric said in her ear. "And I need to check—do you want me to be a part of this too? I'm okay either way." When he pressed a kiss beneath her ear, warmth coiled in her belly.

"Both. Both of you. Like on the beach."

"Well, it won't quite be like on the beach. No sand in naughty places for one." Julia stepped backward. "Shall we take this to the bedroom?"

So odd that humans slept on that flat slab in the center of the room. Shea guessed it would be harder to string up a hammock between walls, but the sacks she slept in were hardly conducive to what they were about to do. Maybe that was the purpose of the . . . what did they call them? Beds.

"Where did you get the clothes?" Eric asked, closing the door behind him.

Shea shrugged. "Stole them off the back of a deck."

Julia laughed. "Good thing. If you'd come down the board-walk naked, you'd have been arrested. But there's no need for them here. May I?"

Shea nodded, suddenly mute as Julia undid the back of the bikini top and bared her breasts. Julia lifted one, her thumb encircling Shea's dark green nipple. The touch made Shea gasp, and even more terrifying, it made her feel something there, in the shadows between her legs. "Oh."

Eric came up behind her and caressed the spare breast, a gentle smile on his face. "Lovely," he told her, before bending down to taste.

Shea didn't know that was a possibility. She didn't expect it, had no frame of reference to prepare her for the way it made her feel, for the wetness that filled her. Her eyes fell closed as she leaned into the touch, startling as she felt hands at her waist, undoing the wrap skirt.

"Oh, nothing beneath." Julia sounded slightly out of breath.

Shea opened her eyes and wondered if she were being rude. "Should I?" She made a cupping gesture with one hand.

Julia smiled. "If you like."

She darted forward, Eric's hands falling away, and cupped both of Julia's breasts. They were slightly larger than her own, with dusky pink nipples. Shea tried pinching one, delighted by Julia's gasp in response. Her skin was soft, so soft, not the tough skin of a mermaid who swam the ocean depths. But even that had changed, with the sea witch's spell.

Eric returned behind her, his hands on her bare hips, his mouth on her neck. "Squeeze them," he told her. "Julia likes that."

Shea found herself smiling as she obeyed. She loved the way Julia's eyes closed in response. There, that was it, the desire she'd seen on the beach, what Shea had so desperately wanted. "I want . . ." She sputtered, unable to put it into words.

"We know, sweetheart." Julia took one of Shea's hands and guided it between her legs. "Feel how wet I am? We want that for you, too."

The folds of her skin were warm and slick. It felt delightful to touch and explore, especially when Julia gasped and threw back her head. Shea memorized the angles of her throat, how she swallowed as Shea continued to stroke her. "Yes," she said. "I want that too."

"Lay down on the bed." Eric's words were nothing more than puffs of breath against her skin.

Shea didn't want to stop touching Julia, but if she didn't, they couldn't move on to more. It took her a moment to figure out how exactly to climb onto the bed. She threw one leg up, like the fence she'd climbed earlier, and then dragged herself on. The bed bounced a bit as she made her way to its center.

"Okay, next time we'll show you how to use a bed." Julia let out a laugh as she climbed on, her own movements much smoother than Shea's had been. She knelt at the edge of the bed, and took Shea's legs between her hands and spread them wide.

"Oh." She'd figured out walking, but having her legs spread like this? Shea had never experienced anything like it. Her tail couldn't be split in such a way. She was conscious of that place between her legs, no longer hidden in shadows, but out in the open, bared for both Julia and Eric. That wetness, the same she'd felt between Julia's legs, dampened her, dripping down her thighs.

The bed dipped as Eric sat beside her, cupping her breasts again. He watched her face as he thumbed her nipples. Shea nodded, trying to tell him that she liked it, to not stop, to never stop, when Julia started to stroke her hands up Shea's thighs. She gasped at the feeling of breath on her center.

"And this, love, is called the clitoris. Remember that." Julia winked at her, and then her lips closed around the place she'd indicated, her fingers sliding up and inside Shea.

Shea howled.

Such pleasure should be forbidden. Her hips bucked up, but Julia pressed them down. She lifted her head to say "stay" before diving in again. Her lips skimmed the edges of Shea's folds, slight mouthing motions that were nowhere near Shea needed them to be.

"Please," she begged.

"Please what?" Eric bent and took one nipple in his mouth; now she could hardly bear it. That want, that desire, coiled up inside her and needed an outlet. Now.

"What you did before. My. My clitoris. Again. Please."

Julia looked up and licked her lips. Her eyes were bright. "My pleasure."

Oh no, it was certainly Shea's pleasure. She thought she'd prepared herself for the sensation to come. But something about this time was different. Julia had a purpose and it appeared that purpose was undoing Shea utterly. She sucked hard, while her fingers kept busy, penetrating Shea and adding to the intensity. As if that weren't enough, Eric kept up his assault on her nipples, one he lapped with his tongue, and the other twisted in his fingers.

She tried to move, but Shea couldn't; every motion put her within reach of either Eric or Julia. Julia sucked hard, and pressed in deeper, impossibly deeper, until Shea couldn't take it anymore.

"Let go." Eric looked up, his blue eyes wild like the sea.

With those words she came apart. Pleasure flooded her, waves upon waves between her legs, pulses of joy that overshadowed everything. Her vision went dark, and Shea could do nothing but feel and gasp and throw her head back onto the bed.

"Easy, easy." Eric stroked her hair, while Julia sat up and massaged her thighs. "You were so good, so good."

Shea blinked. The room felt too bright. "It's a wonder humans aren't doing that all the time."

Julia chuckled. "You'd be surprised." She crawled up until she was on the other side of Shea, propping her head up on her arm. "Do you think you're up for more?"

The remnants of pleasure still throbbed between her legs, and Shea couldn't help but want more. "Yes."

Julia looked over at Eric and pursed her lips—lips that were slick and suddenly Shea wanted a taste. She leaned over and kissed Julia. It was a terrible kiss, their lips mashed together. But Julia smiled and caressed Shea's face. "Like this." She pressed her lips between Shea's, opening them up. She tasted salty and sweet, reminding Shea of home.

"What we did on the beach," Julia pulled away. "When I rode Eric. Would you like to try?"

"You don't have to." Eric kissed up her shoulder, his hair tickling her chin.

Something inside her pulsed. She felt open and aching. "Please."

"All right. We'll just have to do a bit of rearranging. Switch places with him, sweetheart."

Eric took the center of the bed now, and for the first time Shea got to closely examine a human male. He had hard edges where Julia had soft curves, and between his legs beneath blond curls was his . . . she fought for the word, she knew she'd heard it before . . . *cock*. She reached out to touch and he stiffened, as if surprised she could be so forward. It felt warm and hard in her hand, with a bit of fluid at the tip. She lapped at it, wondering if he would taste different. Yes, definitely different, but how she couldn't say.

Eric swallowed. "If you keep that up this will be over far too soon."

"Oh."

"Here." Julia pulled something out of the table next to the bed and handed it to Eric, who slid the item over his beautiful cock. "We don't want to risk getting a mermaid pregnant."

Julia got behind her. "Straddle him like this. I'll guide him."

It shouldn't have felt like a puzzle, to maneuver herself into the proper position, her legs stretched and spread, straddling his waist. Julia's fingers were between her legs, and Eric's hand on his cock, and then, there he was, pressing against her opening.

"Slide down onto him, just like that."

This slow penetration had her gasping. He felt too much, at first, but she was already so slick that she opened readily for him. "Roll your hips." Julia's hands moved on Shea's body to guide her. It took a moment, but like learning to walk, she figured it out. The desire coiled inside her again, this time rising slow and languid, unlike the frantic pace with Julia earlier.

Julia took advantage of the position and moved her hands to Shea's breasts, teasing her nipples into peaks. Shea shuddered and felt caught between the two of them, pushing down onto Eric, and then back up into Julia's capable hands. She could barely stand it. When she thought she couldn't take any more, Julia slipped a hand between her legs, stroking her clitoris.

The pleasure of that, along with the sensation of being filled, was just too much. She felt it again, that rising swirl of pleasure, that built and built until finally it erupted in pulsing waves, made all the more powerful as she gripped Eric's cock. He growled, and grasped her hips, arching up into her. Julia never stopped stroking, leaving Shea shuddering and gasping until Eric choked out a cry of his own and pressed hard against her.

"Easy, love, you did so good." Julia pulled Shea's hair out of the way as she kissed down her neck.

Shea felt so tired, as if she'd swam to the ocean's depths, with all the pressure of the sea pressing down above her. Her muscles didn't want to move, which was okay, because Julia and Eric seemed content to take care of her, wiping her down and tucking her under the covers. Perhaps she could get used to this sleeping in a bed thing after all. It felt so soft and it smelled of what they'd done. She wanted to do it again. Maybe once she'd had some sleep . . .

When the warmth of sunlight woke her, Shea realized she'd slept the whole night through. She sat up with a grin, pushing her hair out of her eyes. It must look like a sea urchin, and she lacked her shell combs to sort it out. She started to braid what she could reach. The door opened to reveal Julia, once again dressed in that delicious-looking robe that seemed only moments from falling off her shoulder. "Breakfast is ready, if you're up for it. There are some extra clothes in the closet." She gestured to another door, one Shea hadn't noticed last night.

To be fair, she'd had other things on her mind. She got to her feet and walked to the closet, throwing it open to reveal a very large assortment of clothing. Nothing looked as comfortable as Julia's robe, however. She pulled a pale gray zip-up hoodie from a hanger and slid into it. It hung on her frame; it must belong to Eric. She looked down at the large selection of shoes and wondered how many variations humans could come up with for something that covered their feet.

"You know." Julia had come up behind Shea so quickly Shea

hadn't noticed, and took hold of the shell around Shea's neck. "I can make the spell permanent if you want."

Shea opened her mouth in shock. How did she know about the spell? "What?"

Julia chuckled. She dropped the charm and stepped back. "I'm a witch. Why else do you think I was so unsurprised to see you here?"

"You're a land witch?" Shea repeated. It made sense. If there were sea witches, then there should be a counterpart up here. But Shea should have known. Julia and Eric had accepted her so completely.

"I guess." Julia laughed. "The offer stands."

Shea cupped the shell in her hand. This wasn't an offer she'd expected. She'd loved everything they'd done last night and her body still craved more, but . . . "I'd miss my home."

"We come back here every summer." Eric had appeared in the doorway. "We rent this house for two weeks in August. If you go back, then we can see you next year?"

She smiled. "Like the whales that return home during the right season."

"Exactly like the whales," Eric agreed.

"You don't have to go home right now, do you?" Julia narrowed her eyes. "It looks like you have a few days left on that spell."

"Three days." Because magic happened in threes and sevens.

"Then we have three more days together," Eric said.

"And then next summer." Now that Shea had this, she wasn't about to give it up.

Julia embraced her on one side, Eric on the other, leaving Shea feeling enveloped and adored. Yes, she'd definitely be coming back next summer. No doubt about it.

THE POSSIBILITIES OF PARADISE

Anuja Varghese
and C.E. McLean

From the moment the plane touched down, Kamalina could feel something electric in the air. Maybe it was the tropical heat, or the smell of the sea, or the way Simon looked at her when she strolled out of the island airport in her strappy sundress and floppy hat, all soft, brown skin, pink straw, and yellow silk. Maybe it was all of those things together and something else too—anticipation.

They said little in the car on the way to the resort. Kamalina reached across the cool leather seats and linked her fingers with Simon's, and in response, he touched his lips to the back of her hand. The car circled a high stucco wall and drove through gates that opened into a long, palm tree–lined road. At the resort's main entrance, they were greeted with fruity drinks and their luggage was whisked away while they wandered into the airy atrium to enjoy a stunning view of turquoise water lapping at white sand.

Kamalina glanced sideways at Simon. His face was serious, his green-gray eyes contemplative behind his glasses. She shifted closer to him and nudged him lightly with her hip. "You ready for this?" she asked. She had intended the question to be playful, but when he looked down at her, his gaze lingering on her lips, there was an intensity to his expression that took the tease right out of her.

"Are you?" Simon asked in reply.

Before she could answer, boisterous laughter across the atrium caught Kamalina's attention and over Simon's shoulder, she saw a familiar face. "They're here," she said. "Should we go say hello?"

Simon took her empty glass. "You go ahead," he told her. "I'll refill our drinks and catch up."

They parted ways and Simon found himself sitting alone at the atrium bar. They had talked about this, planned this, but now that they were here—now that they were *all* here—it all seemed too real, too fast. A hand on his shoulder made him turn and he was met with a Hawaiian shirt and a wide grin. Simon cleared his throat. "Hey, Mike," he said.

"Simon!" The older man leaned in for a half hug, then spread his tanned arms wide. "Welcome to paradise."

It is paradise, Simon thought, already fighting the feelings just seeing Mike again sparked low in his belly. *And you're the forbidden fruit.*

Mike leaned on the bar next to him, so that they were both looking out across the open space of the atrium where they could see their wives chatting amicably in wicker chairs drawn close together. Simon watched their heads come together, watched Kamalina's legs cross and uncross as she shook her head, laughing. He watched her hand rest easily on the other woman's thigh. He might have been imagining it, but he was almost sure he could see the outline of her dark nipples pressed hard to the silk of her dress.

"I see Kam's making herself at home," Mike said. "She and Maggie have been looking forward to this for a long time." Simon wasn't sure what to say. Mike and Maggie had been their neighbors on a quiet side street in Toronto's east end for nearly five years, but it had only been in recent months, over the course of many Sunday brunches, late night dinners, and bottles of wine, that they had gone from being acquaintances to friends. And now, maybe, to something more. After a moment's silence, Mike asked him, "What about you, Simon? Been looking forward to this too?"

Simon had no idea how a question could sound so innocent and so indecent at the same time. A memory came back to him of a late summer evening, nursing beers on Mike's back porch. With Kamalina at work and Maggie upstairs, it was one of the few times he and Mike had been alone.

"I really should be going," Simon had said, feeling buzzed and off balance, and as Mike caught his eye and held it, a little too close to doing something he might later regret.

"Or stay," Mike had countered. "Stay and spend the night with us." The suggestion had been relaxed but the space between them charged with unnamed desire.

There had been a half-second where Simon had almost said yes, had very nearly turned his head into the kiss he knew would be waiting on Mike's lips. But he had stopped, his father's voice in his head. *It's a sin, Simon.* So, he had stammered his excuses and stumbled home, not yet ready to admit his attraction to another man—a man twenty years his senior—was real. When he told Kamalina about the encounter, she had been less shocked than curious, and eventually, had confessed secret desires of her own—desires she believed Mike and Maggie could fulfill. They knew their neighbors spent winters down south, and when Maggie extended the invitation for Simon and Kamalina to join them for a week of fun in the sun, Kamalina had accepted on the spot.

It's so easy for her, Simon thought, watching Kamalina toss her hair over a shoulder. She was naturally beautiful, sensual, playful, at ease in almost any situation. She had been honest with him the first time she had gone to bed with Maggie and Mike and honest as well about wanting Simon to join them. It was Simon who was having trouble being honest with himself.

A hand closing softly on the back of his neck startled Simon out of his wandering thoughts. "Hey, you know this is a no pressure situation, right?" Mike said to him. "Whatever you and Kamalina want to do or don't want to do is completely fine. There are plenty of possibilities here."

Simon laughed shortly. "Do they all result in banishment from paradise?"

Mike's fingers splayed out between Simon's shoulder blades, massaging into the muscle there. He shook his head. "No, Simon," he said. "In our paradise, everyone gets what they want and gets to stay. There are no punishments for choosing pleasure here." His voice went low when he added, "Unless being punished turns you on. Because if that's the case, it can be arranged. That's a possibility too." From across the atrium, Maggie beckoned them over and Mike pushed off the bar. With a backward glance at Simon, he said, "Think about it," and sauntered away.

Simon had to remind himself to breathe. It wasn't the first time he had wanted someone so badly it hurt, but it was the first time he was free to take what he wanted. All the possibilities of paradise were right there in front of him; all he had to do was say yes. "Wait," he called.

Mike turned and Simon closed the space between them. His mouth found Mike's the way a moth finds a flame—on instinct.

He didn't have Kamalina's way with words, but the kiss told Mike all he needed to know. He put an arm around Simon and together, they joined their wives at the table, undercurrents of heat simmering just beneath their casual conversation, all of them waiting to see who would make a move first.

It was Kamalina who finally said, "Mike and Maggie have a cabana suite. They're reserved for long-term guests at the resort. Maggie's promised me a tour of their digs. What do you think, Simon? Shall we go take a look?"

Simon thought about their neighbors. They were an undeniably attractive pair, he lean and tan with salt-and-pepper hair and a close-cropped goatee defining an angular jaw and shapely mouth; she petite and curvaceous with wild silver-copper curls that fell into sky-blue eyes and across full, freckled cheeks. They were comfortable in their bodies and moved with a confidence that made them all the more magnetic. He wanted them. He wanted them both and his wife and all the possibilities this week might have in store. But the sweat trickling down his back reminded him he wasn't ready yet.

"I'm not exactly dressed for the weather," Simon said, gesturing at the jeans and pullover sweater he was still wearing. "I'll get changed and meet you there?"

"Cabana eight," Maggie told him, linking her arm with Kamalina's, as they stood together and headed for the doors. "Ask for Javier at the surf shop if you get lost. He'll help you out."

"Don't take too long," Mike added. His tone was light, but the words sent a surge through Simon's body, straight to his cock. "I hate to be kept waiting."

"Yes, sir," Simon quipped, but as soon as he said it, something shifted between them. In that moment, they both knew that Mike could have issued any command, asked for anything he wanted from Simon, anything at all, and Simon would absolutely have obeyed.

Alone in the air-conditioned hotel room, Simon stripped off his heavy clothes and stared at his reflection in the mirror. His cock was still half-hard, his heart still racing. He turned on the shower and stood under the spray until the water ran cold. *Cabana eight.* He wasn't sure what possibilities awaited him there, but everything in his body said the time had come to leave his fears and his father's voice behind, and finally find out.

Outside the atrium, Maggie, Mike, and Kamalina hopped on a golf cart and headed into the maze of the resort. Kamalina frowned in confusion as they zipped past the main buildings, down what appeared to be a service road. With the resort disappearing behind them, Kamalina questioned, "I thought you said the cabana suites were poolside?"

"They are," Maggie replied.

"But . . ." *The pools are back there,* Kamalina was going to say, but the words died on her lips as they turned a corner and the road opened into a lush spread of palm trees surrounding an oval pool with a bar at one end and a hot tub at the other. Twelve cabanas, each canopied and separated from the one next to it by white curtains, ran along the pool's sides. Behind each cabana stood a small villa, nestled between the swaying trees. Kamalina gasped as Mike parked the golf cart and she got a clear view of the cabanas around the pool. In the one nearest to them, a man was sprawled naked on a bed, reading a book. In the cabana next to him, a couple was making love. A woman in the cabana across from the couple watched them from her own bed, while fucking herself slowly with a large dildo. There was a handful of people in the pool, a couple kissing in the hot tub, and a small group drinking and dancing on the deck of one of the villas. "This is where you live?" Kamalina squeaked as Maggie led her to cabana eight.

Maggie was already shedding her clothes when she replied, "It's a very . . . friendly community." She laughed at the expression on Kamalina's face. "I told you it would be a fun week!"

A man emerged from the villa next door, wearing a Speedo and sunglasses, and set to grilling seafood skewers on the barbecue. He raised a hand in greeting, black skin gleaming in the sun, intricate tattoos spanning his chest and the length of his sculpted arms. Kamalina tried not to stare but found she couldn't look away.

Maggie followed Kamalina's gaze and chuckled. "That's Kwami," she said, waving back. "He's a doll. And let me tell you, I don't consider myself submissive by any stretch of the imagination, but my word, that boy knows how to wield a paddle!" On her knees behind Kamalina on the cabana's big bed, Maggie added, "But maybe you'd like to find that out for yourself." Kamalina turned to look at her neighbor and Maggie took the opportunity to seize the younger woman's mouth in a long kiss. "Don't you worry, darlin'," Maggie said, her voice turning husky as she slipped the sundress straps from Kamalina's shoulders. "Knowing Kwami, he'll be by soon enough. But in the meantime, Mike and I have been dying to have you to ourselves."

Kamalina let herself be undressed, let Maggie pull her back so that she was pillowed against heavy breasts, so her head could be tilted up, her mouth plundered by Maggie's searching tongue. She had all but forgotten Mike was there, until she felt him gently pushing her legs apart.

"If anything doesn't feel right, if you want to go faster or slower, or want more or less—you just say the word," Mike said, before lowering his head to make a sweep of Kamalina's cunt with warm lips. She moaned into Maggie's mouth as waves of pleasure washed over her. It all felt so deliriously good. She could feel her orgasm building, getting closer, closer still, almost there—

"I hope I'm not interrupting. I brought shrimp!" Kamalina's eyes flew open and all three of them turned to look at Kwami, naked as the day he was born and holding a tray of skewers in one hand and a pitcher of sangria in the other. "You can tell me to bugger off," he said with a good-natured grin, a British accent clipping his words. "I won't be offended if this is a party for three."

Maggie looked at Mike and then back at Kwami. "You know you're always welcome to join me and Mike, hon," Maggie said. "But Kamalina here is our guest, so it's really up to her." As she spoke, Maggie reached around Kamalina with both hands and cupped her breasts, a gesture that was both inviting and protective at once.

Maggie's touch reminded Kamalina that she had been on the brink of orgasm and how much she still wanted to come. She licked her lips. "Hi, Kwami," she said.

Kwami's mouth curved into a seductive smile. "Hi, Kamalina," he replied, "it's a pleasure to meet you," as if it were the most normal thing in the world to exchange pleasantries in the middle of a threesome.

"My husband should be joining us soon," Kamalina said. "Maybe we should wait for him before . . ." Kamalina trailed off, but the hungry way she was devouring Kwami's cock with her eyes left no doubt what she had in mind.

"Why don't you go sit next to Maggie," Mike suggested, "and let me get back to work." He turned his attention to Kamalina's still slick pussy and dove back in. He wasn't teasing her this time, but holding her folds wide open and flicking his tongue rapidly across her clit.

Kwami lay back on the bed, turning his head to give Maggie a kiss. "Hello, beautiful," he murmured.

"Hey, hon," she replied. With one hand still fondling Kamalina's breast, she reached the other around Kwami's neck and pulled him in closer. He was happy to oblige, deepening the kiss, while sliding the heel of his palm down his shaft, wrapping his fingers around the head and squeezing gently, then reversing the process. He raised his fingers to his lips to taste the drops of precome there, then brought his mouth back together with Maggie's, so that she could taste his arousal too.

Kamalina was writhing between Maggie's legs as increasingly high-pitched whimpers escaped her lips. "That's it, darlin'," Maggie said. "Come for us, Kam." And Kamalina did come, arching her back with a sharp cry, and coating Mike's goatee in wetness. He took her hand and helped her to her feet, pouring them each a glass of sangria from Kwami's pitcher.

On the bed, Kwami had repositioned himself and was reaching out for Maggie. "Come 'ere," he told her, the sureness of his hands on her body telling of many years of poolside trysts. With a knee on either side of Kwami's head, Maggie carefully lowered herself onto his face. "Play with those perfect tits for me, love," he instructed, and she began pinching and rolling her nipples, pulling them up to lift the weight of her full breasts. Kwami's tongue lapped at her clit as he slipped two thick fingers into her wet pussy.

"Get in there, Mike," Kamalina said, giving him a little push toward the bed. He didn't need to be told twice. He planted his feet astride Kwami's shoulders and gathered his wife's curls in one hand, pulling them back from her face. Maggie parted her lips and took his entire cock into her mouth, and then deeper still, all the way into her throat. The three of them fell into an easy rhythm, each familiar with the other's pleasure, each unhurried in drawing it out.

Kamalina watched as Kwami made Maggie come, his face buried in her juicy cunt; watched as Maggie expertly sucked her husband off, swallowing every last drop that he spurted into her mouth. They came apart as easily as they had come together, Kwami diving into the pool like a sleek fish, Mike doing crosswords in the sun, and Maggie leading Kamalina into their villa. "I really did mean to give you a tour," she said. "Guess we got a little sidetracked!"

Kamalina laughed. "I thought that *was* the tour," she joked. "You're telling me there's more to see?"

"Trust me, darlin'," Maggie said. Her cheeks were pink, a fine sheen of sweat giving her generous curves a dewy glow. "We're just getting started." Maggie toured Kamalina through the understated elegance of the sun-drenched villa, stopping in the arched doorway of the master bedroom. "It's an older suite, but we like it. We have a lot of great memories here."

"It's perfect," Kamalina said. She took Maggie's hands in hers. "Thank you for inviting us—not just here, to this place, but into your lives. I think you know how much we've wanted this. How much I've wanted this."

A smile crept across Maggie's face as she kicked the bedroom door shut, an expression that was half mischief and half indulgence. Without letting go of Kamalina's hands, she backed up toward the bed and said, "Is that so? Care to tell me more about how much you've wanted this?"

Kamalina was on top of her in a matter of seconds, black hair cascading across dark pink nipples that hardened instantly at Kamalina's touch. "I can do better than tell you," Kamalina whispered. Pinning Maggie's body to the sheets with a roving mouth, Kamalina was quick to prove exactly how descriptive she could be.

* * *

It was some time later when Kamalina and Maggie emerged from the bedroom and headed back toward the cabana. The curtains were drawn and when Kamalina poked her head between them, she was not altogether surprised to find Simon stretched out on the bed, Mike laying next to him, running his fingers through her husband's sandy hair.

"Hey," Kamalina called softly. "You found us."

Simon turned at her voice and smiled. He had set his glasses aside, and wearing only his swim trunks he looked more relaxed than she had seen him in weeks. "I got a bit lost," he admitted, "but Javier gave me a ride."

"Who's Javier?" Kamalina asked.

Mike stood up, pulling Simon with him. "Time for some proper introductions," he said. He led them both out to the pool where Maggie and Kwami were dangling their legs in the water and chatting with a bronze-skinned man, soft spoken and smaller in stature than Kwami, with black hair he wore tied back in a bun and intelligent eyes framed by long lashes. "Javier and Kwami, let me officially introduce you to Simon and Kamalina, our neighbors from Toronto," Mike said. "Simon and Kamalina, meet Javier and Kwami, our friends from London."

Hellos and handshakes were exchanged, and the three couples passed the afternoon languidly together, swimming, snacking on seafood skewers, and getting to know one another better. By the time the first streaks of sunset began to paint the sky, Kamalina and Simon felt at ease with Kwami and Javier, as if they had known them for years, rather than hours.

As dusk set in and the lights surrounding the pool flickered to life, Kamalina found herself alone in the hot tub with Javier. Their conversation flowed easily from the friendly to the more intimate and it wasn't long before Kamalina was confessing what she and Simon had wanted from this trip—and from Maggie and Mike.

Javier listened to her intently, then gently lifted the hair from her shoulder and rested his hand on her warm skin. "It is not our intention to intrude on your plans, Kamalina," Javier said, "but Kwami and I want you to know, we like you both—you and Simon—very much."

Kamalina glanced toward the cabana where Mike and Maggie and Simon and Kwami had disappeared behind the white curtains a while ago. "We like you both too," she replied.

Javier kissed her then with a relaxed sensuality that made Kamalina feel as if she was melting into his mouth. It was Kamalina who pushed for more, reaching for Javier's cock under the swirling water. He nuzzled against her neck and murmured, "Should we join the others?"

Kamalina nodded, feeling breathless and hot all over. As they made their way back to the cabana, she could only hope that Simon was as ready as she was for the fantasy they had talked about for so long to finally come true.

By the time Kamalina lay down next to him, naked and dripping, Simon was desperate to be fucked. Mike had been the first to bring it up, earlier in the day, when Simon had arrived with Javier and found his wife otherwise occupied. He had felt the older man's eyes on him all afternoon, had gone with him into the villa to pick from a multicolored array of plugs, finding himself sandwiched between Kwami and Mike, his tongue tracing the lines of Kwami's tattoos while Mike worked the steel plug Simon had chosen slowly into his ass. And now they were here, his wife next to him at last, old friends and new friends all around. The air was fragrant and humid, the way tropical nights can be, and Simon felt the lingering nervousness about what lay ahead slipping away as Kamalina found his mouth with hers. Her lips felt swollen, her pussy wet and wanting when he touched her there.

"Are we doing this?" she whispered.

As if on cue, Maggie re-appeared with a bottle of lube in one hand and a few condoms in the other. She tossed the items on the bed, then lifted Simon's legs and pushed them back, until Simon was grasping the backs of his knees, giving Mike easy access to his ass. Mike twisted the plug, working it in and out, stretching Simon's tight asshole around the hot steel. Maggie positioned herself just above Simon's head, where she could lean forward to play with his nipples, while offering him an open cunt to eat at the same time. He took a tentative taste and found her musky and sweet, her soft moan of pleasure making his cock swell. Out of the corner of his eye, he saw Kwami slipping on a condom, his eyes locked with Kamalina's. Kwami's gaze shifted to meet Simon's and he raised an eyebrow, the question clear but unspoken.

Simon didn't hesitate. "We're doing this," he said, a quiet confirmation that was answer to Kamalina and Kwami both.

Kwami stretched out on top of Kamalina, careful not to crush her under his weight. He pressed the head of his cock to her cunt, teasing her with it, sliding it along the wet slit, until she cried out in frustration. "Please . . ." she begged, thrusting her hips up toward him. "Please, please fuck me."

Kwami entered her slowly and Kamalina gasped at the size, the fullness. "Feels good, no?" Javier said, settling in next to Maggie above Kamalina's head and stroking his cock until it was hard. He guided the tip to Kamalina's lips and when she opened her mouth to moan helplessly as Kwami fucked her, he slid his length inside, murmuring with pleasure as she began to suck.

Beside them, Mike was circling Simon's asshole with his tongue and Simon was groaning into Maggie's pussy. The plug lay discarded on the floor, as Mike rolled on a condom and coated his cock with lube. He let more lube drip liberally into Simon's ass before bringing Simon's legs up to rest on his shoulders. He brushed Simon's hair from his damp forehead and looked straight into his eyes. "Are you ready, Simon?" he asked.

Simon paused. "I probably should have mentioned this earlier," he said, "but I've never actually done this before. Just . . . go easy on me, okay?" He looked from Mike to Maggie and back again, but found no judgment in their expressions, only warmth and desire. Mike lowered his head to capture Simon's mouth in a kiss, and at the same time, began to fill up his ass with his rock-hard cock. "Oh, fuck. Oh, fuck. Oh, fuck," Simon was repeating the words over and over again, barely aware he was speaking at all.

"Simon, look at me," Mike said. "Breathe. Relax."

A soft hand on his cheek made Simon turn and the caramel of Kamalina's eyes drew him in. She alternated between kissing his mouth and sucking Javier's cock, while above them, Javier pumped four fingers in and out of Maggie's cunt.

"Beautiful Kamalina," Javier said, looking down at her. "You're going to make me come."

"Yes, do it, come on my tits," Kamalina answered, and with a short cry, Javier spilled in thick, white streaks all over Kamalina's chest.

Soon after, Javier's hand between Maggie's legs brought her to climax as well and they shared a deep kiss before Maggie moved around the bed to take Simon's half-hard cock in hand. "You know, we've wanted you like this for a long time, Simon," she said, jerking his cock in time with her husband's deep thrusts into his ass.

Simon reached out to squeeze one of Maggie's swaying breasts. His ass felt stretched and a little sore, but Mike was hitting a spot inside him that sent jolts of electric pleasure coursing through his body. Combined with Maggie's sure hand working his cock and Kamalina screaming as she came beside him, it was a sensory overload that Simon had never felt before. He came in Maggie's hand, and as she licked her fingers clean, Mike erupted in Simon's ass. Kwami pulled out of Kamalina and tore the condom off, taking only a few quick strokes to add his load to Kamalina's glistening, come-covered breasts.

The cabana was quiet as they all basked in a satisfied glow. Music wafted in faintly from another villa, mingling with crickets chirping and the smell of a bonfire somewhere nearby. Eventually, they stirred, moving to clean up and get dressed. Javier offered a golf cart to get Simon and Kamalina back to their room in the resort, which seemed a world away from the hidden corner of the cabana suites where anything was possible. Mike and Maggie walked them to the row of carts, arms slung affectionately around each other.

"Good start to the week?" Mike asked.

"Better than we could have imagined," Simon replied.

"You know, we have lots of other friends here who you might like to meet," Maggie said. "There are parties almost every night. Oh, and a club in town—" She paused, catching herself. "Let's just say there's more to the resort than meets the eye," she said. She gave Kamalina's hand a squeeze and said something close to her ear, as the golf cart rumbled to life.

With the sea behind them and the resort stretching out ahead, Simon asked Kamalina, "What did Maggie say to you?"

Kamalina watched the palm trees glowing in the moonlight and leaned into the warmth of Simon's body next to hers. She could still feel Kwami moving inside her, taste Javier's kiss, conjure Mike's mouth between her legs, and hear Maggie's voice in her head. She smiled, soaking it all in. "She said in this paradise, the possibilities are endless."

PTO

Katrina Jackson

I don't need to be told to take my paid leave. Some people I work with have to get that email from Human Resources with the vague threat to take their time before they lose it. Others only learn when they get the notification that they've lost the year's leave with a weak reminder not to let it happen again. And then there are the people who never take it. Maybe they plan to take a little time off, just a week or two, or a long weekend staycation when things quiet down, nothing major, but then something comes up—something *always* comes up.

But so many people I know never plan to take any time away from work. They don't admit it outright, but I've seen the patterns. The people who never take anything more than a few sick days here and there. The ones who never really feel like they can rest because they're scared to leave the rat race long enough to recharge, and there's always so much work to do. And before anyone knows what's happened, it's been nearly a decade, and they haven't had more than a three-day holiday weekend away from work, they're burnt out, hate their job, and don't know what to do.

Not to sound smug, but I refuse to live that way.

I work my butt off for forty-six weeks out of the year, but I never let myself forget that those six weeks of paid time off are coming. I hoard those days like a dragon, refusing to let any unexpected thing nibble away at what's mine. I don't take self-care days. If I catch a cold, I work a full day from home, surrounded by tea and tissues and nondrowsy cough medicine. I have no problem working on weekends and through holidays, and I've had all the passive-aggressive fights with my mother to prove it.

But I don't work this hard because I don't have a life and reject the idea of having work-life balance. I work this way to make sure that when June rolls around, I can disappear. Every summer, I go full radio silence at my job, with my friends, and even my family. My PTO is my time, and I refuse to let anyone infringe on my rest and relaxation. Besides, no one ever taught me how to stop work from bleeding into every other part of my life, so I had to figure it out on my own.

And here's what I do.

At the top of every summer, I hop on a plane from New Mexico to California. I tell everyone at work that I'm going home to visit my family. I tell my family that I'm going on a work retreat. It's no one's business what I do with my time off, but I figure the easiest way to keep people out of my private life is to make them think that it's boring—that I'm boring. Besides, I do get home each summer . . . eventually. But before I stop by my parents' house for a drive-by family reunion, I take a not-so-quick five-week detour to Mountain Vista, California.

Mountain Vista is a small suburb of Berkeley—my hometown. It's just through the Caldecott Tunnel, where there's nothing but small towns connected by winding two-lane roads set inside deep forests. It's like the Twilight Zone—a cute, new-money kind of place, the kind that spells *towne* with that pretentiously superfluous *e* just to be annoying. The architectural firm that planned the layout had taken the California Spanish revival style to the max, practically recreating an old Spanish mission to appeal to the young families looking to live their 1950s nuclear family fantasies in the mountains.

If I were the planning sort, living in Mountain Vista for three years after college wouldn't have been on the list of possibilities. Why would I wish that depth of boredom on myself? But Saint Benedict College had the second-best business school in the region and the only combined MBA and MFA program. They also gave me a full ride for three years of graduate school, and I couldn't say no.

I only wanted to rent a small studio near enough to campus that I wouldn't put too many miles on my old car but far enough away that I didn't have to worry about drunken undergrads throwing a rave next door and puking on my doorstep. When I moved into the apartment over Angela and Kim's garage, I thought I would stay there for a year before I got fed up living in the suburbs. I was wrong. And now, inconceivably, every year, I spend five weeks of my PTO in Mountain Vista because nothing—not even pretentious new-money suburbs and middle-class lesbians with the perfect life—is ever quite what it seems.

There are butterflies throwing a rave in my stomach when I finally turn off El Segundo Circle and onto Sierra Avenue. There's a two-story ranch-style house at the end of the street that looks like every other house in the neighborhood; terracotta roof, warm neutral-colored stucco, low-maintenance, eco-friendly landscaping. But I know the house at the end of this street like the back of my hand—even better than the townhome I own in Santa Fe. I know the way this house smells in the middle of summer when the kids are out of school—a mixture of chlorine and sugar—and in the middle of winter—Christmas tree-scented candles and nutmeg. I know how many steps it takes to get from the front door of the garage apartment that I used to rent to the back door that leads into the kitchen and how to navigate that pathway in the dead of night. I know how many people can fit in the backyard for a quinceañera on a budget. I know how many sweet potato pies can fit in the oven at a time and how many Kim can make before she runs out of counter space.

I also know how loud I can scream before anyone is worried that the neighbors might hear. I know how the carpet feels on my knees and how long before it hurts. How long it takes to crawl up the stairs to the master bedroom without rushing and getting rug burn. But I also know how it feels to have a tongue smoothing over my pussy in languid strokes, taking away the sting of that irritation, at least for a little while. I discovered that the pain was worth it in that house and that I could withstand a surprising amount of it. In the three years I spent renting a garage studio from Angela and Kim Baker-Moreno, I learned that certain kinds of pain are a necessary part of pleasure for me.

And them.

I pull into the driveway, shut off my car, and sigh in relief. All the months of work and stress and too little sleep have been worth it now that I'm here.

The front door and car door open at the same time. Kim hurries down the paved stone path toward me with a smile on her face. "Do you need help?" she calls.

"No, I've got it," I tell her, standing and stretching my arms to the sky.

She ignores me, as usual.

"Are you sure?" Angela calls as if she's going to listen to me. She won't. She's already rushing behind her wife.

I reach into the car to pop the trunk and roll my eyes as they scramble to lift my suitcases out. Without me. I've tried to help in previous years and been rebuffed. It's just easier to let them take care of me since, technically, that's why I'm here anyway.

That thought makes me shiver.

"Come, come," Kim says, carrying one of my suitcases in one hand, too excited to even extend the handle and roll it inside.

Angela smiles at me and winks, silently cocking her head.

I turn and follow them up the stone path to their front door because I want to, but also because ever since the day we met in this very driveway, being with them settles me. Their presence gives me a kind of calm that seeps into my pores, diffuses into my blood, travels through my veins, and goes straight to the pleasure centers in my brain.

And my pussy.

Stepping inside Angela and Kim's house is like hurtling back in time. It still smells the same to me—like cinnamon and kitchen lemon. It sounds the same as well—as if the house is unnaturally and uncharacteristically quiet, like the kids have just rushed out of the door, because they so often have. In fact, just this morning, they headed to summer camp and they'll be gone for the duration of my stay.

My eyes scan the living room to my left while Angela and Kim stash my suitcases along the wall just under the stairs. The sound of their comfortable bickering is white noise as I soak in my surroundings. Sometime in the next month or so, I'll wander around the house and discover all that's changed since I was last here—new art on the wall, new dining room floors, or something. I don't really care about their design choices, but I like to have as full a picture of their home as possible. I want to remember the exact way the light hits their new oatmeal-colored carpet at midday and the feel of it on my knees as I drool around the gag in my mouth onto my breasts and wait and wait and wait for Angela to give me permission to sit on Kim's face. I need to know these things so when I'm alone in Santa Fe, I can crawl into the bathtub with my favorite waterproof vibrator, set a scene in my mind, and fuck myself until the water goes cold.

The devil's in the details. Angela taught me that.

"Do you need some water? Are you hungry? Would you like to rest for a bit?" Kim asks in the softest voice. Her Southern California Valley vocal fry somehow sounds less obnoxious than it should, but that could just be my affection for the way that voice sounds while commanding me to take her strap.

I swallow and shake my head.

Kim's hazel eyes are bright and shining and caring, and her hands are clutched to her chest. She's the perfect hostess. "Are you sure?" she asks again.

Meanwhile, Angela is standing behind her wife like a sentry. Her expression is almost disinterested, and her hands are shoved casually in the pockets of her linen pants as she leans against the wall. I've always loved their contrast, the way they complement one another effortlessly, Kim's effusive charm, and Angela's silent stoicism. The way Kim pets, cuddles, and spanks me while Angela watches, directs, and commands. Kim's mouth. Angela's fingers. It took me a number of disastrous and short-lived relationships before I realized that I needed both. Maybe I can be satisfied with a singular person but that hasn't happened yet.

I shake my head at Kim and Angela takes over.

"Then get on your knees." Her voice is smooth, friendly, casual even, but it's a command, nonetheless. My pussy clenches nothing but air as I comply. Kim helps me to my knees out of a desire to feel me—to confirm that I'm really here. Her left hand brushes my jaw, my breasts, and my stomach. Her smile widens when I shudder against her touch.

Angela clears her throat, calling our attention back to her. She still looks relaxed, but her face is the exact opposite of disinterested. I can feel her gaze on me, and I suck in a sharp breath.

I met Angela first. I'd been corresponding with Kim to set up the apartment viewing, but on the day in question, Angela had rushed home from work to show me the unit when her wife had gotten stuck in traffic. She was precise, and handsome, and intimidating. Her dark eyes had followed me to the four corners of the small studio. She answered my questions in a deep voice that was somehow totally professional but also filthy. Her beautiful accent peeking out when she pronounced the Spanish street names correctly felt like seduction. Or maybe I'd just been horny. I'd felt her silently undressing me with her mind, and I knew it was wrong, but I also wanted it.

The rational part of my brain screamed that I could not take that apartment, even though I didn't have any other options. I couldn't rent an apartment from a married woman who made me wet without even touching me.

I'd been preparing to tell Angela that I wasn't interested as we walked down the stairs toward the driveway, but then Kim arrived. She'd rushed out of the car with a bright smile on her face. She was lovely and incredibly friendly—the complete opposite of her wife, I'd thought at first. But then I felt her gaze on me, undressing me just as her wife had. She talked to me about traffic and the closest grocery stores, nothing special, but the look in her eyes was practically pornographic, and I loved it.

Kim had asked Angela if she'd shown me the laundry room in the garage. When Angela replied that she had, her voice had been closer than I'd expected. And Kim was still holding onto my hand with both of hers. And suddenly, I realized that my nipples were so hard they ached, and I was almost uncomfortably wet, my panties sticking to my drenched folds, my thighs damp and sticky.

Needless to say, they offered me the apartment that night, and I accepted immediately.

I'd barely been in the studio for a month before the kids had a back-to-school sleepover. I don't even remember why I went to the main house that night. All I know is that before I could blink, I was sprawled across their reclaimed dining room table, soft rope sashes from nearby curtains binding my ankles to the table legs, Angela's whole hand inside me to the wrist, and Kim's tongue muffling my cries.

That night changed me. That night is why I'm shaking like a leaf in their quiet foyer on my knees, waiting for whatever comes next.

"You can close your eyes if you need to," Angela whispers.

I exhale and do as she says. "Thank you." I prefer it this way, especially in the beginning. I like to focus on the sounds— my own increasingly ragged breaths, Kim's soft sighs, Angela's slow, calculated steps, their central air kicking on—to ground me in the moment and heighten the experience.

"Have you missed us?" Kim asks. Her voice is close, as if she's kneeled down next to me. Her hand brushes across my left cheek in a soft but possessive touch.

I almost speak. My lips open, and she sucks in a breath, an unintended warning that gives me pause. I press my lips shut. Her hand moves down my neck to caress each of my breasts.

"You can answer." Angela laughs sweetly. Her voice seems

closer as well, but higher. I moan, imagining her standing over me.

I lick my lips, and Kim's finger circles one of my nipples. "Yes," I breathe.

Kim grabs and twists my right nipple hard enough for me to feel it through the layers of my clothing, ripping a cry from my throat.

"Yes, what?" Kim asks. Her voice is always sweeter in moments like this.

"Yes, mistress."

Kim nuzzles into my neck, licking at my skin hungrily. "Good girl," she moans.

I groan at her tickling breath.

Kim's mouth moves back down my neck, her teeth following the wet swipe of her tongue.

I'm shaking and desperate already, and I imagine that Kim can taste that on me—or she will soon enough.

"Come," Angela says abruptly.

I open my eyes and mouth in shock, already fixing my tongue to beg her for just a few seconds or minutes more, but she's already turned toward the living room, expecting Kim and I to follow, because of course we will. We do.

Kim's mouth and hands leave me. She prances after her wife and turns to smile over her shoulder, lifting up her sundress in a teasing peek of her bare light brown ass. No underwear, not even a string between her cheeks.

My mouth is watering as I bend forward and begin to crawl into the living room behind them.

I know from previous years that it'll take a few days for my body and mind to settle into this experience. It'll take a while for me to remember how to move my arms and legs so that I can crawl smoothly, for me to relearn how to settle my weight on the palms of my hands instead of the heels, for me to get comfortable with the heavy swing of my breasts as I move naked in this position around the carpeted areas of this house. It always feels uncomfortable at first, physically and mentally, a little bit degrading, even though I wanted this. Even though just a week ago, I was fingering myself in my sleep, dreaming about Kim leading me across this living room on a leash until I was kneeling between Angela's legs.

But the adjustment is part of the experience. In a few days, I'll probably wake up in Angela and Kim's bed, my body one big dull ache of reverberating pleasure, and smile at how rested I feel—I always do—but knowing that doesn't speed up the process. I need to sink slowly into giving myself to Angela and Kim in this way, so different from all my other relationships. Well, maybe not slowly, I think, as Angela indicates for me to kneel in the middle of the room and silently gives Kim permission to strip me naked. It'll take a few days before that second of hesitation when Angela gives me a command to disappear, before I'm fully submissive mentally, but my body is ready now. In the meantime, I know Kim and Angela will be patient with me. They'll move at a pace that feels good—physically and emotionally—and listen to me and my body. They'll give me what I need because that's what they want.

Because dominating me has been the stuff of their fantasies for the past year.

"We've missed you," Angela says, echoing my thoughts. She's standing in front of me, watching me as she begins to unbutton her short-sleeved linen shirt. My hands are on my thighs, but I want to touch her, and she knows it—that's why she loosens each button carefully. Angela prefers teasing torture. She methodically strips and then neatly folds each article of clothing before placing them on the floor next to her feet. When she's naked, she kindly stands still, letting me drink her in; her small-handful breasts, the geometric tattoo across her hip, the patch of brown, curly hair over her mound.

"Isn't she beautiful?" Kim asks breathily.

I nod eagerly, as much in answer to her question as a silent plea for her to keep touching me. Her hands glide over my shoulders and down to the hem of my T-shirt. I can feel the giddy excitement radiating off her as she diligently undresses me, desperately caressing each new patch of naked skin she uncovers. When I'm naked, Kim hugs me from behind, caressing my breasts before pinching my nipples between her fingers.

I scream.

A small smile graces Angela's lips.

Kim begins to roll my nipples with fluctuating pressure until I'm gasping. "We have five weeks together," she says in a soft, relieved sigh. "We can start off slow if you like. I can let you eat my wife out while I taste you. I know how much you love to come on my face." She moves a hand down my stomach and pushes it between my legs, sliding over my wet lips. No pressure, just an exploratory, teasing touch.

I'm panting, desperate, so fucking wet. I need more.

Kim's soft chuckle makes me shiver.

Angela watches us as she fondles her own breasts. I can feel her eyes burning into me. I beg her silently, and she smiles. "Is there something you want to say?" she asks playfully.

I nod and then groan when Kim sucks my left earlobe into her mouth.

"Is there another option, mistress?"

"God, we've missed you," Angela moans, pinching her nipples roughly.

Kim sweeps my twists behind my shoulder and smooths the back of her hand across my overheated back. "There's nothing but options, honey. An entire year of fantasies we've had about you." Her mouth brushes my cheek, and I watch as Angela moves a hand down her stomach to her own pussy.

Kim begins to lightly circle my clit with two fingers, and I moan loudly.

"We spent our wedding anniversary last month making a list," Kim says, kissing along my jaw. "All the ways we want to tie you up and fuck you and deny you and tease you. All the places we plan to make you come this summer." Kim's other hand is traveling down my back, over my ass, and between my legs.

I can't stop moaning now. My hips jerk forward, trying to get just a little more pressure on my clit. "Oh, fuck," I murmur without thinking.

Kim tsks and swats my clit with her fingers.

The orgasm tears through me in an instant. The sharp sting of that slap as Kim's fingers push into my cunt, her mouth on me, and Angela's hands gliding over her naked body. It all comes together perfectly after months of anticipation in the kind of release I'm going to feel for hours after. I begin to shake violently in Kim's arms and leak all over her fingers.

I worked forty-six weeks for this.

The quiet living room fills with Kim's bright, happy laughter and the sound of her fingers sawing slowly into my drenched pussy. She slaps my clit again and again, enjoying the way my body seizes and my pussy tightens around her digits each time in one long release.

"Give her a break," Angela finally says.

Kim pouts against my cheek.

Her fingers leave my pussy. I sigh, and Kim takes advantage of my parted lips to shove her wet fingers into my mouth.

I groan, tasting myself, licking and sucking my orgasm from her skin, gagging slightly.

Angela watches us for a few seconds before she interrupts. "I said enough."

I shift my gaze from Angela's body to lock eyes with Kim.

Predictably, she greets me with the sweetest smile. I love the way her eyes light up when she dominates me roughly. The excitement she gets from pushing Angela's limits, making her exert control over the two of us at once. The insatiable hunger she takes out on my body, wearing me out physically before fussing over my aftercare with the same focus. I love her. I love them.

Kim stands, and I deflate without her arms holding me up. I feel like I've run a few miles, and we've barely begun.

"Do you need a break?" Angela asks.

I shake my head quickly. "I want to know my other options, please, mistresses."

Kim bends to swipe her tongue over one of Angela's nipples, smiling at me as she does. "She's greedy this year," she says, Angela's nipple between her lips.

"Yes, mistress, I am."

Kim straightens and pulls her dress off in a single smooth motion. Of course, she's completely naked underneath. "We can get our strap-ons," she says, excitedly bouncing on the balls of her feet.

"Both of you?" I ask in a hoarse voice. I press my knees together, trying to get a little more pressure against my aching clit, but I'm too wet, and it frustrates me. Angela enjoys that.

Kim leans into Angela's side, plucking at her nipple. Angela wraps an arm around Kim's waist, and her fingers glisten in the light streaming in from the patio doors. I will absolutely fantasize about this in a few months.

"Both of us," Angela says evenly, hiding the depths of excitement that her fingers have betrayed. "How does that sound?"

I'm so horny I could scream. "Yes. God. Please," I beg breathlessly.

"Told you she'd be excited," Kim whispers.

A soft ripple of arousal pulses from my core through the rest of my body, part lust, part relief.

I shiver as I sink down onto Angela's dildo. It's just a little thicker than the one I use at home, but the girth is the perfect stretch to remind me that I'm not at home. I'm not alone, stretching my legs open and working my abs so I can fuck myself just right after a long day at the gallery. No, this is different. Angela's dick hits me at angles I can't recreate by myself, and I shudder as the tip glides along my G-spot. It's so good I close my eyes and just feel.

Angela is having none of that. "Open your eyes. I want you to look at me while we fuck you." Her voice hits new spots as well.

I open my eyes and twist my hips on top of her, shuddering through a mini-orgasm that takes my breath away.

Angela's fingers dig into my hips. "Come here."

I lean forward, crushing our breasts together before my mouth covers hers. I kiss her deeply and fuck myself up and down on her dick in slow grinds.

And then I feel Kim's hands on my back, pressing me firmly on top of her wife.

Angela smiles against my mouth and pushes her hips up from the bed.

I hear the cap on the bottle of lube open.

Angela's hands smooth across my butt, caressing my skin and pulling my ass cheeks apart.

Kim's slick fingers rub slow circles over the rosebud of my ass.

I moan into Angela's mouth. She kisses me deeper, wrapping her arms around my waist and holding me still while she fucks up into me. Holding me in place for her wife. We both know what's coming, and I can't be sure which one of us is more excited.

It's neither of us, by the way. No one is ever more excited when Kim slips the slightly thinner dildo slowly and carefully into my ass than Kim herself.

Angela stills her hips to let her wife inside of me.

"Fuck, wait," I groan at the intrusion.

They both stop.

I'm full. I'm so fucking full of them that I scream and shudder violently between them.

Angela plants delicate kisses all over my face, murmuring sweet nothings to me in Spanish before dipping her head to lick my throat obscenely.

Kim's fingers replace Angela's at my waist, digging into my hips before smoothing up my damp back. Her hands are shaking with excitement. "It's okay, honey. We've got you," Kim says quietly. She leans forward and places a single kiss reverently on my right shoulder.

I'm so wet now that I can sink just a bit farther down Angela's dick. "Fuck," I groan aloud.

"Are you ready?" Kim asks, her voice full of horny glee.

"Yes," I plead.

They begin to fuck me in careful strokes, establishing a rhythm based primarily on how loud I scream and how hard I'm coming. Sometimes they enter me at the same time, sometimes one pushes in as the other retreats, sometimes one holds in place so I can feel one ribbed dildo rubbing against the other through my thin barrier.

They're practiced in this—practiced in fucking me until I'm a sweaty, screaming, hoarse mess, leaking all over Angela's thighs. And unlike a yoga retreat or beach vacation, I can trust

Angela and Kim to give me what I need, to fuck me until we're all worn out. I can trust Angela and Kim to remind me about the pleasures of letting go.

Soon enough, Kim will carefully gather my long twists around one fist so she can ride me hard. But if she doesn't think to do it herself, I'll beg her. I know Angela will slap my ass until her palm is as hot and sore as I am. I'll probably fall asleep and wake up to their hands and mouths on me. They'll wash me and feed me, and tomorrow, they'll pull out the rope.

I'll spend the next five weeks of my vacation being punished and fucked and loved by Angela and Kim in a way that I've desperately missed. I won't think about work or Santa Fe, but if I do? If I start to fret about all the projects waiting for me back home, I trust Angela to tell me to get on my knees and crawl to her. I trust Kim to whisper the sweetest fucking things into my ear while she slips another dildo into my pussy and fucks away all that stress and worry that I came here to escape.

Maybe one day, in a few years, when their kids are old enough to leave the nest, things might change. Maybe I'll decide that five weeks a year isn't enough. Maybe Kim and Angela will visit me in Santa Fe. But those are considerations for later—much later—and Angela and Kim will fuck away those thoughts as well.

My PTO isn't for everyone, but it works for me. Angela and Kim remind me that I'm not just a cog in a machine. I'm a person with needs and desires that deserve to be met.

CALL ACROSS THE STARS

Lin Devon

Her bike slid through the night like an oiled fist, gleaming quicksilver and midnight black, too intent on destination to slow for traffic. It didn't scream over the city streets, didn't howl like those packs of iron wolves, but hummed with electricity. Streetlights and neon signs cast no reflection in the flat black of her bike or body armor. Leather boots, leather jacket, and black jeans cloaked her like a second skin. At nearly six feet tall with red-brown skin, hazel eyes, and freckles, Max was used to standing out. But on assignment she disappeared. She was a dead space against city shadows, a phantom in the night, harnessed lightning between her thighs.

She shimmied the bike left and right between cars stuck in slow motion. Her waist-length braids lashed across her shoulders like a cat-o'-nine-tails. That felt right. She wasn't a wolf in a pack but a lone panther in a concrete jungle, an infallible hunter. She grinned behind the tinted glass of her helmet and licked her teeth, leaning nearly horizontally to careen around a turn. She shot past the financial district heading straight for the bay shipyards. There and gone in the space of a heartbeat, nothing but a hollow hum in her wake. The glow of the city's man-made twinkle began to dissolve as the gleaming monoliths of glass and steel gave way to wider stretches of undeveloped lots.

She'd gotten the call last minute. She was used to being the last choice. She was good, but she could leave messes the suits didn't want to answer for. Not her problem. She would execute the objective along with anyone who got in her way. She battled creatures most humans only ever met in nightmares. Or fantasies. She knew something about that, too. She always got her man, and the man in her scope tonight was the proverbial "one who got away." And if she wasn't in position soon her prey would be a light year out of reach. Again.

She did a quick mental check of her artillery. At her belt she carried the tools for close-up magic. That was the Sparker with its 80k volt output, her trusted Blueballer, a pair of razor sharp fanblades, and three clips of Titan expanding rounds to accompany the TitanSX pistol grip at her lower back. A small but mighty Series Nine was strapped to her right thigh in easy reach, and a 12-60P gauntlet to her left forearm. That P meant projectile, and boy did it ever. She could make a monster disappear in a puff of gray jelly from a thousand feet away. She twisted the throttle and smiled.

At the entrance point to the shipyard was a twelve-foot gate, padlocked and topped with coils of razor wire. The lock was just a diversion, of course. Likewise the security gatehouse was empty. There was an electrical box beside the booth that did the real security work.

Bike still blasting forward, she tapped a button on her wrist unit, six seconds to impact, five, four. A light flicked green on the electrical box and the gate lights went dark. The suits didn't always have the best toys, but some government tech was damn convenient. With two seconds to impact, she aimed her silenced Series Nine and popped the padlock like an exploding corn kernel. The magnified gates swung wide as her front tire hit them dead center, and bounced back closed behind her. The security system came back on line, but she was a ghost in the darkness by the time it did.

She hid her bike in a shadowed alcove and took off running. The rest would be boots to gravel work. She checked her time. She was cutting it close, and that was only if she was at the right location. It wouldn't be her stupid mistake if the intel was off, but she didn't like the shakiness of it. The other teams had fallen into traps because of shaky intel. Shaky intel is what put the agency in the kind of bind that forced them to dial her in.

The shipyard looked like an abandoned city with huge metal cargo containers, some stacked six high. She bolted into a corridor between crates and listened. No shots fired and there was no sense of a watcher. If they were here they were too few, too trusting, or she was running into a trap. The mission was to confirm the drop off of new alien agents. She was not to engage, but to relay confirmation if she caught sight of them. Send a ping to this location and await backup. If she saw what she thought she might, though, if she saw Xan, engagement was a high probability.

She jogged toward the dock, pausing periodically to peer around corners for sentries. Once waterside she crouched beside the base of a gantry crane. There they were. Not a cluster of alien chimeras squirming over the dock, but a group of men loading an open shipping container with stacks of elongated metal boxes. The intel had been shaky, but in all the worst ways. The ship that was on its way tonight wasn't dropping off but picking up. Those weren't aliens being crated for interstellar travel.

She noticed the massive dark space overhead a second before a blue line of light burst to life at the center of the mass. The crack of a door in an invisible ship hovering fifty feet above the dock.

In that same moment she realized there were eyes on her.

She ducked back between the containers as a noise like squealing tires cut through the night. An alien call. It resonated in her belly, and lower. The first time she'd heard it in the dark woods behind her lakeside home it had changed her life forever. The truth of alien existence on Earth, what it meant, what she had done with that information.

She couldn't retreat if she wanted to. Where was the lookout? She watched the ship. The crack of blue light was widening. They weren't going to call this thing off just for her. The line expanded to form a thin rectangle, a hatch wide enough to allow an entire shipping container. It was the only part of the ship not cloaked, which meant a vulnerable point. She heard footsteps edging in on three sides. They'd flanked her. She had moments, maybe seconds to make an impact and only a few more to see about saving her own life. The lives of whoever had been boxed and crated out there on the dock seemed higher priority just now.

She aimed the gauntlet on her left wrist and fired three shots directly into the opening mouth of the spacecraft. No time left, she spun and flung her Sparker at the thing approaching from behind. She ran past him convulsing on the ground, a million tiny explosions clustered like a swarm of bees around his body. It wouldn't kill him but he wasn't going anywhere either. Another shriek from her left, much too close.

A projectile whizzed past her ear and attached with metal teeth to the shipping container beside her elbow. Not lethal rounds, but damned painful looking. She darted right, then left, but she could feel them closing in. She snatched a rung on a container ladder and scrambled up and over top. Another shot zinged past her ear, much too close.

They were trying to catch, not kill, but death might be preferable. Better than being counted amongst the sorry number bound for stars unknown. She bolted along the top of the crate and leapt to the stack beside it, climbing like a tree monkey up another level.

From this height she could see the damage she'd done, and it was beautiful. She hadn't blown out the walls of the craft, but had severely damaged the cloaking. Now a large segment hung in the sky in full flashing view. It rose soundlessly skyward. They wouldn't get away. The agency had been looking for a slip-up. They would be after it in crafts just as secret and just as quick.

She was nearly at her bike, and on her bike she was untouchable. She leapt for another container, hooked practiced hands on the ladder, and realized halfway down her sliding descent that her body was unresponsive. Something clutched at her back and dug metal claws on either side of her spine. She had time to think her leather had protected her from the worst of the paralyzing agent before she hit the ground like a log unceremoniously dropped to the concrete. She thought, *Well, shit, this is embarrassing*, before someone blurry stepped into view and delivered her to dreamland with a quick blow to the head. *You could have just sung me out, honey, like you did before.*

* * *

The grave was cold and the chairs in hell were incredibly uncomfortable. She'd been rope tied. Not the grave, but it might as well have been. For the first time in her short but storied career as a monster hunter, she'd been caught. Her catlike ferocity rose in frustration, but the hunter in her was already calculating. She was bound to the chair at the wrists, ankles, and waist. She was cold without her leather jacket, colder with her weapons gone. Nothing left but a killer body. They'd even taken her boots.

She squinted to see the room beyond the spotlight overhead. She was in an office. A small window showed the city skyline drifting past. She was on a boat. No, a cargo freighter. She blinked and made out a man in dark clothes sitting on the edge of a desk. He was rooting through her artillery, fumbling with her Blueballer. Just slightly more invasive than your average gynecology visit.

A surge of proprietary indignation caught her off guard and she shouted, "Hey asshole! Those are big girl toys. Ugly little children get hurt playing with those."

He paused, but didn't put it down. He unfastened the latch and let the two chrome balls swing away from each other on a gleaming metal chain. Another man stepped into view and strode to the far wall, staying out of the light. Shit, how many of them were squeezed in this room with her?

A voice from behind her rumbled across her nerve endings. "Humans are so prone to violence."

Familiar hands alighted on her bare shoulders hot as sun-soaked stones and just as hard. Xan. His closeness felt like sunbathing.

He leaned in, swept her braids to the side, and spoke against her temple. "There are better ways to achieve submission."

She clenched her jaw to regain control but memory called her to fall into the purr in that voice, press into that heat, open up, explore. Xan. He'd come from such a very long distance.

"Yeah, well sometimes violence is fun."

He grazed her jaw with his thumb before walking to the desk to examine her things. Indignation flared again. He twirled a carbon fiber dart in his fingers. Standing in front of her he was so tall he nearly grazed the light, shoulders broad enough to block her view. Her weapon gleamed. "If you prefer, we can use your method. Violence. Negotiation of the witless."

He placed the tip at the base of her throat. She held her breath. It was designed to explode into shrapnel on contact, usually halfway through a body. She didn't look away, couldn't think of a useful quip just now. Had she actually told him violence could be fun? Maybe she was witless. That she didn't think he would hurt her was probably proof of that.

She looked up at his face and remembered the first time she'd seen it. Some random white man stumbling out of her woods looking for help. *A crash,* he'd said. *I've been in a crash.*

He trailed the point of the dart down her clavicle and aimed it at her sternum. "We could be done quickly. Is that what you want? A soldier of fortune would be happier dead than captured. And my goodness, Max, we do so want to make you happy."

Her name on his tongue had an effect he could see in her parted lips, her slow blink. Memory rose. He'd said, *Should be easy to remember, Max, even when I'm* . . .

"Yes, I remember you, Max. And I know you remember me. Often." He tossed the projectile onto the table and she winced, bracing for detonation that didn't come. "Don't worry, we've immobilized your charges. We abhor violence, you know. We've evolved past it."

Her voice was surprisingly steady. "Yes, it's so much more

evolved to rape and kidnap. Your methods are just as violent, Xan, maybe worse."

He turned to her again. "We don't rape, Max. We have no need and no interest. The invasion will be welcomed. As you can attest." He bent to look at her very close up. "But we do indeed take some of you with us. You know there are humans who would open a vein for a vampire or lay down on a werewolf's dinner table? Humans are bored. We offer them the journey of a lifetime. They want adventure. They crave the unusual. They want sights and sensations they've never dreamed of. You remember, Max, the sights and sensations you'd never dreamed of." He smiled.

She couldn't help the roses blooming in the caramel of her cheeks, the way her heart had begun to hammer, the slickness hidden behind her inseam. He smelled so good up close.

"I remember you in this ugly human disguise. If you want Earth women to want you, maybe look into an upgrade."

"It worked for you."

It wasn't this face that had done it, and they both knew it. It was that impossible iridescent blue-green one underneath it. She could see a tinge at his collar and temples, itching to break through. If she could make him reveal it, she had other tools at her disposal. She looked at the man seated on the desk and winked.

"He got a better version than you did."

Xan glanced at his compatriot. "You can't make me jealous, Max. There have been many since you."

She blinked up at him, rolled her hips, pretending to make herself more comfortable. His eyes followed the movement.

"None like me."

She spoke to the one leaning against the wall. "Did he tell you about me? Did he brag about the human he bagged that night? How much I was willing to do for a creature finally built to satisfy me?" *My god, what are you, part octopus or something?* The man shifted his feet, stuck his hands in his pockets.

Xan grinned. "Of course, I told them. I trained them. Didn't you realize you were the prototype?" Her heart sank. "Oh, yes. Sweet, insatiable Max, never full enough, always hungry. Before you, the act was more . . . practical. Because of you we know what humans want and we provide it. The human sex drive is perfectly suited to us. As a result, your population is already thick with our DNA."

Her worst fear was realized. She'd taught him too well how to please her and all the ways her body could house all the many aspects of his. She tossed her hair back, regained herself.

"And those people in the crates out there? Heading off to some space rock breeding colony or the exotic pet slave trade? They wouldn't sign up for that if they knew."

Xan was flushing green with every breath. He was trying to maintain his cool, but he was heated, all right. *I'm anything you want me to be.* She caught a glimpse of that iridescent shimmer in both his men. The one with his hands in his pockets was shifting those hands inside the fabric. How uncomfortable to be a creature with so much squeezed into the frame of so little.

"Those people volunteered. They want to serve us. A very special subsect of the human populace, and one we hold in high esteem." He cupped her face in the sudden heat of his palm, his thumb grazing her lower lip. "But no, Max, there is none like you. Which is why when the second ship arrives you will be on it. You'll be prized among humans, and only I will hold your leash."

She snapped her teeth at his thumb and he jerked it back, but smiled. "If you're hoping for backup, it isn't coming. We disabled your locators before we brought you here. Trust me, my backup will be here before yours." Her heart was a triphammer. She was vacillating between the horror of leaving Earth to Xan's conquest and wanting to sink again into the heat of his body wrapped around her every limb, deep inside her everywhere. *I could feast on this alone.*

"They won't let you keep me. I'm too much for you. You found me by accident and I seduced you, remember?"

He licked his lips, and that rippling iridescence cascaded over his features. He remembered, but insisted, "I could have had you any time I wanted. I can feel it when you think of me. I stayed away to keep you starving so that when I whistled you'd come willingly. Anything to feel it again."

Denial would be a lie. She'd been on edge and growing sharper every day he didn't come back. None of the men she'd bedded provided the depth of satiation he had. He licked his lips, his eyes flashing opalescent colors. Oh yes, he was as close as she was.

"You want to feel it again."

His men were flickering blue-green with a tell as obvious as human erections. If he felt it when she wanted him, he could feel it now. He'd made a mistake keeping her so hungry for so long.

He nodded slowly, lenses over his eyes closing and opening like eyelids. His gaze dipped to her nipples, tenting the fabric of her tank top. "Yes." He cupped the swell of her breast, grazed the nub of her right nipple with the glowing pad of his finger.

You're just like a human firefly.

I'm not either of those.

His touch was electric. She hummed an involuntary note. He slid his hand down her belly, over the zipper of her fly. His fingertips vibrated like a purr just slightly, just enough.

She managed, "If you don't take women without their consent, you can't touch me while I'm all tied up."

He halted, blinked in surprise, and after a moment, conceded. He grumbled something to his men who approached and began to unfasten the ropes. They weren't going to set her free. She wasn't going anywhere if they did.

Under the light Xan's skin danced rainbow colors across fine bones and rolling musculature. Almond-shaped eyes swirled opalescent galaxies of color and reflected a mutual need. She was too close to ignore the memory. The way he had come alight in the dark of her bedroom while she discovered his strange and beautiful body. He was right. Anything to feel it again. Her arousal ricocheted through them all.

Please don't stop.

I wouldn't dream of it.

Suddenly she was weightless. Freed from the chair and held aloft. The room existed in a rift out of reality. She drifted above the ground, eye to eye with her towering long-lost lover, wrapped in a living bramble of coiling, twisting, vining blue-green flesh. Their bodies were an unending miracle of form and function. They stood on sturdy legs, they held her with strong arms like those of men, but from their spines each sprouted six prehensile tentacles strong and long as pythons. They coiled around her legs and arms, across her belly, between her breasts. Who needed ropes?

Xan's voice was a growl, his breath coming in hot gusts. "I have felt you calling across the stars for me. A hot flower scenting the galaxy with aphrodisiac nectar. I'm here. So tell me if it's me you want now . . . or is it us?"

She turned her head to the one against whose shoulder she rested. She was rising and falling on the heaving bed of his chest. His eyes were a riot of color when he looked at her. She smiled and asked, "Don't you know?"

She lifted her arms and he slipped her tank top off. His eyes flicked to Xan, but Xan only had eyes for Max, his regained plaything. The man at her side groaned something indecipherable, his hand sliding the length of her thigh.

Xan smiled wistfully. "Yes, she is."

He unfastened the button on her jeans, pulled the zipper down. "We don't take unwilling captives, Max. Your choice, but you have to say the words. Do you want us to take you or should we leave you alone?"

This close he was as beautiful as she remembered. He slipped his hand inside her open jeans and slid his fingertips over the thin cotton lace of her panties, soaked and clinging to swollen lips. "Take you or leave you?" he purred.

The one behind her was humming softly beside her ear, hot breath on her neck. He dipped his head, unable to restrain himself, and licked the salt sweat from the side of her throat. Something heavy tapped against her lower back.

Xan stroked the divide of her sex over the fabric, vibrating her sensitive nerves. The vine of flesh around her waist slid upward between her breasts, coiling like a slim blue boa constrictor to flick her nipple as a hand slid tenderly over the other. Tendrils of muscled flesh were tightening around her thighs, seeking the heat at the crux.

"Just say the word, Max. Say yes. Say no." He kissed her shoulder with impossible tenderness. He smelled like juniper, like pine forest and rain. He kissed her earlobe. "Tell me to fuck you. Tell me to fuck off."

She wasn't going to agree to captivity, but she wasn't leaving here without getting her due either. "Stop trying to fuck with my head, Xan. Just fuck me."

They descended on her as one. Her jeans and underwear vanished. A writhing collection of seeking need searched with curious insistence all the places that made her body sing out.

She was suspended between them, seated reclining three feet above the ground. She welcomed their strength, the way they held and sought her, the cunning in their tentacle tails seeking heat and wetness. Palms glowing heat pressed against the bones of her hips buried under rolling curves. A curl of fingers tilted her face and brought her open lips to an alien mouth. He tasted like a sweet water mountain stream.

Someone kissed the pulse in her neck and trailed hot hands down her torso. Everywhere those electric fingers touched became erogenous. Her body was a cage for atomic lightning. She opened her eyes and locked gazes with Xan. He vibrated pure energy through to her interior with his hands splayed across her belly. Keeping her wet, making her ready. None like her, but none like him either.

She was traveling back in time. The night they'd met. Electric fingers, tongue and cock prehensile in every place climaxing together again and again and again.

Don't stop.

Not ever.

His jism had been periwinkle blue.

She clutched his forearms as he squeezed her hips to hold her steady. His man lapped and lashed her nipples and sent his glowing fingers over the divide of her pussy. Someone, two someones were knocking against the rounds of her ass, sliding self-lubricated dicks along the center to divide the hemispheres, taste the delights hidden deep. Deft fingers parted her prescribed nectar-rich flower.

A mouth came down to catch her nipple between hungry teeth the second a buzzing index finger laid its full length along her clitoris. Her body jerked, her pussy pulsing once, empty then full. Xan swiftly buried himself deep. His cock moved in her like a thick tongue searching for more space where there was none. He gathered her up in arms like trunks and she wrapped her body fully around him. He didn't have to thrust, just held her, explored her with his tongue, with his hands, as his dick swelled and beat against the squeeze in her clutching belly. He covered her moans with his mouth, slid his hand down over her ass, and placed his fingertips against the entrance. He vibrated the tip just inside and sent a shockwave up her spine.

"Just me, Max, or all of us?" he asked again. If they had time Xan could fulfill every need, but times three he might accomplish it quick and dirty.

"I want everything."

A mouth on the back of her neck, arms circled her waist, a body hot against her back, a seeking head nuzzling her ass, then pressing inside inch by stretching inch. Xan watched her face contort in the straining pleasure of housing them both in her narrow body. He pressed her gently backward. She laid out on the bed of an alien body with Xan locked between her thighs. They spun in their tangle of limbs, dancing against each other. She held another around his hips and kissed his cock open-mouthed as he curled around her. All together now. He was sweet as forbidden fruit and scented like moss and woodsmoke. How strange that creatures from so far away would be so perfectly suited to earthling tastes.

The tangle of their tentacles kept her lost to direction, north and south, up or down. She was deep in scratching the itch that had been driving her out of her head for the last two years. But she didn't change her stripes just because of it.

She ground against them, sucked shamelessly into a greedy throat, stroked and squeezed them, harder when they whimpered. In the curling coiling mass none of them noticed when she began to tie a series of slipknots in the discarded ropes.

Groaning between her shoulder blades, the man at her back

suddenly crushed her ass to his lap, and went still. He gasped, bursting magma somewhere achingly deep. The second came tumbling right after. He held her at the nape of the neck for one long greedy moment, sliding his length down her throat before tearing free to splatter his sweetly scented seed over her lips, her chin, in pearls across her throat, and in drops across her sternum. Copious, she remembered that about them. About Xan.

He noticed what the others had not. He knew not to underestimate her, but he had overestimated himself. He'd fought so long to resist her he'd actually convinced himself it could be done. She crossed her ankles behind him and held her pelvis tight to his as he realized that he couldn't detach his hands. She had tied them together behind her back.

Afterward you'll sleep. We both will. It's what happens.

He said, "Oh, no, Max—" but was erupting.

He drew her in and held her close as his climax overtook him. He wasn't going to run. He'd been caught the first night they'd met, the rest was an illusion of control. He kissed her, deep, and his pulse kicked in her belly to explode in a hot wave and fill the narrow space he occupied.

They collapsed at her feet as she stood. The secret he'd unwittingly revealed that first night was that coming sapped their energy. Not a little sleepy but fully undone. As a survival mechanism, it also rendered their partners unconscious after the act. He'd simply forgotten it didn't work on Max. The more he gave her the more she wanted. There were none like her.

She pulled the slipknots tight and huffed, "Now. What was that about holding my leash?"

She smiled down on his beautiful face, humiliated now by capture, and jumped when the door suddenly burst wide. Six men in black fatigues piled in with weapons raised. Then stood blinking at the six-foot naked woman dripping blue cream and standing champion over three naked aliens.

"Uh . . . your locator pinged," the one in front said, his face a sudden flare of pink. "Did they hurt you, Max?"

"Not even a little. Listen, there's a cargo container full of humans out there they've got boxed for long distance travel."

"Yeah we've got 'em. Just in time, too. We intercepted a second pickup after you disabled the first. Good work."

She shrugged off the compliment and crouched to look at Xan more closely. "Those folks might be less than thankful for the rescue if what they tell me is right. These guys will talk with a little persuasion, I think. But this one, well, he's just refusing to cooperate. I can get what I need from him, but I'll need to question him further."

Xan blinked up at her, a touch of admiration for the woman he'd lost the battle to resist.

"You need a box at headquarters?"

She didn't look at him or the others now being restrained and taken from the room, only at Xan.

"No. I've got a place I can take him. I'll send you my coordinates and I'll update you with my progress. Might take a while, but don't worry. I always get my man."

FORGET ABOUT ME

Nikki Ali

Friday morning finds me somewhere I never thought I would ever be: driving in my beloved Mustang along the 5 to Laguna Beach with Hassan beside me and Zubaida in the backseat.

This was my idea: my wife and my ex-boyfriend and I resolving the lingering tension between us beneath the sheets.

"You sit up front," Zubaida said to Hassan as we got ready to leave, slipping her sunglasses over her eyes.

"Yeah, because she falls asleep as soon as she gets in a car," I teased her. She made a kissy face at me. I laughed, so glad she's in high spirits and feeling playful today. We're going to need it.

It's a long drive, from LA to the villa in Laguna Beach down in Orange County, about an hour and a half. I'm thrilled that the traffic gods have smiled down on us today, and the congestion isn't too bad. We make good time.

I drive just the way I like: all four windows all the way down, the car a tunnel of sunlight and sound speeding south down the freeway, too loud and full of sensation even to think, let alone speak. I just turn to smile at Hassan's salt-and-pepper hair tossed by the wind, glance in the back to see Zubaida, of course, asleep, head against the door and her pretty mouth slightly open. I think about what I'm going to put in that mouth later, and I shiver.

At about noon we arrive at the villa, a lovely little place in soft whites and tans, which has escaped being torn down to make way for more luxury rental condos, tucked into a cove with a private beach. It's old, has been in my family for three generations now, and I will leave it to Shamsah. I try to imagine her years in the future, a beautiful young woman with curly blonde hair and the kind of eyebrows popular with the models these days, coming here in twenty years for her own romantic trysts. Or, better, I muse, for solitude, to get to be with herself. I wish I had done more of that, gotten to know myself better. But it is not too late for my baby daughter.

Between the three of us, we carry in the overnight bags, the cooler, the bags of groceries from the Egyptian supermarket. I was just here a few weeks ago—my sister and I rent the place out on Airbnb most of the time, for a rate far lower than most other places in the area, but still exorbitant—to make sure everything was in order, but I still walk through to check on the lights, plug in the fridge, open the windows and air it out. I bring the overnight bags to the master bedroom. A delicious shiver makes my whole body dance as I imagine the three of us there.

"My god," Hassan says as I find the two of them in the living room, bouncing next to each other on the couch, goggle-eyed at the view. "Zubaida and I were just saying how gorgeous this place is, Ashlee."

"Yes." Zubaida unravels her messy bun, shaking out her hair. "This was your grandma's house?"

"Yep." I pick up Zubaida's sandals, abandoned at the foot of the couch, and set them on the doormat. "We rent it out as an Airbnb sometimes, so we've updated all the furnishings, got the latest appliances. You'll love the kitchen, Hassan—Sub-Zero fridge, this amazing Samsung oven. But my nana was old school. She was obsessed with these glass figurines. We couldn't touch anything."

"I can't imagine this being someone's grandmother's house." Zubaida laughs.

Hassan can't stop looking at her. But he glances at me long enough to say, "Do you have any pictures of this place when she lived here?"

I stand on tippy-toes to grab an ancient photo album off the highest shelf of the bookcase, stocked with a couple of recent novels and some pretty knickknacks. "Here," I say. They start to page through the album eagerly, laughing at the '80s shots of my mom, my auntie, my sister, my nana, and me. "Give me your drink orders," I tell them. "I'll pour."

Hassan turns his head to look at Zubaida, and they look so good together, their dark heads close. "What shall we have, Zubaida?" he asks.

She shrugs. "Something light."

"Peach Bellinis?" I raise my eyebrows. "It's brunch time. I bought some gorgeous peaches and a really nice bottle of Prosecco."

Zubaida sighs, looks at Hassan. "Hassan, don't you love how all food is *gorgeous* or *beautiful* to Ashlee?"

Hassan is still getting his footing with her, but after a pause he smiles and says, "Yes. She loves food."

"I'll just go mix those drinks while you sit here and talk about me." I turn and go into the kitchen. I peel and slice the peaches, juice all over my fingers and the delicate tropical scent on the air, mix the cocktails in the blender, and pour, listening to my lovers laughing together.

I bring them their drinks, finding Hassan saying things to Zubaida in Arabic. They're facing each other, her legs tucked underneath her. I decide to settle on the carpet at their feet, where I can look up at them. "What things are you saying to my wife?" I ask him, taking my first sip of the drink. The bubbles make me dizzy, and the flesh from the inside of the peach is so sweet.

"She asked me to teach her some dirty things in Egyptian dialect," he says.

She smiles sweetly and repeats something involving the word *fuck*, probably so dirty it'd make my ears burn.

"*Aywa*," Hassan says.

We sip our drinks in silence for a few minutes. It's not an uncomfortable silence. In the window beyond, the sea is covered in a layer of slow rolling whitecaps in the gentle May breeze, the palms swinging. I imagine us out on the deck later, looking right over the sea, able to smell its salt and feel its cool spray, that's how close we'll be. We'll eat light snacks while Hassan cooks dinner. The thought fills me with such happiness that I wonder if that's what I'm really craving, and not the sex. What does that mean? We'll walk right where the ocean meets the shore at night. We will go to bed together. God, could this be our life all the time?

I tilt my head back to drink the last of my Bellini. It's too much: the two loves of my life here together, the fizzy drink, the angelic light of Southern California, the palm trees swaying against the backdrop of the sea. "I can't stand it anymore, you two," I say. I lift Zubaida's foot to my lips, kiss it gently, lay it back against the couch. "I'm so wet. I'm so ready. I need you to take me to bed, both of you, right now."

Hassan leans over to set his glass, nearly empty, on the blond wood coffee table. "Zubaida," he says, "I don't think we can refuse that request, can we?"

"No, Hassan," she says, "I don't imagine that we can."

My two lovers help me up from the floor at their feet and take me into the bedroom.

In the bedroom, Zubaida pulls the curtains, lilac gauze, over the enormous window, casting the room in muted sunlight. "Look at that beautiful pool," Hassan says, just as the view disappears. He has tucked his hands into the pockets of his pants. He is nervous.

"And a hot tub too," I say.

"Maybe later we should go for a swim," he says. He watches Zubaida as she walks away from the window, toward us. "Zubaida, do you swim?"

"Yes, I swim," she says.

"She swims like a fish." I take her by the shoulders, stand on my toes to kiss her lips, a proper kiss, with lingering tongue. "You should see her."

His eyes watch us with an unwavering intensity. "I have never seen you two kiss like that before," he says. His voice is quiet, but the honesty and simplicity, the vulnerability, of the words resound in the room.

"Did you like it?" I ask, sliding my hands down Zubaida's arms to hold her hands.

He smiles. "I'll show you."

"You should," Zubaida says. "We should get undressed."

"Zubaida always likes for us to just take all our clothes off." I take a deep breath and decide to be brave, as brave as they have been. "The first time we made love, Zubaida took me to my bedroom and asked me to just take all my clothes off." She was nineteen years old at the time; I was thirty-five.

"Really?" Hassan says, his voice barely above a whisper.

I am looking at her as I begin to unbutton my loose, silky button-down. She watches me, hungry, button by button. I have returned us with my words to that long-ago afternoon, the shock and danger of it, coupled with the sweet rightness of our bodies and souls together. I've told people that I knew she was it for me from the moment we first kissed, and that is true.

The two halves open, I toss the shirt aside. I slip out of my pool slides with the feathery fringe, peel off my gray leggings. In nothing but a tiny triangle bra of the sheerest, most delicate black lace, and an even tinier pair of black Brazilian briefs, I slink to the bed in full possession of myself. I sit down against a pillow with one leg tucked under me, my hair tossed over one shoulder, knowing how good I look, and ready to enjoy the show.

"Wow," says Hassan, his eyes all over me. He hasn't seen me in anything like this in many years.

"Yes, wow," Zubaida says. In seconds, she is completely naked, with her usual thoughtless grace and total lack of tease, of coquetry. She joins me on the bed, and now it is her Hassan watches, the knobs of her spine and hipbones, the gloss of her dark skin, the lovely hair between her legs. She sits close to me but does not touch, close enough to let me smell her, to feel the heat of her, to let my whole body salivate for her. She looks over at Hassan, her look, almost surly, quite enough to let him know that he looks only at her discretion.

"Okay, Hassan," she says, tossing her hair, that perfect posture, with the briskness of a chess master. "Your move."

He hesitates a moment, but soon pulls off his white shirt, a stylish, nearly effeminate thing with a blue Greek key pattern around the edges of the sleeves, and steps out of his linen pants and sandals. He comes to the bed in just his black boxer-briefs.

I admire the tightness of his ass in them, and of course the abundant bulge in the front of them. I want to suck him through the thin, stretchy cotton, see it wet first with my saliva and then his come. But he climbs onto the bed with us so gingerly, so tentatively, on the other side of me and as far as he can get from Zubaida, that now my breath picks up, and I too am nervous. Are we going to be able to do this together?

As if in answer, I feel Zubaida's warm palm on my thigh. It travels up but stops before reaching the center of me. I hear myself moan. With her other hand she brushes the curtain of my hair behind my shoulder—and I remember her hand in my hair that day we told Hassan about us, how just that touch spoke the volumes we couldn't say. The memory is finally sweet enough now that I can smile at it. It was not sweet at the time, that's for sure. Telling my on-and-off-again boyfriend of two decades, who had asked me to marry him multiple times, that I was in love with a twenty-year-old woman was one of the most frightening, and the bravest, things I have ever done.

"Hassan," Zubaida says—and her voice gives her away, as short of breath, as nervous, as aroused as we both are. "Isn't her body so beautiful after giving birth to Shamsah?"

"Yes," he says, his eyes warm with love on me, love more than desire, though I do see the rise and fall of his chest under the dusting of delicious silver hair. In his fifties, Hassan is sexier than he ever has been, fully confident in his body. "Though I haven't gotten much of a chance to see it since then."

"That's because it's Zubaida's," I tell him, so emboldened by her hand squeezing the inside of my thigh. My knee bends, almost of its own accord, to try to get her hand where I need it, to bring me some friction, some release. "Today she's just letting you borrow it, baby."

To my delight, they both laugh. "Well, look at her," Zubaida says. "Her thighs. Her belly." She touches my body as she speaks, and I arch into her touch. "Her nipples are so hard in this tiny little bra." I whine long and low as her fingers brush my nipples, and I hear their shared indrawn breath at this. The throbbing between my thighs, my need to come, is so great I could sob. "How her skin looks in the sunlight. Look at her, Hassan, baby."

The small endearment goes a long way. Immediately Hassan is more engaged, shifts subtly closer to us. "I am looking at her, Zubaida." But as he says it, he is looking at her too: the juicy muscles of her arms, the buoyant roundness of her perfect small breasts, and, with a level of want akin to fear, what we can see from here of her cunt nestled inside her hair. She is hard not to look at. Then he smiles at me. "You are driving her crazy, don't you see? She's so close, she wants you to touch her more."

My head falls back on my neck, my breath coming out in a sharp stream. Her fingertips brush the waistline of my panties, and oh, I could cry, I could beg her.

"Sometimes, we do this to each other, Hassan," I manage to say, breathless. The fingers of her other hand trace my lips as I speak. "She tortures me and won't let me come, or I do it to her."

"She's like a dominatrix with me, Hassan," she says, fingers feather-light against my ribs. "You can't come until I say so, Zubaida," she says.

"My god," Hassan says.

"You should touch her too," Zubaida says to him. "He can touch you, can't he, sweet thing?"

"Of course he can."

Hassan puts his hand on the side of my left breast—and it is like an explosion. They are both touching me. They are all over me. Hassan is reaching around me to unhook my bra, and

Zubaida's palms are full of my breasts. He presses heavily against me, starting to trace the line of my body with hot, open-mouthed kisses, nearly too much for me after his distance a moment ago. His lips and tongue are on my ear, my neck, the side of my torso, he is on his knees to nibble on the side of my thigh.

"Let's get her out of these panties," Hassan says.

"Hot as they are, that is a great idea," Zubaida says.

"Open," he says. "Open for her, Ashlee."

I don't need to be told twice. I spread my legs for them.

"Oh," Hassan says, "she is so hot with you, Zubaida."

"I would do anything for her," I say directly into her eyes as she sits between my legs. "She knows that."

"And she owns me." Zubaida thrusts her fingers under my panties at my hips, almost savagely. I love it. "But she doesn't even know it." She draws the sliver of black lace away from my body, and we all watch and gasp at the sight of my wetness clinging to it, a long silver strand between my cunt and the crotch of my panties.

"My god," Hassan says, panting.

"Touch her, Hassan, baby."

Instantly he's touching me, sitting between my legs, his index finger and thumb, so wet and sticky inside me, opening and closing inside my lips. My whole body is so charged that I come right away, a high-pitched whine as if I am in pain, unable to control myself. "Oh, my god, Ashlee," he says. All the times we have been together, he has never seen me like this.

Zubaida grasps my chin in her hand and begins kissing me. In between kisses, she says, "Hassan, sweetheart, touch her more. She can take a lot more than that."

"Zubaida," he says, as he touches the other side of my face, "I think I quite like you telling me what to do."

She laughs against my mouth, and it's so delicious, a sound

that's half laugh, half sob comes out of me. She kisses it away, and doesn't stop kissing me, not for a moment, as Hassan makes his way down my body. I am more and more hungry for her, the softness of her lips with the bite of her teeth, her warm tongue, the liquid silk of her saliva, the farther he travels down my body. He caresses my breasts, my belly, the insides of my thighs, drawing them open with more force than he usually uses.

"Hassan, yes," Zubaida says. "Take her. Open her up. Give her as much as she can handle."

He slips a finger into me, and I writhe like a live wire. They have me so exposed, I am nothing but sensation, energy, nerve ending. She bites my lower lip, and he inserts another finger. My mouth clamps down on hers as I tighten deep inside, the orgasm coming of its own accord, leaving me no choice. My thighs close tightly around his fingers, his hand. I cry out into her mouth.

"Oh, Hassan, she's soaking you," Zubaida says, pausing to lick my lips. "I can smell her from here. Hassan, baby, that's so good."

"You can hear her too," he says. He thrusts his fingers in and out of me, the squelching sound so erotic a few tears leak from the corners of my eyes, my body is out of other options for expressing how I'm feeling right now.

"Open her up, baby," Zubaida tells him. "Let me see her, how wet she is." This time he parts my lips with his fingers, and it's so intimate, the opening of my innermost part so delicious, I come yet again. She kisses me again, and then he's kissing me too, on my belly, and he's slipping down to his stomach between my legs. My body knows what's coming before I do, and every intimate muscle tightens in exquisite anticipation.

"Oh, Hassan, yes, kiss her there," Zubaida says. "Eat her out."

"Oh, I will," he says, "every drop of her."

With every kiss from her lips, I grow wetter, and his tongue inside me can't keep up. He doesn't stop, not even after I come, until I am so saturated from the sensation that my thighs can't stay open, and clamp down on his head.

"Hassan, give her a break," Zubaida says. "Come here, let me see you. I want to see your mouth all wet from inside of her."

He sits up, eyes aflame, hair mussed, cheeks flushed, and his mouth glistening from my wetness. It's one of the hottest things I have ever seen.

"Hassan, oh," she says, letting her breath out along with the word, shifting on the bed in a way that finally reminds me I am not the only one turned on here. "That's so great. I want you to do that to her again. Ashlee?" She strokes my lower lip with her thumb. "Can we do it to you again? Both of us?"

"My god, you're going to kill me," I say, "with pleasure. Okay. Do it to me again."

Zubaida tells Hassan to lay me down on the bed, and he does. They both position themselves between my legs. His tongue begins to lash my clit—and then I feel Zubaida's fingers inside me. I'm so wet it's slippery going for her, but she gets in, turning her hand in a maneuver that makes me scream, the smooth pads of her fingers calling to that place inside me. She presses me until I start to cry, because I just can't take it any longer, and he buries his nose in me and eats me deeply.

"Okay, okay, okay, oh, god," I say. "You guys have to stop. Please stop. I can't take another moment. I'll die, I'll explode."

In a moment I am gathered in her arms. "Ashlee, baby, are you okay? We didn't hurt you, did we? Ashlee . . ." She cradles me, rocks me; and it feels so good to be held, to be comforted, I let myself cry a little more.

I manage to shake my head. "No, of course not. On the contrary. You made me feel so good I couldn't take it."

"Hassan," Zubaida says. "Come over here. Come closer. Can he hold you too, Ashlee?"

"Yes, please," I say, and close my eyes as I feel his arms around me from behind. He kisses my hair, whispers something sweet in Arabic in my ear. In that moment, absolutely everything is all right in my universe.

"You guys drove me crazy," I tell them after a minute, looking at her, twisting my neck to look at him. "You gave me so much. Don't you want me to make love to you too? And don't you want to touch each other?"

Hassan laughs in my ear, a deep, warm rumble that I feel to my bones. "Of course we do, Ashlee. Or at least I do." I can't see him, but I can feel that his eyes are on her.

"Yes, I do too, Hassan," she says. "I want you to kiss me so I can taste her on you."

"Zubaida," he whispers. I feel his erection pulse, nestled where it is in the cleft of my ass.

"Oh," I say. "I just need to feel like I'm not the only one. You guys have me so exposed, crying, screaming, squirting all over the bed. But you seem so calm."

He laughs again, pressing his hard dick into me so I moan. "I am not calm, baby. I'm so hard it hurts. I feel as crazy as you do, believe me."

"We do want each other," Zubaida says, and my gaze whips to hers. "But you are the link that brings us together, Ashlee."

"Yes, don't you see?" Hassan brushes my hair aside to kiss my neck. "We both love you so much that now we want to make love to each other."

Overcome, overwhelmed, we decide to take a break. It's early evening by the time we return to the bed. I peel the sheet free and drape it lightly over my lap, cuddling against a pillow as I watch them. From my makeup bag on the bedside table I retrieve the vibrator I brought.

"Now it's my turn to watch the two of you, and sit here and play with myself and let you entertain me," I say, tracing my lips playfully with the vibrator.

"Your wish is our command," Hassan says. He joins me on the bed, and she follows. I watch them looking at each other, his strong chest rising and falling, the lovely sharp angles of her face framed by the curtain of her hair, the barest outline of her hard abs underneath the skin. I flick on my vibrator on a low setting and begin to tease my outer labia, getting ready.

"Zubaida," Hassan says. "I like the idea of us being honest with each other. So, I must tell you, I am terribly nervous right now."

"I . . . yeah," Zubaida says. Hassan waits for her to say more, but she doesn't. I shake my head. He should be happy he even got that out of her.

"I really want to make you feel good," he continues. "I think we should take it slow."

"Slow is good." She nods. "I think."

"Let's see where it goes, and be honest with each other." She nods again. I let the vibrator trail lightly, so lightly, over my clit, and my limbs tremble.

"I want to hold you," he says. "Can I?"

"Sure," she says.

Hassan shifts closer and draws her into his arms. Immediately they grow close, his arms around her waist, hers around his shoulders. She rests her head quite naturally against his chest and, after a moment, closes her eyes and breathes deeply. It's such a beautiful sight every cell inside me sharpens. He whispers something to her, too softly for me to hear, and she replies, also inaudible. I find I like the idea of them having a secret together from me. I trail the head of my vibrator against my wet slit.

He pulls back to look at her, to hold her face gently in his hands. I love him more than ever for being tender with her. She shifts, slips one leg out from underneath her and snakes it around his waist.

He closes his eyes. "Put your other leg around me."

She does, and gets closer to him, cradling him in the circle of her legs, the head of his penis grazing her pubic hair.

"Is it okay if I kiss you?" he says.

"Yes," she says, "kiss me."

He pecks her lips gently at first, but when he returns for more she opens to him, and I watch them fall seduced by their own kiss, the tangle of their tongues, her slender hands gripping his forearms with a strength that reveals her desire. I watch their hips slide closer together, the tip of his cock disappearing amidst her hair. His penis is turgid, swollen, enormous, a nearly angry red. He parts her with the fingers of one hand and begins stroking her, gently, with the head of his cock. She grows coated with glistening wetness. She white-knuckles him. The rhythm of her breathing drives me insane; when she starts to groan, I lose it, and come powerfully.

"Oh, god," she says.

"Yes," Hassan says. "Even when we are not touching her, she is coming."

She's so turned on I can see her clitoris growing more swollen and larger, engorged. He runs the slit of his penis over it, lightly, experimentally, and then harder and with more purpose. "Yes," she sighs. "Yes, yes, just like that. Harder. I want to come, Hassan. I've been waiting all day."

I turn my vibrator to a higher setting. His breathing, too, becomes fractured as his hand pumps his cock to move it faster and faster over her. He sighs with relief, releases himself from his fist, as she comes, the sound of abandon in her voice bringing me over the edge again too.

"Put it in me," she says. She brings one knee up, resting her leg against him, opening herself to him wider.

"Okay." He lets all his breath out with the word, takes her knee in one hand and his penis in the other, and notches it inside her beautifully. He slides in, and they both sigh. "Ride me," he whispers. "Set the pace. However you want it."

He closes his eyes, his brow creased as he absorbs what she's doing. It takes her a few tries, but she sets their rhythm, rocking their hips together, pulling back to unsheathe his cock, drawing forward to consume it again. It grows a wet, full, brilliant red from the inside of her body. Her hand finds his shoulder for traction, and she rides him. Watching her take her pleasure from him undoes me, moment to moment.

"Touch me," she tells him, when it's clear that he is getting close. He grips her thigh, which is resting beside his body, and with the other hand rubs her clit. He does it like he does it to me when he wants me to come, in quick, concentric circles. By now, the noisily vibrating dildo is deep inside me, so I touch myself with my fingers like he is touching her.

"Zubaida," he says. "I am going to come. Is it all right? Do I have your permission to come?"

I am shocked, delighted. I thought I knew Hassan so well, knew him as well sexually as anyone could, had seen him at his dirtiest and most wild. But now his voice is strangled, moaning around my wife squeezing him inside, and he's pleading and playful at the same time. Maybe it's Hassan and Zubaida who should be together, forget about me.

We come together, the three of us, an extraordinary thing. I'm sure they can hear us all up and down the coves of Laguna Beach.

DISHING IT OUT

Sienna Crane

I might have been named after Julia Child, but my flambés fizzle and I can't tell a crimini from a porcini, so I have no idea how I made the cut for season twelve of *Kitchen Gauntlet*. Even less idea how I came to be the last female contestant on my team. But one thing I do know for sure—that blind panic you see from the throng of quivering contestants whenever Chef Marius is around?

It's absolutely, unfailingly, one hundred percent real.

You know how they say people on TV look smaller in person? They haven't seen Chef. The man is at least six foot four, with hair black as beluga caviar and eyes the vivid green of Genovese basil. He has a big voice and an even bigger personality.

But your average TV viewer mainly thinks of him as the guy who, in his lyrical German accent, popularized a certain scathing insult.

"Is that the best you can do, Dickless?"

A gentle giant named Eddie was on the receiving end of the tirade. Eddie's knife skills were laughable, but maybe his painful earnestness had inspired the producers to keep advancing him.

Or maybe he'd just managed to successfully evade the wrath of Chef Marius.

Until now.

Chef grabbed a slice of pork loin from Eddie's plate and waved it directly under the shaking contestant's nose. "Look at this." Chef's accent grew thicker the more upset he became. "You don't even need to cut into it to know it's raw. Just feel it." He shoved the loin chop into Eddie's hand. "Feel it."

Eddie dutifully gave the pork a squeeze. His eyes were wide with shock and his pallor was alarming. If he didn't breathe soon, he might very well topple over. And he'd probably take out half our team if he did.

Chef Marius narrowed his eyes and said, "Well, Dickless?"

Eddie's lips moved, but only the smallest sound came out. Like the squeak of a mostly deflated balloon.

Chef got even closer, toe-to-toe, eye-to-eye. They were a pair of titans facing off, one strapping and muscular, the other a big squishy teddy bear. A very frightened teddy bear. "What was that?" Chef prompted.

Eddie swallowed convulsively. "It's raw."

Chef snatched the pork from Eddie's hand and flung it dramatically to the floor. "It's raw! Raw! Raw!"

If ever I thought these dramatics were all for the camera, I'd been sorely mistaken. Everyone froze but Eddie, turned tail and ran . . . and he moved faster than any guy his size had any business moving. The other chefs fell aside like bowling pins as he barreled away, red-faced, with tears running down his bristly cheeks. Eddie was a team player who'd never once thrown anyone else under the bus. Not one of us had anything snarky to say about seeing him cry.

None of us contestants did, anyhow. But the guy wielding handheld camera number four? He was another story.

Steve-o was one of those typical art school hipsters who thought way too much of his own taste. His tattoos were over-the-top. His hair was dyed black with at least an inch of reddish-brown roots, and his taste in band T-shirts was ironic. He was a douchebag of epic proportions—and, disturbingly enough, he was also kind of hot.

When Eddie burst into the back room so hard he damn near tore the door off its hinges, Steve-o was right behind him, speaking in a low, sinuous voice that would never be picked up by the microphone. "What's the matter, Eddie, not used to having your pork insulted?"

Audiences love it when people on reality shows cry. I know I used to. But when you're actually here, it's not so fun anymore. Especially Eddie, of all people. He was the last one who should be reduced to tears.

Once Chef Marius stepped aside to explain the dangers of raw pork to one of the jib cameras, my shock wore off. It was replaced by anger. The sight of Eddie with tears running down his cheeks not only broke my heart, but it made me want to give that art school dropout a piece of my mind.

The back room was a real, functional storeroom, not just a place for weeping contestants to blubber to the cameras. But Eddie wasn't going on and on about that maudlin stuff that always makes me roll my eyes. He was trying to hide. "Just leave me alone, Steve-o."

"I'll bet you want to stand up to Chef Marius. Those are tears of frustration, aren't they? Marius intimidates everyone, but how is it anybody intimidates you?"

"Go away."

"Unless you're just a big softy. Dickless? Maybe what you're actually missing is your balls."

"Hey!" I poked Steve-o hard in the shoulder and he swung

the camera around on me. The little red light was on, but I didn't care. "You're way out of line."

Maddeningly, Steve-o just answered with an infuriating grin.

I said, "You're nothing but a bully. Someday you'll take it too far—and you'll really get what you deserve."

"Maybe someday," Steve-o smirked. "But not today."

Livid, I clomped off to try and find a producer. Instead, I caught a glimpse of chef whites at the opposite end of the hall, where Chef Marius was now rinsing pork marinade from his hands. Dare I say something? Off-camera, Chef was surprisingly down to earth. Still terrifying, but there was an everyday quality to him, too. That's what I was telling myself, anyway, as I changed direction and approached him.

"Excuse me, Chef." I was surprised at how even my voice sounded.

"Julia. What is it?" He was focused more on toweling off his hands, but I still got a little rush whenever he said my name.

"It's about that cameraman—Steve-o."

"Who?"

"The obnoxious one with the lip piercings. You know, the one who smells like patchouli."

"Right."

"Look, I get that they all have jobs to do, but he takes it way too far."

"You can't expect the world to coddle you, Julia. If you want to be a successful chef, you need more than just exquisite knife skills and a trained palate. You need backbone."

The other contestants would have thanked him for his time and slunk away. But I just couldn't. "I know a chef can't be thin-skinned when it comes to their cooking. But Steve-o takes it too far. Not just insults, but sexual harassment. You wouldn't tolerate this kind of behavior among the cooking staff in your restaurants. So why does some random cameraman get away with it?"

Marius gave me his full and undivided attention now. The power of his flashing, dark eyes nearly took my breath away. I'd never been subject to his extended scrutiny, and it took everything in me to keep myself from slinking away. But I held my head high and met his gaze. Not with arrogance, but with confidence. I might not have actually felt that confidence, but I was determined to fake it. For Eddie's sake.

"Where is this Steve-o person now?" Chef asked.

"The storage room."

Without a word, Marius turned and marched away while I jogged along behind him to keep up. When he opened the storeroom door, Eddie had crammed himself into the corner behind a stack of tablecloths while Steve-o shoved the camera lens over his shoulder.

"Come on, Eddie, it's your fifteen minutes of fame." Steve-o clearly enjoyed taunting poor Eddie—who could have crushed him without thinking twice. But dominance is a funny thing. It's more about attitude than size. And Steve-o had attitude in spades.

But he wasn't the top dog. Not with someone as exquisitely alpha as Chef Marius around.

In front of the cameras, Marius hollered and yelled and made a big show of being upset. But behind the cameras, at least in this tiny space, he didn't even need to raise his voice. "Hello, Stephen. Care to tell me what, exactly, you're doing?"

Steve-o's whole body language went submissive. He cringed back and set the camera aside. "Just picking up some footage for the B-reel." He laughed nervously. "You know it's not an episode of *Kitchen Gauntlet* until somebody cries."

Chef crooked his finger. "Get over here."

Steve-o swallowed. His Adam's apple bobbed. But he dutifully stepped forward.

Chef Marius leaned forward from the waist so his eyes were level with Steve-o's. "What gives you the right to shove the camera in his face like some kind of unbridled paparazzo?"

"But I was told to—"

"Do you take me for an idiot? You know what you did."

Steve-o wasn't stupid. He stopped arguing and simply nodded.

Marius gazed down into his eyes for a long, squirmy moment, then echoed his nod. "Good," he said simply. And while it was gratifying that the obnoxious cameraman had received a verbal warning, it really seemed like the reprimand should have been more dramatic.

I guess it wasn't my show.

But then, instead of walking away and getting back to the rest of the contestants, Chef Marius dusted off the front of his whites and said, "Well, go ahead, Stephen. Apologize."

We all turned to Eddie, who was swabbing at his face with a damp paper towel. He looked like he wished he could be anywhere but there.

"I'm sorry," Steve-o said.

"Now say it without smirking," Chef told him.

Steve-o rolled his eyes. "I'm very sorry for following you . . . though how could anyone resist when you carry on like that?"

"One more chance," Marius said testily.

"I'm truly sorry, from the very bottom of my heart, for goading you to keep on crying . . . like a big ol' baby."

"Right," Marius said. "That's it. On your knees."

That part where I said Marius wasn't as scary behind the camera as he was in front of it? I was entirely off base. Marius stood over Steve-o, rigid and unyielding. The fact that he hadn't raised his voice was suddenly infinitely more powerful than any yelling, screaming, or name-calling could possibly be. Funny thing was, Steve-o didn't seem particularly surprised by the request. Dutifully, he got to his knees in front of Eddie, then looked up at Chef Marius for further instructions. Still smirking.

Marius turned to Eddie and casually said, "Well? You've got a big fondness for raw pork. Pull out that slab from your trousers and make Stephen do his penance."

Wait a minute. Had he just . . . ?

Eddie looked as confused as I felt. But when Marius said, "Now," there was no arguing. The sound of Eddie's zipper coming down filled the small room.

It seemed like I should look away, but I couldn't help but steal a glimpse. Eddie's dick? Just as oversized as everything else on him, even at rest. But I wasn't about to add to his humiliation by gawking. I turned to face the wall, but flinched when I felt a hand fall on my shoulder. "Julia," Marius said—and there was that illicit thrill over him actually knowing my name again. "Don't look away. You're a reality show contestant. You know better than anyone how everything is magnified when it happens for an audience."

He slipped an arm around me and turned me to face the two men—one on his knees with his hands clasped loosely behind his back, the other towering over him, redder than an heirloom tomato with his dick in his hand . . . a dick starting to swell and lengthen.

"Now," Marius said. "Stephen is paying Eddie his restitution. But he needs to learn his place."

Was this actually happening? Maybe the mushrooms in *Kitchen Gauntlet* were the psychedelic variety and I'd tasted my competition omelette one too many times. But no. There was a level of reality here that went above and beyond reality TV. The sight of the sweat glistening on Eddie's brow. The smell of Steve-o's obnoxious patchouli. The muffled, wet sound Eddie's fattening dick made as it pushed past Steve-o's lips.

"That's quite a mouthful," Chef said to me conversationally. "You have a decent palate . . . how do you suppose it tastes?"

Well, we'd been running around the kitchen all afternoon trying to make sure our pork was at the correct temperature . . . "Salty?" I ventured.

"Indeed. And umami. Always. Even if it's drizzled with honey or covered in spunk. Genitals always taste of umami."

Whatever flavor that monster cock might be, it must be hitting the cameraman's every last taste receptor. Eddie was ragingly hard now, and his dick was so girthy I could practically hear Steve-o's jaw creak from two yards away. It wasn't just a big dick, it was gargantuan. Now Eddie wasn't the only one turning red. Steve-o's cheeks were flushed too, possibly from lack of air. But his hipster old-man trousers now had a distinct peak forming behind the fly.

Marius pressed his mouth to my hair—oh, my god—and murmured, "Stephen gets off on you watching him. Haven't you noticed he fancies you?"

I shook my head. I highly doubted Steve-o cared much for anyone but himself.

"It's true," Chef said. "He's always following you around. We have more footage of you than any other contestant."

"I just thought he was being annoying."

"Oh no. You're his type. The perfect blend of sweet and spicy. Soft but firm. Innocent but world-wise. I've seen his eyes on you. And he would like nothing more than for you to indulge yourself in the umami between his legs." My heart raced faster. Was Chef going to tell me to suck this obnoxious cameraman's dick? "But he's being punished. And traditional gender roles are so tedious, don't you agree?"

I had no idea what he was talking about but I nodded along anyhow, dazed, and still half-convinced that this was all some bizarre psychedelic dream.

"Look inside the sous vide machine and bring me what you find inside."

Every season, some show-off contestant decides to get fancy and poach something in the sous vide—a big water bath. Chef Marius is never particularly impressed, but that doesn't stop people from trying. But the process is fussy and takes a lot of time, so the bath doesn't usually get used more than once or twice in a season. Why he wanted it now, I had no idea. Until I opened it, and discovered a tangle of leatherette straps inside . . . and a glittery purple sparkle dildo attached.

"Come now, Julia. Don't dawdle. You know I hate dawdlers."

I scooped up the strap-on, and the bottle of lube beneath it.

Chef gestured at Steve-o, and told Eddie, "Strip him."

Steve-o got to his feet. His lips were swollen and pink from sucking cock, and I'll bet his jaw was killing him. But he didn't resist when Eddie unbuttoned his shirt with big, clumsy fingers. He had a nice body underneath those insufferable thrift store garments. Tight and muscular, with artsy tattoos covering his entire left arm and part of his chest. And while no one's dick could possibly compare to the whole pork loin hanging between Eddie's legs, the hard-on that was revealed when Steve-o's briefs were pulled down was pretty impressive, for a human-sized man. And it was pierced through the slit, a Prince Albert.

Of course it was.

"Do you know the proper technique for lubricating an asshole?" Chef asked. I shook my head mutely. He took the lube from my unresisting fingers and flipped open the top with his thumb, then gave naked Steve-o a shove to the shoulder so he bent at the waist, ass in the air. "You might want to warm the oil so as not to shock your partner. However, I think Stephen hasn't quite earned that right." He squirted a glistening glob of oil on his first two fingers, then slipped them into Steve-o's ass with the same sort of confidence he would use to extricate the giblets from a game hen.

Steve-o groaned, a loud, guttural sound that sank into me, right down to the bone. Eddie too. He caught his breath in response, then took his monster dick in hand and stuffed it into Steve-o's waiting mouth.

"Never skimp on the lube," Marius told me. "It might get messy—but a proper chef should never be squeamish."

"No, Chef," I answered in a daze.

Marius's long, strong fingers plunged into Steve-o's tender pink asshole, disappearing and resurfacing, gleaming with lube. Steve-o gurgled around Eddie's fat dick, while his balls swayed and his own hard cock bobbed up and down with the force of being fingerbanged. His pierced cock was as red as his cheeks now, and leaking profusely at the tip.

"If you care about your man's pleasure," Marius said, "locate the prostate." He pulled his slick fingers out with a gentle, wet slurp and held his oily hand out for mine. Dutifully, I put my hand in his, and he slicked it with lube from his own hand, then extended my forefinger. Hands clasped together, his piggybacked over mine. With both forefingers pointing, he pressed our fingers up that obnoxious cameraman's ass and aimed them toward the floor. "There, maybe you can feel it. Maybe not. In this case, it doesn't matter. Filthy sluts like him will get off on just about anything."

He plunged our fingers into the slippery hot tightness, over and over, and I reveled in the feel of breaching a man's body. It was unexpectedly intriguing, and left me wanting someone to plunge into me.

"I don't suppose I need to tell you he's ready," Marius said after a few minutes of focused thrusting. I looked at Steve-o. His tattooed body was taut and quivering. His breathing was coming in shallow gasps. A shimmering thread of fluid connected the pierced tip of his dick to the tile floor between his feet.

"No, Chef," I said, "I can see it."

"Very good, then equip yourself." He gestured toward the purple strap-on. "Whether you prefer to shed your clothing is up to you. Although the sensations are much heightened on bare skin."

I would never dream of taking off my clothes for the camera. But if I was getting naked not to titillate some nameless, faceless reality show binger, but to accentuate my own pleasure? Yes. I should do it.

I shucked off my herringbone pants and squirmed out of my jacket and T-shirt. The bra I had on beneath was black and lacy, and I'd be lying if I said I didn't get a charge out of the way Chef Marius's pupils dilated when he saw it. "Leave that on," he murmured, and his voice was low and rough. I nudged away my discarded clothing with my foot and turned the strap-on help-lessly around in my hands. Marius took it from me, not with impatience, but with the quiet focus he gave the contestants when he was showing us a technique for the very first time, from filleting a turbot to coaxing a mussel from its shell. "One foot through here." He helped me step in. "The other here, and buckle it like so."

The sparkly purple dildo should've looked ridiculous dangling there between my legs . . . but it didn't. It looked powerful. I could tell Eddie thought so too. He was staring at it as if he didn't quite know what to make of it, but it fascinated him nonetheless.

"A bit of lube," Marius said. As he slicked the purple dick, I tried to wrap my head around the fact that he was lubing my fake cock. "And then you ease it in." He gestured toward Steve-o's gleaming, tender asshole. "Not too hard. The silicone isn't as forgiving as human flesh. And pay attention to what's going on in front of you—as always. It's just like a hot pan. You don't want to bang away on autopilot. You pay attention to the meat. You listen to what it's telling you."

Eddie was obviously as baffled as I was . . . but even more turned on. Veins stood out in high relief around the base of his thick shaft, and he had taken a handful of Steve-o's dyed hair in a loose fist, guiding his head.

I stepped up behind Steve-o. If I closed my eyes, it almost felt like a flesh-and-blood dick in my hand, too. I guess that's why they made these things out of silicone. It felt foreign for it to be facing away from me . . . but not in a bad way. I stroked the head across the quivering pucker of that slick asshole, and Steve-o moaned deep in his chest. The reverberation carried through his throat, and Eddie gave a tiny gasp as it played across the base of his massive cock. I fondled the asshole again, getting a feel for its resilience and shape. Chef was right. It was a lot like cooking. Being aware of how much pressure was the right amount. How much tenderizing the delicate cut of meat could take. And with that, I wielded my tool, and I sank in.

All four of us made an appreciative sound as that purple glitter dick breached Steve-o's ass. The dick had no nerve endings, obviously, and at first I really couldn't tell how it must feel. Too hard. Too soft. Angled too much up or down? And yet, when I really thought about it—when I really got in the flow, like I did when I was in the kitchen—the strap-on became an extension of me. Like a whisk in my hand, fluffing up the eggs for a soufflé, one that would actually rise this time. No, I couldn't really feel the dick. But plunging it in and out of that hot douchebag's splayed asshole, I almost thought I did.

It turned me on as if it had nerve endings, anyhow. With each plunge, I grew wetter and wetter. My nipples strained against the lace of my bra, and when I opened my eyes, I saw that Chef Marius was gazing hungrily at the sharp peaks. I paused in my thrusting and eased my breasts over my underwire. The black lace framed them gorgeously, and my nipples were taut and flushed. I should have been too intimidated to say anything— you don't make a suggestion in *Kitchen Gauntlet* unless you're damn well sure of it—but I was giddy with arousal. And so I said, "The only way to be sure of your ingredients is to taste them." The tiniest flush appeared across Chef Marius's cheekbones. I'd never seen him at a loss for words, but he didn't say a thing. Just bent and took one aching breast into his hand and swiped his tongue across the hard nipple.

Need raged through my body at the feel of Marius's tongue on me. The four of us found some kind of rhythm together. Tongues and breasts and dicks, and all of us breathing hard. The scent of our arousal filled the small room with umami. But I wanted more.

"Chef," I said tentatively—and it was really hard to make my voice sound casual. "I'm not sure I have exactly the right rhythm here. Maybe you could show me."

At first I thought I might've overstepped my bounds. But then Chef Marius's eyes grew even more intense, tumultuous, with an edge to them that was part frightening and part thrilling. He unhitched his herringbone pants and said, "It's never shameful to ask for help."

He positioned himself behind me, hands firmly on my hips. It was just like the way he treated so many of the other contestants in the kitchen, pausing to demonstrate exactly how they should handle the ingredients. Except I'm guessing the other contestants didn't feel his hard cock pressing into the curve of their ass. And I'm guessing none of them were naked except for a bra and a sparkly purple strap-on.

Marius slipped a finger inside me—and his touch was just as deft as I always imagined it would be. Long, strong, and just forceful enough to make my body quiver.

But I wanted more.

And Marius didn't disappoint.

A condom wrapper crinkled, then I felt his stiffness pressing up against my hungry pussy. No, not just hungry—famished. And no one ever walks away from Chef Marius unsatisfied. He pushed in, and filled me utterly. The long, hard, silky stiffness glided in with just the right amount of friction. Filling me, and filling me, and filling me. He thrust in with both precision and abandon. And all the while, Eddie watched as if he'd never seen a woman get fucked doggy style before.

Maybe he hadn't. Not in person. By Germany's top TV chef. The world's top TV chef.

With each powerful thrust, Marius bumped my hips, shoving me harder up Steve-o's willing ass. At first, I jostled him forward with the motion. But when the shock wore off and Eddie gathered his wits about him, he realized that we were bookending the obnoxious cameraman. And that if anyone could stop another person like a brick wall, it was him. Eddie started timing his thrusts with mine. Sinking into Steve-o's mouth with each time the purple glitter dildo drew out. If I felt full, I couldn't imagine how Steve-o must've felt. He was being spit roasted as effectively as any suckling pig, with an unyielding slab of dick pinning him from either end.

Marius fucked my aching pussy. I fucked Steve-o's quivering ass. And Eddie jammed his humongous cock relentlessly into that wide-open, aching mouth. We moved together, the four of us in concert like an experienced kitchen team that's been working together for years, thrusting and grinding, whipping the four of us into a frenzy. Sweat flowed freely as if we were laboring over a hot stove. Salt slicked my bottom lip. The air was thick with umami—saline like the catch of the day, fresh from the sea and still pulsing with life.

Marius bent over my back and cupped a hand over each of my bared breasts. He shed his chef coat, and his chest hair tickled between my shoulder blades. He pressed his mouth to the nape of my neck and said, "We could go on and on, ride the knife edge of pleasure all night long. But there comes a point in every meal where the ingredients become overworked. A good chef knows when the batter is ready."

"Yes, Chef," I said through my broken gasps.

Marius slid a hand downward and eased a finger behind the glittery purple dildo. His touch was as sure on my throbbing clit as it was in any other ingredient. He slipped the finger between my gushing folds and found that sensitive nub with as much adeptness as he'd separate an egg yolk.

My body bucked in shocked pleasure, but Marius anticipated the movement, just as he might anticipate the spatter of hot grease on a fresh slab of bacon. He moved with the motion and rode the wave, turning it into a deep, satisfying thrust. The dildo was buried in Steve-o all the way to the root, and he gave a deep, broken groan around Eddie's fat dick. Arousal spiked between the four of us, suddenly dizzying. Before I realized what was happening, I was coming. Surge upon surge of cleaver-sharp orgasm, tearing through my body, driving it into Steve-o's needy asshole. The feel of him trembling beneath my hands was hotter than any seasoned skillet. It was almost as if I had a dick of my own, filling him with my bittersweet seed. He bucked beneath me, spilling his pleasure on the floor. His groans of pleasure changed and thickened as Eddie broke, coating his gullet with thick, salted cream.

Chef Marius treated me to a single caress on the shoulder as he pulled free and his hot seed spilled down my thighs. He wasn't an effusive man. But maybe I had learned to read him in those subtle gestures and wordless nudges of encouragement. He pulled on his clothing. Without being told, Steve-o got to work, naked, swabbing up the mingled fluids cooling on the pantry floor. Eddie was still pretty stunned. He needed to be told to put his clothes back on before the cameras spotted him.

We left the back room one at a time so as not to give the other contestants anything to gossip about—though, frankly, I don't think anything they might dream up could possibly be as crazy as what actually happened. Chef first, then Steve-o, and finally me, since Eddie looked like he was still processing our little tryst. The producers must've herded everyone else back to the dorm while we were spicing up the pantry. When I crept out into the hallway, the contestants and camera crew were gone and the lights were low. All but the light at the far end of the hall, shining from the doorway to Chef's office.

As quietly as I could, I stole a glance . . . and a glance was all it took. Steve-o was on Chef's desk. Not with his butt in the air being spanked with a belt, either. Just sitting there, easy as you please, with his feet swinging lazily. Contestants wouldn't so much as lean against Chef's desk, let alone sit on it. Chef was making himself a cappuccino for the road from the fine Italian espresso machine on the credenza. At least, I thought it was for him, until he handed it to Steve-o, and I saw the way their fingers brushed.

In the media, Chef Marius was notoriously private about his

private life. Now I knew why. Were Eddie and I the first contestants who'd ever joined the two of them in a little off-camera fun? Doubtful. But one thing was for sure. Even if I didn't end up taking home that prize at the end of the season, I'd learned an entirely new technique for pounding meat.

THE LIGHTNING ROUND

Alexa J. Day

*C*ome on. *Come for Daddy like a good girl.*

Oh, god, I'm so close. His voice pushes me closer to the edge, so close to falling or flying. Say it again, Daddy. Say anything.

Cullen's stopwatch interrupts us with a loud click. "Time."

The men shift in their chairs, and frustrated sighs surround me. I'm just as frustrated. No, actually, I am more frustrated than they are, because none of them expected to have an orgasm in the last few minutes.

I should have come by now. They can all sense it, even if they don't know why. They can't know how hot this game makes me, getting myself off while they leer at me and take turns talking dirty to me. They don't know how much I love being center stage, an object of lustful curiosity, my arousal growing as they watch me. They definitely don't know the little fantasies I weave about the four of them. They only know that they can look but not touch, that I won't touch myself, and that the one of them who comes closest to guessing how long it takes me to come will win the pot of money they all contributed to. Tonight, even the most generous of guesses was not enough time, and now they're all antsy, wondering what will become of their money.

The cash might have distracted me tonight. It doesn't usually get to me, but my cut of the pot will mean the difference between a quick weekend in Vegas and ten long days of pampering and decadence. It's a lot to think about.

Cullen enters the circle of chairs with a bottle of water for me. I'm slouching a bit in mine, and I bring my knees together as he approaches. His fingertips graze mine when I take the bottle from him.

"You okay?" His voice is barely audible. I'm on his stage, in his club, and this is his game, but if I say the word, everything will stop, no questions asked. He'll send everyone home with what they brought in, and I'll go home with a little cash for my trouble.

It won't be decadence money, though. I can practically feel cool, chlorinated water around my toes. I smell the warm massage oil.

And frankly, I didn't go through all this trouble to go home without an orgasm.

I drink some of the water. "I'm okay."

He gives my shoulder an attagirl squeeze, and I straighten up in this uncomfortable-ass chair, smoothing my skirt down over my thighs. I always wear this outfit for the game. I know what the skirt does for my legs and my hips and my ass. The shoes make me feel ten feet tall. The blouse slides over my chest just enough to attract men's eyes. I love taking this outfit to my dry cleaner, knowing that I wore these pricey things to this circus of perversions.

The youngest of the men, his eyes wide with anticipation, pipes up with a question. "What happens now?"

"Now?" Cullen favors them all with a wicked grin. "Now we go to the lightning round. Come on. Let's get started while she's warm."

The stage creaks beneath them as they close in around us. I saw them before we began, to verify for Cullen that I didn't know any of them. Junior, with his round, inquisitive eyes, has porcelain skin that glows with good health or an ever-present blush. He came with a friend who dresses like a lawyer. Shadows stand out beneath the lawyer's eyes, and he wears that expensive suit like a skin. The one who calls himself Daddy has been sitting to my right. His shoulders fill out a dark pullover, and a dense beard covers his square jaw. The last guy, seated behind me, has a tweed jacket and a pair of horn-rimmed glasses. He looks like the sort of man who doesn't own jeans or watch American television.

Cullen's blue-blooded pedigree shines through in his cultured Southern accent, which he uses to further charm the men as he explains the new rules. "The objective is the same, but the rules are a little different. Each of you has thirty seconds to touch one part of her body, above her waist or below her knee." He lifts one finger. "Use one hand. Once you touch her, you can't move. If your hand is on her breast, it stays on her breast. We'll draw to see what order you're going in. If she comes with your hand on her, you win."

The lawyer pulls out his wallet. "We can still talk to her?"

Junior looks at me and smiles shyly, as if apologizing for his friend's abruptness.

"Yep," says Cullen. "But just during your thirty seconds."

"Same buy-in?" asks Daddy.

Cullen nods.

"And for the lady?" The professor's British accent elevates the question. "Same rules, she can't touch herself?"

"Same rules."

"Can she touch us?" the professor asks. Everyone goes still. Apparently, they hadn't thought of that.

"Sure." Cullen chuckles. "If she likes. Same rules, though. Over the waist or below the knee."

"Damn," says the lawyer.

The four of them are counting out their money now. I close my eyes to the sound of the bills unfolding and changing hands, flapping softly like wings. I kick off my shoes and grind the balls of my feet into the stage. My toes grip the gritty surface. My calves flex and release, and then my thighs follow suit. I breathe in deep, focusing on my spine, the long line reaching up into the heavens and down into the earth's hot, liquid center. My muscles relax as I exhale, toes uncurling, calves unlocking. My thighs ache as if longing to be separated by firm hands. My own center grows hot and liquid. The cool fabric of my blouse rises and falls against my breasts, suddenly warm in this bra made of intricate lace.

Daddy's voice cuts through the thickening air. "Shit."

They've decided on the order, then. Anticipation kicks my pulse up, and I try to control that energy without dampening my excitement. They'll be here soon, all of them touching me, at war to see who will bring me to climax first. My arousal swells, fluttering and thumping in a rhythm all its own. This weightless sensation reminds me why I'm here, on a stage surrounded by strange men. The money is nice, and tonight it'll be nicer than usual. But this is why I love the game.

I open my eyes as they take up position around me. Daddy is at my right again, standing close enough that I can rest my head on his thigh. The lawyer is in front of me, with his friend Junior

and the professor on my left. From his position between Daddy
and the lawyer, Cullen pulls his stopwatch from his pocket.

"Ready?" he asks.

Daddy nods brusquely. No wonder he was annoyed. If he's
going first, he's least likely to make me come. I can't help but
smirk at him. His eyes narrow just a bit in response, and the
whisper of fear that rises in me makes me a little hotter.

"And . . . go."

Daddy reaches for me swiftly. His big hand seizes a handful
of my hair. The aggression sends a flash of sensation through
me, and I gasp. I twist my hips on the unyielding chair to try to
magnify the heat building in me.

When my eyes meet his, his features harden. His mouth is
set in a firm line. I sense the tension flowing through his body,
all the muscles flexed in this primitive assertion of dominance
while he decides what he wants to take from me. I'm his now.
I'm an object for him to subjugate at this forbidden crossroads
of terror and desire.

My knees rub together. I imagine his thighs between them,
thick and hard beneath the worn denim. I want his crude, angry
mouth on mine. I want him to shove his thick fingers into me,
hard enough to make me cry out.

Cullen's voice intrudes. "Three."

"Dammit," says Daddy.

"Two. One." Daddy releases me, and my scalp has just begun
to tingle when Cullen points at the lawyer. "Go."

He leans over and pulls me toward him by my left calf. My
legs part as my skirt rides way up over my thighs, where the air
cools my heated flesh. My ass slides right up to the edge of the
seat, and I hang on to the chair with both hands.

He guides my leg up until my knee is level with his waist,
carefully, so that no part of me is touching him. I relax into

his surprising strength. His frosty gaze glitters with some dark intent. He's the sort of man who might host an orgy in the posh hotel suites he's used to, as long as he can watch from a place high above the free-flowing alcohol and the tangle of tightly entwined bodies. My skin heats under his silent scrutiny. I want so badly to close my legs around him. I long to feel the silken fabric of that suit on my hypersensitive skin. I want him to lift both my legs high, so that he can lose a little of that iron resolve with each balls-deep thrust into my tight cunt.

"Three. Two. One." The muscle in the lawyer's jaw works as he sets my leg back down. Cullen points to Junior. "Go."

He seems startled, as if he didn't know he was next. He blinks his wide blue eyes at me, as if asking for permission before he places his hand on my breast. His touch is tentative at first, his hot, sweaty palm resting squarely on my nipple, but then he curls his fingers around the full roundness of my breast. He's not quite squeezing. It's as if he's trying to pick something up using only his palm. I push myself up into his hand and he responds by closing his fingers around me. It's hard to believe he and the lawyer have ever met each other.

I wouldn't mind putting him into this chair. Hiking my skirt up so that I can straddle him. Grinding myself against him until he's hard and ready. I want his hands under my blouse, those fingers trembling and awkward on the hooks of this bra. I'd lift my tits up to his mouth and take his soft hair in my hands. His smooth skin, flushed pink, would be so hot against mine. Those lips shivering against my flesh before I teach him how to flick and twirl his tongue just so. I want to ride him hard, until he takes over and pulls me down onto his shaft. I want to see his face when he gives himself over to primal, animal need for the first time.

He's thirsty, too, in his way, wanting more than any lover

has ever offered him. With the right hands to tease him into exploring his dark side, a man like him would flourish. Something hides beneath that boyish awkwardness, and I want to capture it and put it to use before his friend infects it with the privilege of their world. But right now, Junior's innocence is something sweet, dissolving in the heat of my mouth, and my hunger for more surprises me.

"Time," Daddy demands.

Cullen chuckles. "Three. Two. One." He points at the professor, who waits for Junior to withdraw before he drops to one knee at my side. His slender fingers slide over the back of my neck.

His touch is cool. It feels heavenly, but I can feel myself falling into it and away from that ever-elusive climax.

Then he whispers to me.

"You could have any of them. Or all of them at once."

He's so close to my ear. His breath tickles the fine hair on my cheek, and it slowly rises in a tingling wave. His scent reminds me of pipe tobacco or well-conditioned leather. I shift my weight on the chair, and the fabric of my panties, so hot and wet, stretches over my engorged clit. My breath catches. I'm winding up inside at the thought of his lips closing on my earlobe, his teeth and his tongue teasing me.

"Who would you have first? The lumberjack? He wants you almost as much as I do. Or this eager young fellow? There's something in his eyes. Or this other one. You could teach him something."

I want to be spit-roasted by both of them while the others look on. Or spread open for Daddy's rough beard on my swollen mound as he pushes his tongue deep into me. Or the lawyer's soft hand on the back of my neck while he pounds into me from behind.

The professor's hand massages the back of my neck. I put my palms on my knees and bear down on them, leaning back into his touch.

"All of them—all of us—are yours for the taking. What might we accomplish together?"

I only have a moment to think about it. Daddy's big, hard body pushing my legs apart so he can feast on me. Junior pinning me down before he lowers his blushing face to one breast. The lawyer curling the tip of his sharp tongue along the periphery of my other nipple before they both start teasing me, making my juices flow right into Daddy's mouth, as the professor looks on, seducing me with his indecent whispers.

I pull in a long, deep breath, and my body opens up, pleasure extending from my crown through the center of me, rooting me to the earth and then bouncing me skyward to hover in space for an instant before dropping back down. It's a perfect sensation, and I greet it with a perfect sound, something pure like song.

"That's it," says Cullen. "It was close. You had two seconds left."

The professor waits for me to catch my breath before releasing me. For a moment I can barely hear anything over the velvety crush of my pulse in my ears. He touches his lips to my temple, and he feels just as I imagined he would.

"Thank you," he says. He helps me sit up, and I realize what a disheveled mess I must be. My whole body aches when I get out of the chair.

Cullen approaches with a roll of bills. Somehow the bills sound crisper than before when he counts out the professor's winnings. Daddy has already stalked off toward the door, I guess; I don't see him anywhere. Junior is chattering away with his friend, who smiles indulgently back at him. I can't help but grin as I watch them. Junior's discovered a new obsession, and he doesn't seem to mind that he's lost a good bit of money in the process. Oh, well. That enthusiasm is always a joy to behold.

The professor waits for the others to leave. He takes my hand between his and holds it until I look up at him.

"I meant what I said," he says. "Yours for the taking."

I blush like Junior. "Thanks. I'll remember."

He runs his thumb over my knuckles and then pushes his glasses up on his nose before heading out, leaving me with Cullen. The long night in the chair is starting to catch up with me, and it must show on my face. The two of us are quiet for a moment, and it's enough just to be with him in this place he's made into a home.

"You all right?" Cullen asks.

I nod. It's late enough to be early. It won't be light outside when I leave, but the birds will be singing. "I just want to go to bed."

Cullen nods and peels my Vegas money off the roll of bills. I fold the thick stack over my thumb.

"I'll stay if you want to shower in the back," he says. "Let you borrow some sweats. You could even take me out to breakfast."

Cullen is a master seducer, but he knows the power of a nonsexual proposition. The only thing more tempting than a long shower is going to sleep on a full stomach. It feels good to think of food after everything that's happened. Besides, my purse is safely tucked away in his office. I have to go back there anyway.

"Okay." I peck his cheek and gather up the water bottle from its place beside the chair. When I look up, he's touching his face like he's been kissed by a movie star. I roll my eyes at him. "You're buying next time."

He chuckles as I head toward his office, pinching that Vegas bankroll between my fingers and daydreaming of long massages, luscious facial masks, and the promise of fantasies waiting to come true.

ABLE BODIES

Michelle Cristiani

"Optic chiasm" were foreign words to Kira. But "car accident," she understood. And, "concussion." And "blindness." Sure, she was lucky to be alive. Alive, to nurse endless bruises from furniture she constantly bumped into. Alive, to forget where she'd left objects, and knock other objects over when she looked for them. Alive, to give up her favorite things like cooking and classic comedies. Alive, so she could relearn her entire journalism job orally.

At least, Kira thought—as her body healed from broken ribs and cranial stitches—she didn't have to see anyone's pitying faces. She could see blobs, only. She could tell whether the person in front of her was her brother or sister by the size of the blob. She could maybe, with practice, tell how the light fell *on* versus *in front of* the toilet, so she wouldn't trip over it, like she did at least once a day.

Everyone brought food she couldn't identify until she tasted it. They recommended audiobooks and podcasts. Of course, yoga. And carrots. Good for the eyes. Always with the carrots.

The only worthy adviser was Kira's sister Nicole. "After Matthias was born, when I had postpartum depression," she said, "the only thing that helped was a support group."

Kira shook her head. "Online groups, Nicole? I can't handle that tech. And in person? I can't drive anywhere, and I can't figure out that damn cane."

"Let me look into it. The ride service will take you. It may be the only thing that keeps you afloat."

If there was anyone Kira wanted to believe, it was her big sister. "All right," she said. "You find it, I'll try it."

Two weeks later, Kira sat in (what they told her was) a circle, at group therapy for those handicapped from car accidents. Light and shadow showed her about ten blobs.

When they introduced themselves, there was a long pause before Kira realized it was her turn. She wasn't in public much anymore, but when she was, every minute held cues she couldn't respond to. The girl who'd just spoken, describing her new wheelchair, must have turned and smiled. But the room was silent until Matt, the leader, said, "Your turn, Kira." She shyly introduced herself, then nursed her shame while the room moved on. She listened to their voices carefully. Some were old, some young; she fell somewhere in the middle at thirty-two.

After her clumsy introduction, Kira stayed silent, but had to admit she felt slightly better after the ninety minutes. Some of these people were so damn positive that they sparkled, even to the blind. And here's a bonus, Matt said before Kira left with her ride: she didn't have to stack chairs, since she couldn't see them. She was sure he was smiling when he delivered the good news. She smiled, too.

The next week they talked about independence; inspired,

Kira attempted the voice typing programs from work. Tears flowed; she couldn't remember where she put the tissues, and finally found them next to her pillow, when she climbed into bed.

The next week they talked about unwelcome advice. Kira shared for the first time, describing how people always recommend carrots because they're "good for the eyes." She could tell they were laughing. She laughed, too. After the meeting, three of them invited her to the bar. They guided her to and from the booth, and someone drove her home.

The next week they talked about support. The next week they talked about post-traumatic stress. The next week, the girl in the wheelchair (Anita) brought up sex.

"I'm not paralyzed down here," she said. Kira imagined Anita gesturing between her legs. "I used to turn heads. But now," Anita said, "people try *not* to look at me."

Kira added, much more chatty now than the first few weeks, "At least you can tell. For all I know I'm getting checked out constantly, and missing out." Everyone chuckled loudly for her benefit.

Anita sighed. "Am I ever going to get laid again?"

"For me," said Beto from the far right side of the room, "I'm afraid to have sex again. I feel like, with these scars all over me . . . it'll crush me to see pity on their faces."

"What you need to do," said Anita, "is have sex with one of us. We already know you."

"Pick me," said Kira. "I'll never see your scars."

"You'd feel them," said Beto, "and I can see *your* face. And anyway, I'm gay."

"Damn," said Kira. "You sound hot." They laughed.

Bruce piped up quietly from the right. "Anyone thought about . . . hiring someone? Just to get out the jitters? Like losing your virginity again?"

He continued, "I'm thinking about it. I've got the eye patch, and girls always want to see under it, and someone I pay never would."

Matt the leader, himself disabled with a near-useless leg, said, "I would like, maybe, to live out fantasies I never thought I could have."

Kira couldn't see any of their faces, but surely they could tell she was thinking, hard. Later at the bar (after Kira heckled her friends while they put away chairs), Anita said, "I could smell wood burning from your deep thoughts about sex. Out with it."

Kira knew she was blushing. And looked down on habit, though it changed nothing for her.

"You got me thinking . . . I actually always wanted to be blindfolded." She let out a sad, sarcastic chuckle. She pointed to her face. "No blindfold needed."

"Now that's seeing the positive," said Matt. "I thought I could try BDSM and maybe carry a special cane in my cane."

"Or a flogger inside the cane," said Beto.

"I'd love to do that," said Matt. "I'd feel in control even if no one ever knew it."

"Do it, man," said Beto.

"Let's all come up with something to do," said Anita. "Then we can report back."

"I know what I'm gonna do," said Beto. "I'm gonna hire a guy to lick every single one of these scars."

Anita sounded like she shrugged when she said, "I'd do it for free, you know that."

"I. Am. Gay."

"Doesn't mean I can't lick you." She nudged Kira's other arm. "You're spot on, Kira. He's hot."

Kira smiled. "Did I just actually hear an eyeroll?"

"Stop changing the subject, Anita. What are you gonna do?"

"Hmm," she said. Kira could hear her long nails tap the table. "I want my legs over some guy's shoulders. I want my legs in super high heels, all over the place."

"What's yours, Kira? Just a fake blindfold? Cheap."

Kira tried for blank face. "I have some ideas."

"Girl, I'm your driver," said Beto. "You're not getting home unless you spill it all."

Kira wouldn't see their faces when she told them. What did it matter, anyway?

"Once I was with two different guys in one night. But they didn't know each other or anything, it wasn't like—"

"So you want two guys at once," said Anita.

"I get it," said Beto. "I always say, I have two holes for a reason."

"But," Kira said slowly, "I have three."

She felt a silent beat. Surprise? Simple math calculations? An exchanged look she'd never know about?

"Damn," said Matt.

"Why not?" said Beto.

"Do it," said Anita.

"I could have died," Kira said. "And after, I wished I had. I don't anymore, thanks to you three. But if we're alive, we've got to *live*. Right?"

"Right," they all said at once. For the first time, Kira was inspiring *them*.

"A month," said Anita. "Enough time to get ourselves off?"

Kira nodded and realized they must have been, too. Sometimes they still forgot to speak out loud. But her three friends all piled hands on hers, to show solidarity. She put her other hand on top and so did they. She squeezed. "We're going to live," she said. "No," she corrected herself. "We're going to live *well*."

* * *

"I want this easy," she said, when she met with the three escorts beforehand. "I don't want names, even your fake ones."

"We get it," said the first man. His blob looked a little taller than the other two. "It's not about that."

Kira cocked her head, thinking. "What exactly do you think this is about?"

He paused. "I think it's about good sex—great sex—with four senses instead of five. Comfort in being played with without the control that comes with seeing it happening. And when that pleasures you, you'll own your disability."

She smiled. "I gotta pay you for therapy, too?"

"You'd be surprised," he said. "We're therapists as much as we are escorts."

They decided the men would be called X, Y, and Z, when she had to call them anything at all.

Kira thought hard about the setting. It wasn't part of the fantasy; she was always in her very own personal darkness. What Kira wanted most was a setting she couldn't predict—the exact opposite of what she tried to create at home. She wanted to be immersed in foreignness. Let space be the wild card.

So X, Y, and Z chose a hotel. She wouldn't know whether the bathroom was on the left or right, whether there were mints on the pillow or roaches under the footstools. Why even pretend it made a difference?

Kira described to Anita the clothes she wanted—satin swing dress, sheer bra, low heels, and thong underwear—but didn't want to know what colors her friend picked. Her pleasure wouldn't lie in that. It would lie in the chill on her skin, the swish of the skirt, the click of the heel. Kira was going to jump headfirst into what senses she had.

XYZ, as she'd come to think of them, arrived on time; Kira

made it to the door without bumping into anything. Funny: they didn't comment on her appearance. They, too, knew it didn't matter tonight. Instead Z said, "You smell good." And one of them placed her hand on his arm, and off they went to a limousine.

In the car, Kira sat on the lap of one man and spread her legs out on another, while the third leaned across to kiss her. By the end of the ten-minute drive her arms clutched his broad shoulders, and six hands roamed her body. Kira felt every one of those thirty fingers: each seemed to have an electrical pulse all their own. She didn't need to, but she closed her eyes, and gave in to touch, and the sound of breath.

When the car stopped, XYZ righted her, and helped her straight to an elevator, where it dinged five times before they led her out and right, right again, then left. A door clicked open, and they walked to what could have been the center, the corner, or the closet. It was dark enough that Kira perceived no blobs; she kicked off her shoes and thick carpet embraced her toes. The heater faintly hummed. That hum, her breath, and her feet were all that anchored her.

XYZ were either robots or well-timed, because they each ran one hand over her simultaneously. Kira's back and both her arms tingled; one pair of hands pulled her in for a kiss. Another mouth found her neck, and another found her breast through the thin fabrics. The endless hands got her dress off easily and quickly, and turned her from man to man, kiss to kiss, tongue to tongue. She was just dizzy enough to stop tracking her space, twisted and wanton and nurtured at the same time. Her bra came off slowly, straps first, then cups pulled down where two mouths grazed her nipples as the bra was undone. The mouths were random, uncoordinated. It was impossible to predict when or where they would bite, or suck, or switch with a hand.

Kira's own hands had at once too much and not enough to touch. She was forever left wanting because she couldn't predict any placement. She was always reaching, but she didn't know what she would hold when she touched skin. Eventually, she stopped trying to replace her sight. What if she just sat within the senses she retained?

Touch was obvious; touch was unavoidable. But she could hear endless breath, skin sliding on skin, the pop and moisture of sucking, and so many moans like atonal melody. Kira could smell her own arousal, her own rose perfume, and a slight mint on the air above the masculine scent around her. For the first time since the accident, Kira felt full. Not lacking. Complete as she was.

As hands and mouths reached lower, Kira's own hands learned the men's topography, her hips bounced, pinball-like, from X to Y to Z. The men weren't the same height, so she writhed against different parts of each of them. One of them—X, she guessed— was just the right height for his cock to line up perfectly; they could fuck right there standing up, no problem. She found herself on tiptoes when she pushed against the other men. When she faced one, her ass faced another. Desire supported her from every side. They closed in. She became nothing but sensation.

Before long XYZ picked her up and rested her on a mattress. Kira couldn't feel the edge—who knew, and who cared, if she was diagonal, or this bed was gigantic, or this wasn't a bed at all. Y took her mouth with his, X took her nipples in his hands and tongue, and Z lifted her legs and licked his way from thighs to pussy. Z's fingers threatened, but didn't quite reach inside her yet. Kira arched her back for more, one arm each around Y and X. One of Y's hands reached up to grab and pull at her hair. At that same moment, X bit one nipple and pinched the other, and Z pushed two fingers inside her, tongue never slowing.

Kira came within seconds, surprising herself since it usually took her much longer—three times as long, in fact. All four of her senses had sharpened to a point. Her moans magnified, harmonized with theirs. The cotton blanket under her was a trillion threads massaging her back. She writhed under endless skin, the men's tenderness waxing as she rode back down in their care.

As she settled, moans faded and condoms opened. Kira reached out her arms to only air, but for the first time felt no panic. She knew they were still there because she heard them breathing. And she knew they weren't done with her. Content and patient, Kira closed her eyes, and gave in to the darkness forced upon her.

Y flipped Kira to her stomach, and pushed her hair away as he licked down her back. Z pulled her hips up so Y could slide under Kira, who was now on all fours. Y's hands encased her face and dragged her down to his lips, as X settled at her head and Z at her back.

Y took her first. His cock slid easily into her wetness, while his tongue plundered her mouth. He filled her with such force that her hands flew out; X caught them with one hand and her chin with the other. Kira's moans filled X's mouth as Y pumped into her from below. She heard the squeeze of lube and shivered at the cold drip between her ass cheeks as Z massaged her from above. Her tongue swapped rhythms with X while Z pushed a finger into her back hole. Overcome with finally being filled in two places, Kira arched her back and mewed into the black air. X bit her neck as Z stretched her farther, in time with her thrusts onto Y's cock.

On one of Kira's gasps for air, she felt X's thumb at her mouth. On instinct, she sucked it, and heard his groan mingle with Y's below her. He released his thumb with a pop that rang in her ears, and on her next breath, his dick was at her mouth instead. She gulped him in like oxygen, still tasting his mouth as she swirled her tongue around his width and grasped his balls underneath.

Once Kira had established a rhythm with Y and X, Z removed his fingers from her ass, and replaced them, inch by inch, with his cock. Her muffled pleasure was still loud and clear, and they joined her in broadcasting how they each loved where they were. Each time Kira rocked forward, she took X a little deeper; his hands still pulled at her hair, keeping time with her, forward and back. And when she'd gone forward far enough, Z pulled her back onto Y and into him, filling her all the way and gripping her tight. The four of them were connected with Kira as the conduit, the focus and the center and the source of all this pleasure. With what thought she could form, Kira was certain she could never release like this if she could see them all. She'd be thinking, maybe, of how she looked when she moved, if her hand was in the wrong place, if X wanted or didn't want eye contact. This, here, was about her and only her: what she could feel, and what she could make these men feel. She fell into it—no, she jumped into it—and she flew.

Kira rose and rose to a height she thought was orgasm, then higher, and higher yet, until she burst apart with a wince then a yell. She thrust harder in and out and out and in, riding out her pleasure until she shook and trembled. Kira reached around to X's ass cheeks and pulled him deep in her mouth, even less inhibited now that she'd crumbled apart. Her raw moans and squeals around him, plus how deep she took him, made him come with a growl that had her digging in her fingers while the other men's fingers dug into her hips and breasts.

Z came next, filling her even more as he swelled and released. X was smoothing her hair in front while Z reached feverish deep thrusts in back. When Z came, he grabbed her hips so tightly Kira knew these were bruises she'd planned for, and would be happy to remember.

X and Z kept hands on her even after they pulled out, spent and panting. Kira took Y to the hilt over and over, as she kissed and rubbed hands across his chest. He pulled her in to nip at her neck. Until now, there had been no talking; but in her ear he spoke then, deep and ragged. "The way you moan, the way you smell. The way you touch us. The way your pussy tastes. You're beautiful, Kira." Even while floating off on a pleasure cloud, she got his meaning. Her beauty, to them tonight, had nothing to do with sight either. She moaned back into his ear, clutched his shoulders hard, and picked up the pace. Y came with a grunt, feeling her aftershocks. He nipped her neck again as Z and X pulled her up and turned her over, cleaning her off and licking her gently. She put out her hands and caught two chins; a third leaned in to meet her cheek. "Thank you," she whispered. "I feel . . . whole. I feel . . . lucky. This kind of surrender, I got to have it, because of what I lost. Thank you."

XYZ squeezed her with their hands, and each gave a last kiss on her cheek before tucking Kira under the soft sheets. She knew they had left her a voicemail telling her everything she needed to know about her location. Safe, spent, and satiated, Kira slept for the first time free of that fist around her heart. The fist that swore nothing good would ever come of her life again. That the loss of sight was only pain. And here she was, holding what she could never have understood before: deep within her loss, she gained. She wondered before she fell asleep whether it was she, or the others, who were dis-abled. She had access to so much that they didn't.

* * *

Kira and her friends hadn't revisited their pact all month; they gave each other space to sort out their own journeys. But those four weeks later at the bar, they were each ready to share.

Matt did indeed procure a hollow cane, in which he hid a small crop. He had such a good time with his new submissive that he was planning to learn more from her. He even talked about having different canes for different crops. There was a lightness to his talk about these plans: Matt now had control over a part of his life that his bum leg could never take from him.

Beto's confidence was soaring, after spending time with several men who worshipped his scars. He learned that several scars were highly sensitive, even erogenous. As if in a new body—and in a way he was—he was learning it could work for, instead of against, him.

Anita was practicing being more verbally proactive in bed. But she also indulged in a photo shoot of her legs, a series of beautiful shoes in beautiful, erotic positions. She started a collection of "fuck-me heels" that made her legs feel sexy even when they didn't touch the ground. And was working on a website to display these new poses proudly.

When it was Kira's turn, she took a deep breath. "I won't lie; I wish I could see. But there is plenty of pleasure in a world without sight. Sometimes, even *more* pleasure. There's so much wonder in what we can't see. When I could see, I didn't even know that wonder was there."

Kira put her hand out, and her friends put theirs on top.

"So," she said with a sideways smile, "what's our next challenge?"

SNIP, SNIP

Misty Stewart

His breath was warm against her cheek, arms strong, encircling her from behind. A solidity she could rely upon. Right now, with her heart beating so fast she could near taste it at the thought of what was to come, she needed that anchor.

She met his eyes in the bathroom mirror, the two of them together in the glass.

"Ready, Beth?" he said, voice seductive by her ear.

She nodded, not trusting herself to speak. She wasn't sure she was ready for anything, but she was doing this anyway.

He ran a hand through her hair. Long, blonde. The one physical attribute she'd always been proud of, even back in her turbulent adolescent years when hating everything else about herself had been commonplace. Back in high school, several years behind them now, her hair had been the envy of all their friends and even Caleb said back then how much he liked it. She hadn't cut it since, though it'd been far less fashionable once she got to university. It was too much a part of her, too embedded in who she was. Even if these days, at almost twenty-five, it inevitably got in the way and she always wore it tied up in a messy bun.

As she watched in the mirror, he wound her hair hard around his fist, then pulled suddenly tight, yanking her head back. She cried out at the shooting pain, arching helpless in his hold and gasping fast breaths. Vulnerable to his dark smile and that hungry spark in his eyes she could see in the mirror. She loved it when he held her strong like this, like he'd never let her go. When he looked at her like he did now, predatory and needful and full of lust.

When he let her hair drop again, releasing her without warning, it fell to her waist. Effortless blonde locks with enough kink to make things interesting. Herself all over, really. Caleb, too.

He pressed his lips to her earlobe. "Tell me the safeword."

"Game over."

"Last chance to call it before we start. It'll stop things once we're in, but it can't undo what's already been done."

She shook her head. She knew the stakes. "The decisions are yours." She turned in his arms. "I want it to be up to you. I'm in your hands."

His sharp intake of breath was subtle, but there. That slight widening of his eyes. His desire flared when she gave him such power. He loved it. And she loved that he loved it. The control he took. That she wanted him to take.

They'd never been like this back in high school. Those days, fumbling innocent kisses had been the extent of it. But the four or five years apart while in university had taught them both a lot, given them time to try out other people. And other things. Given them each a chance to grow up a bit before coming back together as adults.

And boy, had Caleb grown up. Broad shoulders and a swim-mer's physique, with a journalist's sharp, enquiring mind and a genuine self-assurance he'd only pretended to as a kid. Which she still didn't have even now. Sometimes it felt like he'd outstripped her in these last eight or nine years, while she floundered around still trying to figure out who she was in life.

He gave her a dark, wolfish grin. Ran a hand over her hair like a possession. "You got it, sweetheart."

From somewhere beyond the bathroom sounded a knock. A structured rat-a-tat-tat from the vicinity of the front door. He took her hand, winding his fingers through her own, and led her into the hallway.

But before they reached the door, he pushed her instead into the living room.

"In there," he said. An order. "Now."

She obeyed without hesitation, never able to resist the rough command in his voice. Her palms sweaty, she absently playing with her hair while she waited for him to answer the door, but was unable to make out the low murmur of voices once he had. He had the fire burning strong already, so there was a pleasant warmth to the comfortable room. She put another log on it anyway to ensure it wouldn't die down too soon and so she had something to do with her hands. There was too much energy in her limbs for her to sit on the long couch, pushed back to make room on the rug before the fire. Winter's cool sunlight filtered in from behind curtains already closed.

A room prepared. He'd put thought into this. She straight-ened from feeding the fire, smoothed down her pale green blouse, and fixed her knee-length, dark brown skirt. It brushed against her bare buttocks underneath. No underwear. She'd put thought into this too.

She waited, wiping those clammy palms against her hips.

The crackle of a log falling in the fireplace accentuated the silence and just how little she could hear of whatever was being discussed outside the room. But finally the living room door slid open and Caleb came in, showing another person in after him.

A woman. Beth's breath caught. This was a woman she'd only ever seen before across a crowded room, but one she'd long stared at.

Delia.

Tall, brunette, sharp pixie cut. Black leather all over. Gloves to her elbows, tightened corset emphasizing every delicious curve and black boots going all the way up, to be lost beneath a close-fitting black skirt.

Beth couldn't help the way her body warmed. It was hard to resist the urge to go down on her knees right then and there. Delia had dressed the way she did for the club where she'd so captured Beth's attention and where Beth would gaze unwittingly, but never get up the courage to introduce herself. She'd always loved leather.

Delia didn't greet her. Delia didn't even look her in the eyes. Instead, the tall woman strode into the room and walked straight up to Beth with one eyebrow raised and an appraising expression raking her over head to toe. Judgment made obvious. Beth froze, caught in the other woman's sights, feeling desperately underdressed in her simple cotton skirt, yet way too overdressed at the same time. Delia took her time, walking around her in a circle, behind, to the side, pausing in front and cocking her head as if critiquing a tool, a piece of furniture, an object.

Beth let her eyes drop. How could a mere gaze turned on her bring such heat to her body? How could a look and an attitude alone push her into such a hot, panting mess? She had never understood her own desires, though at least since reuniting with Caleb she'd stopped fighting them. It'd taken her a long time to stop feeling scared of herself and learn to embrace who she was. Or start to, at least.

Delia completed the full circle around her, before glancing back to Caleb.

"Do you mind if I touch?" she asked him, clinical in every way.

"Go right ahead," he said.

The woman's leather-gloved hands took hold of her hips. Beth's bones near melted at that alone, except the woman held her still. She hardly dared to breathe, let alone allow her knees to fold under her. Those hands rose up her sides, palms firm against her waist, ranging along her ribs, the sides of her breasts. Lingering with intent while Beth didn't move or look up, unable to meet the woman's sharp, penetrating eyes. She stared instead at the leather of the other woman's corset, tight-laced, with glinting silver catches. Tried not to wish the hands at her breasts, caressing gloved fingers across her nipples, would pull her in harder and crush her against those leather-clad curves.

Delia did not do that. She simply continued her inspection, hands ranging higher, leaving Beth's breasts and moving over her shoulders, up her neck. Beth leaned her head back automatically, so the gloved hands curled about her throat. She willed them to tighten, needing to feel this sensual woman's power and control in a way that burned her from the inside out. But Delia didn't stop there, instead pushing her hands further, winding them through her hair and scraping her fingers against Beth's scalp, until she was shivering with it.

Holding her by the hair, Delia leaned forward, lips by her ear but not quite touching. "Safeword?"

It took Beth a moment to find her voice. "Game over."

"Caleb stays in the room. Ask for him if you need to." The

woman pulled back and met her eyes directly for the first time, with a dark twist of her perfectly painted blood-red lips. "But you're in my hands now, little one."

Beth gasped. Delia only smiled and held out Beth's long hair, letting it run through her fingers, before suddenly turning her back and stalking away, leaving Beth unbalanced with want.

Caleb brought in a large leather bag from the hall and put it on the side table; Delia must have brought it with her, the equipment of her profession. She might be dressed for the club they all frequented by night, but by day she ran her own business. A salon. The woman went to the bag, stripping off those fine leather gloves that had caused such a frisson along Beth's skin, to reveal long fingers with red-painted nails. She pulled implements out of the bag. Flashing silver, sharp and menacing.

From the bottom of the bag, a tablet. Delia and Caleb conferred over it, swiping through images on the screen, comparing and contrasting and discussing each, ignoring Beth entirely. From where she stood there was no way for her to see what they were looking at.

"I'd suggest something like this," Delia said, one painted nail lingering on the tablet.

"No. More like this one." Caleb tapped the screen, pulling up something else. "That's what I want for her."

Delia's fine eyebrows raised. "That's a radical change," she said and Beth's stomach turned over at the woman's mild hesitation. "Don't get me wrong, I like it. But your girl might not."

Caleb was unmoved. "It's my decision. Not hers. That's what I want."

Beth's chest was so tight it was hard to pull in enough breath. She stared at Caleb wide-eyed, but when he finally glanced her way his return gaze was hard, dark. Not giving an inch. Her knees quivered at that look in him, wanting to throw herself at his feet and let him take everything, let him take her. Give in to it all.

Yet even still the words were almost at her lips. *Game over.* Her hand at her hair, fingers shaking. Perhaps this was too much, too big a step. Perhaps she would falter partway in or struggle to know herself afterward. It wasn't like she fully understood her own need for this; she'd never been able to make any sense of herself. Desiring this and frightened of it at the same time. Wanting it all the more because it frightened her so.

Delia shut down the tablet with a dark smile. Caleb fetched a dining room chair. They pulled away the rug, leaving only the polished floorboards beneath their feet. Caleb plonked the chair down in the middle of the room. Then he took her by the arm and pushed her into it with real force. She sat with a thump.

He crouched in front of her, running his hands up the outside of her thighs, grounding her with a touch.

"Still with us, girl?" he said and she nodded, gripping at the chair's seat on either side of her thighs. "Anything you'd like to say?"

She pressed her lips together and shook her head, as firm in gesture as he was in tone. He grinned and caught the hem of her skirt, pushing it up her thighs and tugging it out from under her so her bare buttocks were against the cool wooden seat. She tried to press her thighs together, as if that would help conceal the urgent need between her legs, but he didn't let her get away with that. He forced her thighs apart, holding her open and exposed.

"Do not move," he commanded, then stood up, leaving her gasping and on edge. Her skirt barely covered any of her. Her hands gripped the chair, but she didn't close her legs, no matter how wanton or vulnerable or exposed it made her to be displayed so openly before them.

"She's all yours, Delia," Caleb said. "She won't move. She knows better than to disobey me."

"She is a sweet little thing," Delia said. "Wet as fuck already, I see."

His grin was dangerous. "Beth loves it when someone takes control away from her. Fortunately for her, I love to take it."

He caressed her cheek almost gently. She leaned into the touch, him standing tall above her on one side, Delia on the other, the two of them crowding her in. She tilted her head back as he ran his hand through her hair, stretching out the length of it, those beautiful blonde locks she'd always prided herself upon.

Caleb held out her hair, while Delia picked up her scissors.

The first cut came slow, even loud. Beth uttered a small cry with it. Gripping onto the hard wood beneath her bare thighs while the length was cut away. Her identity, her sense of self. If Caleb hadn't been standing so close, the surety of him giving her courage, she'd have given way to a rising anxiety in her chest. With the leather-clad Delia close on her other side, she was trapped between them with no chance to move or pull away.

They held the control. They held the power. Her fears faded in the face of it.

Something clicked inside her; her anxiety dissipated as she put herself in their hands. Trusting Caleb, and this woman he'd brought to her, Delia, entirely, made her ability to resist slip away and her limbs weak for the need inside her.

Each cut, each snip of hair, brought blonde chunks falling to the floor. They fell across her shoulders, down her front. She didn't move; Caleb had ordered her not to and it was increasingly impossible to even consider denying him. With each lock of hair cut away, she slipped further into the headspace she craved so hard, trusting him to take it from there as she lost herself to his commands.

After the first few snips, Caleb stepped back to let Delia have space to work, but he stayed within her field of vision, so she could always see him there. Her eyes held on him, an anchor, the only fixed point in a floating world. He sat across the room, watching with dark, hooded eyes filled with his own enjoyment and need. His own breathless wonder. She was his girl, to be remade to his choices, his taste. She held his gaze as Delia worked so he would know that, feeling her own burn down low to be made the object of his lusts.

Was that why she got off so hard on having her hair cut off? On giving up all choice about something she'd so long clung to? The ultimate act of control. Her head began to feel weightless. The hair was still falling over her front, her back; there had been no gown wrapped over her shoulders, just as there was no mirror before her to see what was being done. This was no salon and she was no customer. They took her hair, Caleb choosing it, Delia doing it, and her body trembled with the heat rising inside her for them to do so. A wetness dripping between her legs, snip by snip.

As her head felt light, Delia stood back to survey her work. The woman glanced at Caleb with eyebrows raised.

"Yes?"

His eyes raked over her, considering. "Oh, yes. Delia, you're a master with scissors."

"Mistress, please." Delia's fingers on her head scratched across her scalp, the long painted nails sending a shiver down Beth's bones. "Not quite done yet. But the poor girl is covered in cutoffs."

Caleb's grin turned dark. "I'll deal with that."

He came over to crouch in front of her, brushing hair from her shoulders, arms, and bare thighs with firm hands. Then he was undoing the buttons on her blouse and pushing it over her shoulders, while Delia's fingers ran through her now shortened hair. Beth gulped as Caleb pulled the blouse down her back so it trapped her arms in place, pinning them behind her. Her skirt was pushed even further up, over her hips, until she was all but naked before him, eyes wide and panting, vulnerable and exposed.

His hands caressed her bare belly, her thighs, her breasts, pinching the nipples suddenly hard. She cried out, clenching her teeth against the volume of it, her need spiking with the sensation.

"She likes pain," Delia noted, from above.

"She does," Caleb said, squeezing harder until she whimpered. "She also loves her hair being pulled. I trust that's still possible?"

"Of course." A hand went through her hair. "Just do it like this. Close to the scalp." And the hand gripped so hard Beth cried out, her head pulled back in the vice grip of the leather-clad woman above.

Delia held her head back as Caleb kissed each of her abused nipples in turn, flicking them with his tongue. Soft and wet sensation to contrast to the hard, sharp pain he'd inflicted on them before, which Delia still inflicted even now on her scalp. The woman continued to hold her head as Caleb kissed his way down her belly, yanking her hips toward him. Her thighs were already forced open for him as his tongue traced its slow way down, further down, right to the center of her. She was naked and made to keep still, unable to move, unable to stop him, and . . . and . . .

And holy fuck, but his tongue on her clitoris nearly brought her to orgasm in an instant. Swirling across each contour of her, licking strong with a sure knowledge of what she liked and what brought her to an edge so damn quickly. She could barely hold on for the want of it, uttering a half-delirious cry as his tongue pushed deep inside her, while Delia kept pulling back on her hair so painfully, dreadfully hard, keeping her in place while Caleb worked her sex.

She couldn't last, wouldn't last. It would take her in a bare moment. But Delia shifted, pulling her head to the side and holding up her scissors right before Beth's eyes.

"I will finish this cut," the woman said. "And I'd advise you to keep very still. These are sharp and we don't want any accidents, do we?" Delia smoothed a hand over her shortened hair. "That means no orgasms, understand me, little one? You don't get to come until I say so and that means not until I've finished cutting."

Beth uttered a plaintive cry, for how could she do that? How could it even be possible with Caleb so insistent between her legs? She couldn't hold on. But Delia's scissors were back at her hair, snipping loud in her ears even as Caleb's tongue continued to run the length of her, a firm-wet sensation between her legs. Her body trembled, unable to move, arms pinned back. Trying to keep impossibly still and obey, whimpering with each exhale, screwing her eyes shut and hanging on. Holding off climax with everything she had.

While the scissors snipped on, and on, and on, and the burning inside her built higher and higher for it. Snip, snip.

Snip, snip.

"Please," she whispered, words almost impossible to form. Only the snipping sounded in response. "Please, mistress. Please, sir. Please . . . "

But further words were lost and her mind began to float. There was only sensation. Being held tight in place. The pleasure from Caleb's tongue, thorough and skilled. The sound of the scissors forever snipping. The desperate need to give herself

up to others, to their control, their decisions. The world dropping away and only feeling, only sensation, remaining.

A final loud snip.

"Done," the woman said.

The orgasm took her as if she'd been commanded to it,
flooding her limbs in a rocking, pulsing, rolling wave, unable
to think, unable to speak, unable to know. Unable to worry,
unable to question. Only able to feel and ride with the stretched
moment of it.

Gasping as she came down from that high. Slumping in the
chair even as Caleb sat up, wiping his face, smiling. Not his dark,
commanding smile now. His sweet one instead. Well satisfied.

He rested a gentle hand against her cheek.

"Happy, my girl?"

She still wasn't up to forming coherent words yet, so she
just smiled and nodded with exhausted satisfaction and leaned
forward to kiss him, tasting herself on his lips.

When she had strength to move again, he helped her slip her
blouse off so her aching arms were no longer pinned in position.
His fingers rubbed feeling back into her shoulders.

"Would you like to see your new haircut?" he asked.

She managed to find words this time. "Yes, please." Still
breathless, but her grin broadening. "But maybe not yet. Can I
thank our guest first? Can I thank you?"

The glint in his eye turned dark. His lips twisting, pleased
and hungry. "Well. Far be it from me to deny that request."

He reached up an inviting hand to Delia, who put down her
scissors at last and came to join them on the floor.

Hours later, she finally got to see her new haircut.

Standing once more before the bathroom mirror with
Caleb at her back. Each of them clothed again, cleaned up and

satiated. His arms around her, solid and grounding, as he finally let her see her surprise new look.

Long locks gone and with them the safety and comfort of the familiar. The length was something of a revelation: it was so short. So sharp and modern. Undeniably a very cool cut very well done and more fashionable than she'd worn her hair in years. But different. Like nothing she'd ever have chosen for herself.

Who was she, if she wasn't that awkward girl of many years ago, who'd received a compliment or two on her hair and clung to it ever since? Who was this woman in the mirror, now grown up, with her strange kinks and fetishes and needs she couldn't always understand, but neither could she deny? A woman who might retain a sense of identity tied up in a hairstyle and yet get off so hard on having another take it away from her?

How did that make sense? How did she make sense?

A smile twitched at the corners of the mouth of this woman in the mirror. A smile growing on her own face broad and strong. Maybe the new haircut wasn't the real surprise; maybe it was how well it suited her. Maybe it was how little a haircut actually changed anything after all. Whoever she was, she was certainly no longer that awkward girl; she was adult and experienced and growing in self-assurance. She might not entirely know herself yet, but she was going to have fun figuring herself out.

"Okay, sweetheart? Not too much of a shock?" Caleb said, with perhaps a hint of his own nerves. It'd taken him time to accept himself too and sometimes he needed the reassurance from her, just as she needed it from him.

She turned in his arms with a happy shake of the head, new short hair light and flicking.

"Caleb, I love it." She kissed him. "Best haircut ever."

HUMAN
OUTREACH

Adrian Amato

'm an alien prostitute. Whether that means I'm a prostitute for aliens or an alien that's a prostitute is a matter of perspective. For my clients, I'm an alien who is a prostitute. For members of my own species, I'm a prostitute for aliens.

Actually, to both I'm an Extraterrestrial Liaison Officer, or ELO (pronounced "ee-low") for short. Few other humans know what I do for a living. Not all ELOs have sex with aliens.

According to the air force recruitment website: *A career as an Extraterrestrial Liaison Officer (ELO) can provide you with the exciting opportunity to be an integral part of building positive relations with Earth's newest neighbors.*

After ten weeks of the Basic Military Officer Qualification (BMOQ) course you will complete a six-month Extraterrestrial Cultural Education Course (ECEC) at Canadian Forces Base Shilo in Manitoba. After ECEC, you will specialize in either Human Outreach or Cultural Outreach. Human Outreach involves embedment in the daily lives of the Ganni-

*tans, living amongst them, and establishing a positive rapport
with them. Cultural Outreach involves exchanging and partici-
pating in traditional practices with Gannitans and establishing
and maintaining a presence in their cultural institutions. Both
subtrades carry the possibility of deployment to Ranteranan,
the Gannitan home world.*

Not only did I go through basic training to become an alien
prostitute, I get saluted for it because it's an officer position.
Four months into ECEC (pronounced "ee-sec") I had a meeting
with Major Doe to discuss which subtrade I had the intention of specializing in. "There's no delicate way to put this,"
he began before I could get a chance to start in on awkward
chit-chat about the cookie-cutter family framed on his wall.
"Human Outreach involves more . . . um"—he made a circular
fanning motion with his freckled left hand—"intimate aspects
of building relations than you were probably anticipating. Do
you understand?"

"I think so," I said. Heat rose from my heels to my neck like
I was sitting on a vent connected straight to the Earth's core.

"Just to be sure, what do I mean?"

Intimate, a word that can have more than one meaning, but
only one that begs for clarification, requires asking if the other
person *understands,* wink wink, though Major Doe didn't
wink. He didn't even blink. He kind of looked constipated.

"You mean that I'll be fucking them, sir?"

"Yes," Major Doe said.

I tilted my head to the side, looked at the picture on his desk
of him shaking hands with Ranteranan's president.

"I know you're wondering whether I've ever—ahem—*been
with* one of them. I mean on the one hand"—he held up his left
hand, like one side of a broken scale—"I'm a Human Outreach
ELO, but on the other"—here he held up his other hand—"I have

a desk job. I mean, I was a major before I even transferred into this trade. Well, the answer is 'yes,' once. . . . It was quite strange, they have a different way of doing things, but it wasn't unpleasant."

I had no idea what their "different way of doing things" was at the time, but now I know it's gangbangs. They're really into gangbangs, though I suppose to Gannitans they're just regular bangs, because they need three people to reproduce.

Let me give you a rundown on Gannitan reproductive biology. It's absolutely fucked. Don't worry if you don't understand. It took me three lessons and labelled diagrams to get it. Gannitans have two sex-coding chromosomes, just like us, but they have three sexes; TY, TT, and YY. TY Gannitans are what we might consider male, in that they have what we might see as penises and produce what we might call sperm (though theirs is light blue and tastes like the milk left over when you finish a bowl of Froot Loops). However, they are the only ones who pass on their genetic material. They create T- and Y-coding haploid cells. TT Gannitans are what we might consider female, in that they grow fetuses inside their wombs, except these fetuses don't contain any of their genetic material. TT Gannitans have sex with two different TY Gannitans. One of the haploid cells from one TY Gannitan will combine with one of the haploid cells from the other to create either a TY, TT, or YY zygote. YY Gannitans aren't involved in the reproduction process at all, though they still go through puberty and have a sex drive.

To Gannitans, it's kinky just to be one-on-one. It's more intense, more intimate, like a secret. It used to be considered a form of sodomy for them, to have sex with just one person. It's still taboo, incomplete, "promotes unhealthily strong attachment and isolation from society within a codependent coupling."

And that's just the *way* they do it, not to mention the *way they do it.*

For example, they don't do blowjobs, probably because of the big, pointy, tusk-like teeth protruding from their lower jaws. I tried giving a blowjob to two of them once. One liked it and the other seemed bored. One thing that really gets their rocks off that doesn't do anything for me, doesn't even feel like sex, is rubbing the raised bumps of flesh that run in a line down either side of their torsos. Those are sensory receptors for their sense of direction. Gannitans are like walking compasses, attuned to magnetic north. Somehow, they can distinguish its location from magnetic interference. Magnets feel fake they say—metallic, hollow. Magnetic north is richer, mustier, full. According to them Earth's magnetic north feels rusted. I have no idea what that means.

Don't get me wrong, having sex with aliens isn't the only thing I do for a living. I help prepare events, office spaces, and living quarters for Gannitans on Earth, and I do the reverse when I'm deployed on Ranteranan; I help to accommodate humans working and living there within the bounds of what is culturally acceptable to the Gannitans.

I guess that's one thing that separates me from a traditional prostitute. Another is that I'm salaried. I don't get paid per dick or vagina. No matter how many Gannitans I fuck, how much overtime I put in, I get paid the same amount.

I might seem blasé about this now, but I was nervous as hell the first time around. Sex is about communication, and it's hard to communicate effectively when you don't even speak the same language as the person you're doing it with.

That's why I asked for a translator to be there.

A man in camo, a second lieutenant with a nametag that read "Perez," led me to a room down a side hallway on the top floor of the Extraterrestrial Liaison Unit building.

"The most important thing to know is 'chet' means 'stop.' As long as you remember that word, you'll be fine. I'll be there for all the rest, ma'am."

"Just call me Carrie," I told him. "You're about to see me naked; I think we can be on a first-name basis."

"Okay, I'm Juan," he said. He opened the door to a room made up to look like a dimly lit hotel suite, except there was no TV, no indecipherable art on the wall, nowhere to store clothes. I was the entertainment, what they were meant to look at, and if I did my job right, where they put their clothes wouldn't matter.

"Make yourself comfortable, they'll be here in a few minutes," Juan instructed.

I sat on the bed, took off my heels. I wasn't used to wearing heels. I was more used to combat boots, but Major Doe said not to wear the uniform.

I heard footsteps in the hall and wiped my sweaty palms on the cotton bedspread.

The door opened and two Gannitans entered. One was tall and had a big belly, the other was around my height, skinny.

The tall one walked over to me, hand outstretched, and said something in his language.

"I know it is the custom for your people to do this upon their first meeting with someone," Juan translated.

I grabbed the tall Gannitan's hand and shook it firmly. When I let go he said something else.

"May we take our clothes off now?" Juan interpreted.

"Yes," I responded, and Juan repeated it in their language.

They sloughed off their boots, pulled off their shirts, and stepped out of their pants. The tall one was already hard. He placed his hand on my leg, ran it up my thigh, then spoke in a low voice.

"Is this okay?" Juan translated.

"Yes," I responded.

The tall Gannitan reached under my dress with both his hands and slid my underwear down my legs. I pulled my dress up over my head and, looking the tall Gannitan in the eyes, I dropped the bundle of cloth on the floor beside the bed.

He grabbed my waist with one hand while the other slid a finger into me, back and forth, back and forth. So slowly it was infuriating. I bucked my hips into his hand for more purchase.

His fingers were shorter and fatter than human fingers, meatier, softer. Comparatively, human fingers feel skeletal. Ironically, every time I've been fingered by a human since has felt like being prodded by an alien.

He pulled his finger out, then grabbed his cock and pushed it into me, so fast that it made me gasp, but his earnestness was contagious. I wanted it as fast as he'd give it to me. *I want to be used.* I could feel my face burning red at the thought. I didn't usually see sex that way and the women's lib class I took in university reminded me I wasn't *supposed to* think of it that way. But that was really what this was, at the core of it, wasn't it? Even if I liked it, I was being used, used for these Gannitans' pleasure. And besides that, this was a job, and—like any other job—my employer was using me for something. In this case I was being used to build rapport with a new culture. A noble use, I suppose.

The tall Gannitan started thrusting fast right away, his belly slapping against my legs. He gripped onto my hips and I bunched up the bedspread in my fists. Just as I was getting close, he pulled out. That's one thing I'll never get used to. The way Gannitans like to tease their lovers. I can never just get an easy O with them.

Not even five seconds after the tall Gannitan pulled out, the shorter one was putting his cock inside me. This one stared into my eyes, unblinkingly. At first it was unnerving. I felt like an object under scrutiny, especially since his eyes were a piercing orange color unlike his companion's green ones. But then he leaned down and pressed the space between his tusks to my forehead, and I felt seen instead of watched, warmed instead of burnt by his fiery eyes, connected to him beyond the barriers of language. I reached up and wrapped my arms around his back.

"He said he wants you to run your hands up and down his side," Juan said. I was so focused on the eyes in front of me that I hadn't even noticed the Gannitan saying anything. It was hard for me to distinguish their foreign language from their grunting and moaning. I wished we could do this without speaking, without having a nonparticipating observer there repeating bedroom talk in a monotone devoid of sensuality. I wondered if they'd trained him to speak like that when translating, or if the Gannitans just didn't have as much inflection in their language.

I looked over to Juan. His uniform couldn't camouflage his erection. I locked eyes with him and smiled as I ran my hands up and down the raised bumps on the Gannitan's sides. The Gannitan groaned loudly and fucked me harder. Then he pulled out and the other one came at me again. This happened five or six times. They would fuck me just long enough for me to start getting close, then they would stop and switch. Toward the end I could feel that they were getting close too. Their sweaty palms left prints on my sides, their cocks twitched inside me, pressing up for a torturously miniscule moment against that sweet spot.

"Please just let me come," I said.

"Um, hold on a second, I need to think how to translate that . . ." Juan paused before continuing. I had a sudden urge to laugh. I hadn't even meant to say it, but was that not one of the common phrases taught in Gannitan Language 101? I feel like it should be, because anyone who bottoms for a pair of Gannitans will surely think it.

The skinny Gannitan grunted in response to Juan's translation and kept going. I wrapped my legs around him to make sure he didn't go anywhere. He grabbed my hips and pumped even harder. It would have been too much if I wasn't already so close. He was partially lifting me off the bed, his grip on my hips so tight I couldn't move them to his rhythm. Normally, I like to be able to thrust with my partner, but the way he took control was freeing. It allowed me to just lie back and hold on to him for the ride. I couldn't keep my eyes open and locked to his anymore as I felt my whole body tighten around his. He kept going as I came and writhed against him. I felt his cock spasm inside me as he slowed down. When he pulled out, I was wet and sticky with his come. Then the tall Gannitan grabbed my legs and placed them on his broad shoulders. For a moment he was unmoving inside me. He hummed and closed his eyes, riding the aftershocks of my orgasm still pulsing around his cock. Then he thrust hard into me a few times before groaning loudly and saying something.

"Thank you," Juan translated as the Gannitan pulled his cock out of me.

The two Gannitans got dressed slowly and lazily before leaving, pausing to talk between themselves. Juan said they were talking about what to get for dinner. The skinny one wanted to try shawarma.

"Looks like you're having a *hard* time there," I said to Juan as the door closed behind the Gannitans. I hadn't gotten dressed. I was wearing nothing but the lacy red bra the Gannitans hadn't removed.

"Sorry," he said, covering his crotch with his hands.

"Don't be sorry," I said. "You just watched a hot girl get

fucked. Your dick doesn't know I'm a superior officer. I take it as a compliment, really."

He let his hands fall back to his sides.

I got up and walked over to him. The Gannitans' come ran down my leg.

He had a strong jawline and deep brown eyes. He'd recently been on vacation somewhere warm; his skin was bronzed and glowing. Sweat beaded on his upper lip.

I took his hand and placed it on my breast. He swallowed, leaned forward, and touched his forehead to mine. His breathing was shaky. I had no intention of having sex with the translator when I'd asked for one to be there, but now I really wanted to.

I reached back and undid the clasp on my bra. His hand was now the only thing holding it to me. He moved his hand and let the bra fall to the floor at our feet.

I pulled him back toward the bed, let myself fall backward into it. He stood over me, unzipped his pants. He looked away from my face, at my crotch where the Gannitans' sky-blue come was oozing out of me as he pulled his cock out and pumped it a few times with his hand.

"Turn around," he said.

I flipped over.

"Let me know if I'm being too rough," he said.

"I will," I affirmed.

He slid his cock into me, thrusting slowly at first, not putting all of it in. He ran his fingers across my back, then his nails. He dug them in. He went deeper into me. The way his nails were running up and down my back tickled a bit, electrifying all the nerves in my body.

"Mm," I said.

"Yeah, you can take it, can't you?" He grabbed my arms, held them down.

"I can take it all," I said.

He was going all the way in with every thrust now, speeding up.

I could feel my pussy getting tighter around his cock. This surprised me because I'd never come more than once during sex. But I'd also never been fucked by more than one person at a time, and never turned someone on so much that even the risk of losing their career couldn't keep them from wanting me. I would be lying if I said the risk didn't turn me on, that this had to be fast and furtive for the possibility that that door could swing open and we'd be caught.

"You gonna come again?" he asked as I bunched the sheets up in my fists.

"Yes," I said.

"Yeah, come for me."

"Yes," I said again, then I said it again and again and again as I came around his cock.

His voice was shaky as he asked, "Can I come inside you?"

"Please," I said.

And he did.

Afterward he waited while I cleaned myself up in the bathroom attached to the mock hotel room.

I didn't see Second Lieutenant Perez again until three years later at a mess dinner on Ranteranan. By then he was Lieutenant Perez and he was married. He introduced me to his wife as an old friend. She smiled at me like she knew, a little too big, like she was on the verge of giggling, but otherwise she was nothing but polite.

I like my job and I'm not ashamed of it, but if any human ever asks what I do for a living I just tell them I'm an officer in the Canadian Armed Forces. Humans don't get it. Prostitution is still illegal on most of Earth, and where it's legal it's not seen as a favorable occupation. But my job is necessary and fulfilling. It helps to build a connection between two exceedingly different cultures. We don't speak the same language or even really eat the same food, but sex is something we share. The overwhelming majority of us like sex, and sex builds bonds. When two cultures that are as different as ours come together there can be a lot of tension, even war, if we can't find something to bind us together. You're much less likely to make war with a culture if the people in your military and government and society in general have intimate bonds with the people in their military. You're just not going to want to fight them if you're getting into bed with them. That's why my job is a military occupation. It's part of not only national, but international defense, more directly even than most. So, no, I don't feel weird when I'm saluted for being an alien prostitute.

HER NEXT
ADVENTURE

Lucy Eden

I

"Yes," I replied in a low voice. "Table for one." I swallowed nervously before taking a deep breath, squaring my shoulders, lifting my chin, and striding with what I hoped looked like confidence after the host led me to an empty table in the restaurant in this luxury five-star resort that I was dining in, alone.

I wasn't supposed to be alone, but of course, when I'd spent months researching beautiful island getaways before settling on The Sterling Beachfront Paradise, I had no idea that my husband was planning to leave me for our marriage counselor. The vacation had been her idea. It was supposed to reignite the spark that had extinguished in our relationship. I wondered if she thought Mark would bring her instead of me, once he dropped the bombshell that he was destroying the life that we'd spent twenty-six years building.

"You're just not exciting anymore, Kat. I need adventure and passion."

Well, what's more adventurous and exciting than hopping on a plane and jetting off to a tropical paradise alone, Mark?

I was also wearing a two-piece bathing suit, something that terrified me despite my daughter's insistence that my body was "sick" due to a diligent thrice-weekly Pilates routine, which was apparently a good thing. I was determined to enjoy myself on this trip, though any competent therapist would tell me that running away from my problems wasn't the answer, I didn't have a competent therapist. I had a shitty one.

"Your table, ma'am." The host pulled out a seat for me. My table was perched close to the edge of the cliff where the resort sat and overlooked the ocean. The view was so beautiful I could weep, but I'd done enough of that over the past few months.

"Thank you," I replied and slowly lowered myself into the seat. He nodded and turned to leave. "Excuse me!" I called to his retreating figure.

"Yes, ma'am?" He raised an eyebrow.

"May I have two dirty gin martinis with extra olives?"

"Certainly. Will someone be joining you?"

"No," I said, maintaining eye contact.

"Very well," he replied with an amused expression and headed toward the entrance to the restaurant. I heard a deep chuckle over my shoulder that made me instinctively turn.

A pair of gorgeous golden-brown eyes greeted me. They were attached to a man with an equally gorgeous golden-brown face. He had salt-and-pepper hair and a dazzling smile. He was aiming the smile at me. My throat went dry. I answered his smile with one of my own before quickly turning back to stare at the ocean.

It had been quite a while, and I was a bit out of practice, but I was quite sure that man might have been interested . . . in me. I turned around again to be sure, and there he was, still smiling at me. My heart began to race. He motioned for me to join him at his table. I hesitated for a moment. Then I wondered what an exciting and adventurous woman would do in this situation.

"Hello," I said as I sank into the chair opposite the first man I'd flirted with in almost thirty years. "I'm Katherine, and you are?"

"Henrí," he said in a delicious accent that I couldn't place. Was it Italian, Portuguese—"French." He gave me a knowing smile. Was I that transparent? "And where are you from, Katherine?" The way he said my name made things happen in my chest and between my thighs that I thought didn't happen anymore. I wondered if I'd just had my first hot flash.

"I'm from the US."

"Where in the US?"

"Um, New York." I kept smiling while willing someone, anyone, to materialize holding two martinis. "So, are you on vacation?"

"Isn't everyone?" Henrí chuckled softly. "Yes, my wife and I love this resort. We come here at least three or four times a year. Ah! Perfect timing," he called to the approaching server carrying a tray laden with four drinks. I recognized half of them as mine.

I grabbed one and lifted it to my mouth, not caring how I might look, attempting to down the entire thing while I processed his last sentence. He insisted on adding my martinis to his tab, and I didn't stop him. He watched in mild amusement as I succeeded in draining my glass.

"*Mon dieu,*" he said. "I see why you ordered two."

"I'm sorry," I cleared my throat, trying to speak past the burning in my chest from the gin and rampant global infidelity. Was any man faithful these days? "Did you say you were married?"

"*Oui.*" He nodded as if I'd just asked him what time it was.

"And your wife is here?"

"*Oui*." His smile widened. "Here she is now."

I turned to look in the direction he pointed. My breath caught in my throat at the sight of the tall, voluptuous, equally golden-brown-skinned woman wearing a white bathing suit approaching the table. She was wearing an oversized sun hat on top of waist-length braids that were black tipped with purple.

She didn't look surprised to see another woman sitting at a table with her husband. She looked amused, making me more confused and uncomfortable.

"Is this for me?" She reached for the fourth cocktail on the table, something pink with a wedge of lime. I was surprised to hear an American accent.

"Of course, my love," her husband replied warmly before kissing her on the lips.

II

"Hello." The wife giggled and turned toward me. "I'm Mina, but you can call me Mimi. You have to forgive my husband. He forgets how to act in the presence of beautiful women." She patted Henrí's stubbled cheek.

I smiled nervously but didn't speak. Her compliment made my cheeks warm with heat. Mina wasn't young, but she was certainly younger than I was. Her body was like a work of art. She was beautiful in a way that was indescribable and unattainable. She also knew it. No wonder the sight of another woman pretending to have an eighth of the confidence she possessed naturally didn't bother her.

"My apologies," he said with a mischievous smile. "Katherine, allow me to introduce you to my clever wife, Mina. Mina, Katherine is also from New York."

"Really? We live on the Upper East Side." Her eyes lit up. "Where are you?"

"Well, I grew up in Harlem, but I got married and moved to Elmsford. I'm considering moving back to Manhattan, though." I felt like I was rambling. I probably was. I was nervous, the martini started to kick in, but something about Mina put me at ease.

"You definitely should." She reached across the table and placed one of her soft hands over mine. "We could make plans to get together again." She smiled and raised an eyebrow.

"Slow down, Mimi," Henrí chuckled. "We've only just met Katherine."

"You didn't invite her?"

"I haven't had the chance." He smiled sweetly at his wife before caressing her shoulder.

"I'm sorry, invite me to what?"

Mina shot her husband a mischievous glance before leaning forward and taking my hand.

"Henrí and I are polyamorous."

"Polyamorous?" I asked. I could glean the word's meaning, but I had trouble wrapping my mind around the concept. "You cheat on each other."

Mina laughed, and Henrí gave her a knowing smile.

"My husband is my best friend and my partner in life. There is no one else I would want to navigate this world with." Henrí brought his wife's hand to his mouth, brushing his lips across her knuckles. "But we have appetites that can't always be filled by each other. We like to explore and experiment. Sometimes with each other and sometimes with other people." She leaned forward and reached for my hand again, and squeezed. "But, Katherine, there is no cheating. We're open and honest with each other, and this lifestyle works for us."

"Don't you get jealous thinking of your husband making love to another woman?" I was too curious, and possibly too inebriated, at this point to be polite; I was also projecting. Perhaps I was trying to make sense of my situation because I asked, "Do you ever wonder if you're not . . . enough?" My face flushed with heat, I looked away from them and took another sip of my martini, wondering if I should have ordered three.

Mimi engulfed my hand with both of hers and smoothed the pad of her thumb across the bare ring finger of my left hand that still bore an unmistakable tan line from my wedding ring.

"Katherine," she asked earnestly. "When was the last time someone told you how utterly breathtaking you are?"

"Never." I stammered and met her eye. It was the truth. I was sure Mark had complimented my appearance at some point in our marriage, but he'd never looked at me the way Henrí had or the way his wife looked at me now.

"Well, you are," Henrí said. "You are absolutely stunning. That's why I wanted to talk to you. That's why I wanted my wife to meet you."

"I'm sorry. I'm confused." My instincts told me one thing, but logic and forty-eight years of societal conditioning were telling me another.

"Katherine, you are beautiful and sexy. We want you."

"You want me?" I squeaked.

"If you would be open to it."

"No," I stammered and shook my head. It was a knee-jerk reaction. This didn't make sense. It wasn't right. Wasn't I sitting at this cliff-top café because my husband wanted to sleep with someone else? At least the idea of Mark wanting to sleep with one person at a time made more sense than what Mimi and Henrí were proposing.

"Listen, *mon cher*," Henrí began. "I know the concept can

sound uncomfortable because it's like nothing that you're used to, but it can be incredibly liberating. There is no pressure, and it only works if you are completely at ease and enjoying yourself."

"You don't have to decide anything now. Take some time. We're a part of an online community called moreamour.com." She wrote the website on a napkin. "It's a global group of people just like us. There are quite a few of us in New York." She smiled at me and raised an eyebrow.

"I'm sorry. I don't think that would be something I could do," I whispered nervously. My body's reaction to this conversation and my words were in direct opposition. My heart was racing, and I felt myself take slow, labored breaths as I watched Mimi's long, manicured fingers wiggle as she wrote something else on the napkin.

"We're having a party tonight," she slid the napkin over to me, "in our suite."

"We would love it if you could come." Henrí gave me a smoldering look and clever smirk.

"You don't have to do anything that makes you uncomfortable, and you can leave any time you want." Mimi reached for my hand again, and I found that I loved the feel of her soft skin as it caressed my palm. "Please think about it."

"I'll . . ." I swallowed nervously and heaved a deep sigh. "I'll think about it."

But I was sure that I wouldn't be attending Henrí and Mimi's sex party and definitely not joining some sort of online orgy community.

III

Katherine Samuels, what the hell are you doing here? I asked myself as I paced back and forth in front of the door to Henrí and Mimi's suite. Truth be told, I was asking myself that question since meeting Henrí and Mimi. I asked it as I masturbated in the shower after their invitation, while I imagined Mimi's soft hands roaming my naked body as her husband made love to me. I asked myself that question while I Googled "polyamory," "open relationships," and "swingers." I questioned my sanity as I shaved and groomed my most intimate parts, a clear indication that I'd made up my mind to accept their invitation. I was still second-guessing my decision as I left my room and made the long slow walk to the resort building that housed the larger suites.

I was about to return to my room in defeat when the door opened, and I was face to face with Mimi. She was wearing a long robe made of see-through lace. There was nothing underneath, and it made my heart race. I had to lace my fingers together to stop myself from reaching and stroking the soft fabric.

"I was hoping you'd come. Henrí and I had a bet going." She opened the door wider. "You owe me a hundred dollars, baby."

Henrí joined his wife at the door and wrapped a hand around her waist.

"Money well spent, my love." He planted a kiss on the side of her head. "Come in, gorgeous. Everyone is eager to meet you."

"Don't make her nervous, honey," Mimi chided and wrapped her hand around my wrist, gently pulling me into the apartment.

Too late.

"There is absolutely no pressure." She put an arm around my shoulder. "Help yourself to food or drinks." She indicated a small buffet. "You can play by yourself or with anyone else who's willing, or you can just watch." She indicated a table full of what looked like sex toys, bottles of lubricant, and a bowl of condoms. Finally, she turned me to face her and clasped my hands. "You're safe here, Katherine. Let go and enjoy yourself." She brought my bare left hand to her lips and kissed the tan line on my ring finger. "You deserve to feel good."

Mimi released my hands and backed away from me. She winked at me before another man hoisted her over his shoulder with a squeal, carrying her into one of the apartment's bedrooms. I scanned the room, looking for Henrí. He was seated on an oversized couch, completely nude with his legs spread while being pleasured orally by a woman with long red hair. One of his hands was moving between the legs of another woman leaning over the couch, fellating another man. Henrí caught me watching him and smiled at me, holding my gaze. I should have been embarrassed, but I couldn't look away. He seemed so powerful and at ease. It made the muscles between my legs throb with arousal and my heart race.

"First time?" a deep voice with a British accent called from beside me, making me startle. I looked up to see a tall, brunette man with startling green eyes and a dazzling white smile. He looked like he was in his mid to late thirties.

"Is it that obvious?"

"It is, but it's no cause for shame. Can I get you a drink?"

"Sure. I'll have a white wine." I chose something light so I could keep my wits if I had to. He pressed a cool glass of pale yellow liquid into my hand, and he sipped on a beer. "Have you been to a lot of these?" I asked.

"Yeah. Celeste and I have been in the lifestyle for a few years." He tipped his bottle at the woman moaning and writhing on the couch with Henrí's hand between her legs.

"How do you handle it?" I cast a glance at his wife before I turned to look at him again. He raised an eyebrow. "Seeing your wife with other men." Every time I imagined Mark making love with Dr. Finch, my blood boiled, and I wanted to commit felonies.

"Our main objective in our marriage is to make each other happy and be honest with each other. As long as we never lose focus on that, everything else is simple." His easy smile made me relax.

"That's beautiful." I smiled at him. We clinked glasses and sipped our drinks.

"Do you know what would make me happy right now?" His smoldering look that made my chest quiver.

"No," I whispered. "But I have a feeling you're going to tell me." I smiled, suddenly feeling light, giddy, and incredibly aroused.

"Putting my face between your legs and tasting the beautiful pussy that I know is under that dress."

"Oh, my. You are honest, aren't you?" I said with a slight giggle.

"It's the only way to live, beautiful." He smiled. "That is, if you're willing, of course. This being your first time . . ."

"I am willing," I heard myself say a little quickly. "But does it have to be out here, in front of everyone?"

"Of course not." He slid a large warm palm across my shoulder, down my arm until he interlocked our fingers and pulled me down a hallway toward the bedrooms, planting a kiss on his wife's shoulder on the way.

"Should we know each other's names," I asked, "before we . . ."

"Whatever makes you comfortable." He smiled at me before opening the door to an empty bedroom.

"I'm Katherine, but you can call me Kat if you want."

"It's a pleasure to meet you, Kat." He stroked my face. "I'm Peter, but you can call me Pete."

"Nice to meet you, Pete." I returned his easy smile.

"Shall we?" He gestured into the bedroom.

"Yes." I nodded and stepped inside.

IV

Pete didn't waste any time once we got inside the bedroom, and I was thrumming with excitement.

"You're in charge, Kat. Nothing happens in this room unless you want it. I'll go as fast or as slow as you want. You want to stop this, just say the word, and I'll stop." He led me to bed and motioned for me to sit. I took another sip from my glass before Pete slipped it out of my hands and knelt between my legs. "I just want to worship you."

They were the sexiest words I'd ever heard. I'd never imagined myself worthy of worship, but here I was in a tropical paradise with a gorgeous man kneeling at my feet, eager to make love to me.

"Lay back, beautiful." He purred as he eased the skirt of my dress over my thighs. "I'm gonna make sure you enjoy this as much as I will." His fingertips pressed into the flesh of my waist as he hooked them into the waistband of my panties and slid them down over my legs. My heart pounded in anticipation as Pete dragged his lips over the inside of my thighs.

"I knew this pussy was going to be beautiful." He pressed my thighs apart and leaned forward. A sound I'd never made before escaped my lips as Peter's tongue curled around my clit, a cross between a grunt and a squeal.

All nervousness and self-consciousness had disappeared. Ecstasy replaced every other feeling. Pete was so adept at using his tongue, lips, and fingers to bring me to the point of oblivion that if nothing else happened in this room, or hell, on this entire vacation, it would have been worth the trip.

"Oh, my god. Oh, yes." My thighs were over his shoulder, my heels digging helplessly into the muscular flesh of his back. I was mindless with pleasure, and couldn't tell if minutes or hours had passed since we'd entered the bedroom. The only sounds were my moans and desperate slurping sounds of Pete working between my legs. "I'm coming. Oh, my god. I'm coming." I wasn't sure if I was talking to Pete, myself, or trying to communicate with some higher power.

Peter tightened his grip on my thighs and pressed his face between my legs, intensifying my climax and working himself into a frenzy. I didn't know there was such a thing as too much pleasure, but after a few moments, I pushed his head from between my legs, gasping for breath.

He rose from his knees, wiping his mouth, and crawled next to me on the bed wearing a huge smile.

"How are you feeling, Kat?" His breath carried the scent of my arousal with every word he spoke. I reached out and slid my fingers over his lips, still slick from tasting me.

"Amazing," I said. "You're amazing."

His face spread into a lazy grin, and he brushed my cheek with the backs of his fingertips. "So what do you want to do now?"

"I don't know. I kind of feel like I can do anything."

"You can, gorgeous." He folded me into his arms and held me, just held me, and it felt so good and free. I'd never been held like this before.

"Are you sure your wife is okay with us . . . doing this?"

Peter let out a small chuckle and held me closer. "I appreciate your concern, Kat, but I assure you, Celeste doesn't have a problem with what I do at these parties. She encourages it."

"Really?"

"Yes, really." He nodded and planted a kiss on my forehead. "Excuse me if I'm prying, and feel free to tell me to fuck off if I am, but does the reason you keep asking about my relationship with my wife have something to do with this?" He picked up my left hand and smoothed the pad of his thumb over the pale brown tan line on my ring finger. I didn't answer him, but I was sure the expression on my face told him everything he needed to know because he kissed my forehead again.

"He cheated on me," I whispered. "With our marriage counselor."

"What?" He let out a shocked chuckle. "What a fucking idiot." He laughed again. "The pair of them."

I stared at him in confusion for a moment. I'd just disclosed the worst thing to have ever happened to me, and he was laughing about it. I opened my mouth to protest for a moment before I felt my lips spread into a smile. It *was* funny, in a way.

My husband left me for our marriage counselor.

Before I could stop myself, my laughter grew raucous and loud. Soon we were both howling. We were startled when we heard a loud knock at the door.

"Petey, babe?" a woman's cheery voice called through the door. "What's going on in there? We can hear you laughing down the hall."

"That's Celeste," Pete whispered to me. "I think you'd like her. Shall we invite her in?" he asked. I shot him a mischievous smirk.

"Come in," I said loudly.

Celeste poked her head in the room and didn't look the least surprised to find another woman in her husband's arms.

"Celeste, baby, this is Kat." Pete grinned at his wife. "Kat, this is my wife, Celeste."

Celeste stepped into the room and stole my breath from my lungs when I saw that she was completely naked. She was all curves and softness with full heavy breasts and wide hips. She had ample dimples and stretch marks but not an ounce of shame. Her waist-length soft brown curls made her look like a

Botticelli painting. I was mesmerized and still aware that I was half-naked and cuddling with her husband. I felt giddy, excited, joyful, and untethered. Henrí had warned me that the polyamorous lifestyle could feel "incredibly liberating," and he was right. That was precisely how I felt, lying in Pete's arms, with Celeste's hungry eyes devouring me.

"My husband left me for our marriage counselor, and Pete and I were just celebrating," I said with a residual chuckle. "Would you like to join us?"

V

I'd never made love with a woman before, but I'd spend the rest of my life wondering why I waited until I was nearly fifty to start. I loved the feeling of Celeste's body moving over mine. I loved the softness of her hands as she methodically and gently undressed me. Her gentle moans as she ran her tongue along the curves of my breasts made me come undone.

"I want to sit on your face while I watch my husband fuck you, Kat." She brushed her lips over mine. "Would you like that?"

I smoothed my tongue over her plush pout, tasting her sweet skin before I nodded. "Very much," I managed to whisper. "I would like that very much." She crawled to the edge of the bed and reached into a bowl of condoms, withdrawing one and handing it to her husband. I watched as Pete unwrapped the condom and sheathed himself with slow, lazy strokes as he watched me. Katherine reached over to the bedside table again, retrieved a small bottle of lubricant, and held it up to show me.

"Yes, please," I said in a relieved sigh. Despite all of the things that happened in this room, I was still too self-conscious to ask. Celeste coated her fingers with the liquid before caressing me between my legs until I was warm and slick.

"She's so ready, baby," she said to Pete before turning to me. "Aren't you, Kat?" I was only able to nod before I felt the thick head of Peter's cock pressing into me, stretching me and making me moan in pleasure. "How does she feel, Peter?" Celeste asked as she smoothed her palms over my breast and stomach while Peter began to work himself slowly in and out.

"She's tight, baby," he said between clenched teeth. "She's so fucking tight."

"You're so beautiful when you're getting fucked like this, Kat." Celeste was gazing at me like some long-lost treasure. "I could watch this all day." She traced a finger over my lips, then slid it over my tongue so I could suck it.

"Mmmm," she said and swung one of her legs over my face, so the heady aroma of her sex engulfed me. I stretched my tongue toward the junction of her thighs, but I was too far away to reach. I wrapped my hands around her thighs, digging my fingers into her flesh to pull her closer to me. "Tell me what you want, Kat. Just ask for it, and it's yours."

"I want to taste you, Celeste," I said as Pete continued to pound me into oblivion. "Let me taste you."

"As long as I get to return the favor, beautiful."

"Yes," I said breathily as she lowered herself onto my face and began to grind her sex onto my tongue. The flavor was tart, sweet, and velvety. Her flesh was soft and slick like a ripe peach.

Celeste flattened her warm body against mine, parted my labia with her fingers, and began to smooth her tongue over my clit in rhythm with Pete's thrusts. The sensations were delicious and overwhelming. I was being carried over the edge again.

My jerking and spasming set off a chain reaction. Peter withdrew himself and snapped off the condom so his wife could greedily catch his release in her waiting mouth. She turned to me with her eyebrows raised in invitation. I sat up and grabbed the back of her head, pulling her into a hungry kiss where we shared the product of an exhausting night of fucking as if our lives depended on it. We swallowed and collapsed in a sweaty tangle of arms and legs, lazily kissing, caressing, and tasting each other while our heart rates slowly returned to normal.

"Hello," a voice I recognized as Mimi's called into the room. "It smells amazing in here." I picked my head up to look at her and saw that she was still wearing her lace robe, but it was open. Her perky dark brown nipples were standing at attention, and there was a perfectly groomed black triangle of curly hair peeking from between her golden-brown thighs.

"Did we miss all the action?" Henrí was standing behind Mimi, massaging her shoulders.

"I don't know," Celeste said with a lazy chuckle. "I feel like I'm getting a second wind. Kat?" She smoothed a palm over one of my bare breasts and squeezed.

I'd never felt more tired in my life, but also never more alive. I grabbed Celeste's hand and brought it to my lips before Henrí and Mimi joined us, where we proceeded to make love all night.

VI

I woke up in Henrí and Mimi's suite cradled between Mimi and Celeste. We spent the morning making love before Henrí and Peter joined us.

I made it back to my room just in time to shower, change, and pack for my flight back to JFK. The thought of leaving Barbados and all that I'd discovered made me sad, but I was eager to start my new life. I'd spent the last two months wondering how I would survive the destruction of the only life I'd known for the past three decades. Mimi and Henrí's simple party invitation opened my eyes to a new world of possibilities.

When I got to the airport, I upgraded my ticket home to first class. Once in the lounge, I opened my laptop and logged into the wifi.

The first thing I did was email my realtor and ask her to start looking for apartments and townhouses in Harlem and possibly, the Upper East Side.

The second thing I did was email my divorce attorney that I was ready to move forward with the dissolution of my marriage.

The final thing I did before I boarded my plane to New York was visit the website moreamour.com and start a profile.

Username: Wildkat1973

Location: New York, NY

About Me: "Looking for my next adventure!"

TELL THEM THANK YOU

Lilith Young

Somehow the week managed to drag on, while at the same time Friday night came quickly, and just like that we were walking down the stairs of the club to movie night. Ash, my partner, owned a queer bar with a private BDSM club in the basement. Once a month, the community did a clothing optional movie night, and we hadn't been since Ash got out of the hospital. Everyone was doing just a little extra to welcome Ash back. The space was beautiful. Candles lit all around the room, a beautiful table of drinks and food, and all my favorite people lying about scantily clad. I walked over to my new friends and gave them all hugs.

"Y'all, the space is amazing."

"Girl, it has been way too long since we all had fun. A celebration was necessary," Michael said as he winked.

"Tell me about it," Sam chimed in.

"Please tell me your cute ass is putting on a scene tonight, Mel. My life is empty without watching your ass get smacked," Michael said as I fell over laughing.

"You know that would depend on the big boss over there, but I will see what I can do. I don't think she's recovered enough for a real show."

Ash had been shot by some homophobic drunk neighbor a month ago and still had a long recovery ahead of her. If it weren't for the shoulder brace, you wouldn't be able to tell she was even injured. Her perfectly gelled, short, dark hair was perfectly in place. Her dark jeans were pressed to perfection. Even now, months into our relationship, I struggled not to stare at her beauty.

Michael got a twinkle in his eye as he ran over to Ash and whispered in her ear. I saw her smirk as her eyes darted over to meet mine. A lust-filled fire was burning through those eyes. Clearly Michael was asking for a show. It still shocked me that this was my life now. Six months ago, I was a simple kindergarten teacher with terrible luck dating men, and here I am in a members only kink club, hoping to have sex in front of my new friends. I kept thinking this was a dream that I would one day wake from. Michael winked as he scurried over to his partner John. I walked over to Ash to try and find out what they were up to, but before I could say anything, she wrapped her arm around me as she said, "Let's go change, Sunshine."

"Yes, sir," I replied as I leaned into her. She smacked my ass as I walked in front of her. We made our way to her office to strip down. She tugged her sweater over her head, and it got stuck on her shoulder brace. Seizing the opportunity, I slowly licked up her chest, teasing her.

"Sunshine, this is not funny. Help me get out of this shirt."

"Hmm. I don't think so."

I slowly unbuttoned her jeans, sliding the zipper down tauntingly.

"Sunshine, if you continue this, I'm going to make your ass so red," Ash growled out.

"Is that a promise?" I asked as I slid her jeans down to the floor. That was quite enough for Ash, as she finally got free of her sweater. She gently pushed me back toward her desk.

"Strip," she ordered.

"Yes, sir," I answered as my body shivered. I pulled my shirt over my head right when I heard a knock at the open door. Ash looked up to the door as she wrapped a toga around her naked body.

"Come in," Ash said as she sat down on the couch. Michael crawled in, followed by John. I looked questionably back and forth between everyone. Michael was already nude, his cock hard and bouncing as he slowly crawled toward me. My eyes met John's while he searched my body language. Feeling like he was reading my soul, I couldn't look away. He was breathtakingly handsome. His dark skin glistened in the light, making him seem young at first glance, only to be given away by the sprinkling of gray hair that he didn't bother to hide.

"Ash?" I questioned, unsure of what was about to unfold.

"I know you needed a good scene, and Michael and John need someone to play with. Are you interested?"

"Yes, thank you," I whispered as Michael's smile grew.

"I thought you told your slut to strip, Ash? Getting soft in your old age?" John announced, masterfully walking the line of joking, but also being deadly serious.

"Fuck off, John. Sunshine, you have ten seconds," Ash snapped.

I stuck out my tongue at them both and slowly pulled off my lingerie, watching annoyance grow with each passing second on John's face. Two minutes later, I finally stood naked and raised my eyebrow in defiance as I awaited my punishment from Ash.

"John here is going to give you thirty spankings for deliberately disobeying me in front of my guests," Ash told me as I gulped. I had never played with someone else. I trusted them all, but it still felt like a milestone.

"Yes, sir. Sorry, sir."

John walked up to us and looked into my eyes when he spoke. "Melissa, before we start let's make sure we're on the same page. I like to use colors, so please use yellow or red if you need to stop."

"Okay," I replied.

"I would like you to call me sir."

"Yes, sir."

"Ash and I have discussed your limits, but please speak up if you need to stop," he repeated calmly.

"Yes, sir. Thank you, sir," I answered with a shaky voice.

"Get on all fours on the couch next to Ash, facing me," he said with so much authority that my body just moved on its own. I could not stop myself from doing what he wanted.

"Yes, sir."

I quickly climbed onto the couch, settling onto my hands and knees as my long brown hair hung over my face.

"I want you to count for me."

"Yes, sir."

His hand came down in a rush against my skin. The sharp sting on my ass burned. God, I had missed this.

"One," I counted as his hand came down again on my quickly reddening cheeks. I wished I could see Ash's face, but I dared not turn.

"Ash, you are lucky with this one. She reddens beautifully."

"Lucky bastard for sure," Ash said as the spankings continued.

"Eight, nine, ten," I whispered as the pain radiated across my body, and I found it harder to keep counting with each smack. My arousal began to take over the pain as my pussy began to drip.

"If you think a dripping wet pussy will stop me, you are

out of luck. When I am done with you, you won't sit for a week."

I gulped as his hands rapidly rained down on my ass cheeks.

"Nineteen. Twenty," I called out. I was unsure if I was going to make it when Ash spoke to me.

"Melissa, what's your color?" Ash asked. I thought about it for a moment.

"Green," I said as I turned to meet her eyes. John smiled as he began my last spankings. I could feel an orgasm building. Not knowing how John felt about it, I began to panic.

"Yellow. Sir?"

He paused.

"Yes, Lissa."

"I . . . I . . . Please can I come?"

He laughed, "Yes dear, you may come but not until number thirty. Hold it in."

"Thank you, sir."

Smack. The sound of my bruising skin resonated in the room.

"Twenty-nine."

I braced myself for the last hit. As his hand struck my ass, I felt the orgasm I'd been holding onto wash over me. A moan escaped my lips as I collapsed onto the couch. I felt Ash tuck my hair behind my ear and whisper something to me. I blinked a few times, making sure I'd heard her correctly.

"Sunshine, I'm going to plug your ass for the rest of the night," Ash repeated.

"Mhm," I nodded, not really understanding what I was agreeing to. I quickly jumped when I felt hands on my ass that I didn't recognize.

"Whoa, what?" I stammered.

"Sunshine, Michael is going to prep and plug you up. Okay?"

I looked back and forth between everyone in the room. Their eyes were all on me, waiting for my decision.

"Okay."

I rolled back over, bracing my hand on Ash's thighs.

"Don't worry, Melly. I will make your ass very happy," Michael said, then giggled. He then pulled my cheeks apart and began licking my puckered hole.

"Shit," I moaned out.

I could feel his tongue circling my hole, teasing me as he gripped my bruises, adding just a touch of pain. He knew exactly what he was doing. I could feel his fingertip begin to trace my hole. I looked up at Ash, and seeing how close she was to me, I leaned in and kissed her neck. She ran her fingers through my hair, gripping it at the base and yanking me off her neck. This was hot, but I wanted more. My eyes met Ash's as she winked.

"Oh, we can up the play if you want, Sunshine."

"I want."

Ash motioned to John, an unspoken conversation passing between them.

"We are in," John said, and Michael nodded in agreement. Ash lifted me up and set me on the floor in front of her between her legs. Michael pulled me up to all fours, and he lined up behind me. John stepped up behind him. I ran my hands up Ash's thighs as I got closer and closer to her center, just as Michael's tongue dove inside me. I knew John was likely behind Michael. Fucking him. I honestly didn't care. I just wanted to keep feeling this good. Ash's hand rested on my head as I sucked her clit in between my teeth. Tormenting her. I felt a thick finger pierce my ass, and I cried out.

"Oh, fuck," I mumbled into Ash's cunt.

"Maybe I should stretch you out big enough for some of Ash's big dicks. You played with any of those yet, Melly?" Michael asked.

"Oh. Mhm. No . . ." I stuttered out in between moans, quickly latching back onto Ash.

"Ash?" Michael looked up, questioning as he slid a second finger into me. I accidentally bit down on Ash, wondering if she would say yes. Did I want her to?

"Not tonight, Michael."

"Boo."

"Michael," John said firmly as he pulled out and slapped his ass.

"Sorry, sir."

"Apologize to Ash."

"Sorry, Ash." Michael sighed.

"Just plug her up Michael," Ash said as she tossed a large vibrating plug over my head.

"Oh! Yes, sir."

I felt the cold drizzle of lube on my skin. The hard cold plug pressed into me. Slowly, he teasingly pushed it in.

"Ash, that feels really big," I said in a panic. She grabbed my chin and looked me in the eyes.

"You got this, Sunshine."

I felt my ass pop as the rest of the toy slid in. Michael leaned in and gave me a kiss on my cheek. He pulled my back flush against him.

"I'm going to fuck you now, Melly, while Ash watches and your sweet ass is plugged up. John is going to pound into me, and you, my slutty friend, are going to love it."

I nodded my head up and down as I stared into Ash's brown eyes. She had slid a harness on and was rubbing her cock as she watched Michael line his dick up at my entrance.

"Oh, fuck!" I yelled as Michael slid in. I fell forward onto my hands as he quickly began to pound in and out of me.

"Mel, god damn you feel good. So fucking good wrapped around me."

Lost in the moment, all I could do was brace myself as he

stretched me over and over. Ash stepped up in front of me, guiding her dick into my open moaning mouth. Threading her fingers through my hair and holding my head still, she thrust down my throat. I was mortified at the thought of how I must look, my pussy dripping wet, all my holes stuffed full and stretched to their limits. My eyes watered as each passing moment I became more and more aroused at my own degradation. Quickly lost in the sensations, I allowed pleasure to rush through my body.

"Oh, god, Mel!" Michael yelled out as his fingers gripped my hips, leaving tiny bruises. "I just can't stop myself. You feel too damn good." He shuddered as his orgasm ripped out of him, his body trembling into me. Ash stepped back and sat on the couch, watching our climax as she smiled. Each final thrust pulsed a new layer of orgasm out of my cunt. Lost in pleasure, I slowly pulled away from John and Michael. I crawled up onto Ash's lap and turned around to see Michael and John still fucking.

"Tell them thank you, Sunshine," Ash said.

"Thank you," I managed to whisper.

John was completely unfazed as he continued to pump into a whimpering Michael.

"Anytime, Ash. Hell, you need entertainment, call us," John called out as he wrapped his hand around Michael's neck. I rested my head on Ash's shoulder and watched them finish. I buried my face in Ash's shoulder, suddenly feeling like I was intruding on a moment between them. John thrusted into Michael slowly and roughly in a most poetic manner. John closed his eyes as he twisted his fist over Michael's cock, time pausing as he shot out across his hand. Bringing his palm to his face, John licked Michael's come off his hand and winked at me. Quickly, he scooped up a limp Michael and turned to walk toward the door.

"We'll save you a seat on the couch," Michael called out as they left the room. Suddenly the weight of what we'd just done hung heavy in the room.

"Sunshine, come here," Ash said as she turned me around to face her and wrapped me up in a blanket. "That was a lot. I want to know how you feel."

I paused for a moment and replied, "I'm surprised how much I enjoyed that."

"Me too. John and I have been doing scenes together for years. I was nervous to see if we would be able to continue to do that with you."

"Can we do it again?" I asked, smiling.

"Sunshine, we can do whatever you want." She laughed and kissed my forehead.

"Now. You want me to fuck you in here or out there? Because I cannot go a single second longer without being inside that pretty pussy."

"I've put on enough shows for tonight. Take me right here love, just us."

Ash lifted me up by my hips, and I set myself across her lap, feeling the plug push deep within me as I ground against her.

"Watching you writhe against John as he spanked your ass was divine, Sunshine." Ash's hands ran up and down my torso teasing my nipples.

"It felt divine. He's an intense man."

"I could have come just from watching you," Ash said as she leaned in and bit down on my collarbone.

"I do like putting on a show for you," I said, leaning my head back in pleasure.

"Did you like being fucked by all of us?" Ash said as she slid inside me.

I groaned as the cock filled me up, "Yes, Ash, yes I love being fucked by all of you."

"Damn, woman. I will never get tired of this," Ash said as

she shook her head and slowly began to thrust up into me.

"Never," I said. I leaned in pressing my forehead to hers, roughly kissing her lips. A whimper escaped my lips with each pounding my sore cunt took. Our tongues battled as I felt her large dick fill me up. Already having orgasmed more times than I could count, I didn't think it was possible for me to come again. But I could feel it building in my toes and spreading pleasure through my body as Ash bit down on my nipples and slid deep inside me over and over.

"It's like you were made just for me. I am addicted to your sweet cunt," Ash said breathlessly.

"Ash. I. Oh. Oh. Please let me come," I said in between each bounce, when Ash stopped abruptly. My eyes flashed open.

"Please," I begged as I stared into her soul, her eyes lighting up.

"All right, my love. Come for me."

She reached her hand in between us and pinched my clit and rubbed as she pulled in and out of me. My orgasm crashed out of me, seeming to pass between us in a ripple. We collapsed in a tangle of body parts onto the couch, silently breathing as the moment washed over us. I snuggled into her chest as she pulled a blanket over us. She slowly began to cover my face in tiny kisses. I kept thinking we should get up to go and watch the movie with everyone, but I just couldn't make myself move. And I wasn't sure I wanted to.

THE UNICORN

Shay Mitchel

Pete has been nursing the same cocktail for an hour; meanwhile, I'm reaching the bottom of my third. The alcohol is easing away my inhibitions, and I've become more handsy and flirty since drink number two. It's dark out on the rooftop terrace of the bar save for a glowing strand of lights suspended above the seating area, and the heavy summer air makes the open space feel intimate. A minute ago I was leaning against Pete in a fit of laughter over his story about bartending in the Florida Keys and I found myself turning in toward his neck to capture more of his masculine scent. I need an exit strategy before I embarrass myself. Pete has a boyfriend at home.

"I should go," I say out loud to commit to departure. My intention to assume an upright position is thwarted by a combination of gravity and rum. Instead I rock forward and then collapse back and end up practically sitting on Pete's lap. Now not only could I lean in and taste the skin on his neck, but if I just moved my hand up a few inches I could run it up his inner thigh and . . .

"Should you?"

"No I . . . sorry . . ." *So much for not embarrassing myself.* I whip my hand back into my own lap and shift off of Pete, ungracefully rearranging myself at what feels like a safer distance on the couch, until Pete moves closer so our knees are touching.

"I meant should you leave?" Pete's hand comes to my back and his fingertips trace circles across my shoulders. His touch initiates a trail of tingles that travels down my spine.

"Oh . . . ummm . . ."

"I don't think you want to." His fingers brush over the bare skin of my neck and even with the comfortable numbness that comes with my light buzz, my nipples peak and a warm pulse heats the root of my cock. Despite my journalism degree, I can't string together a succinct phrase that summarizes *I don't know what's happening here but I'm getting turned so what do you want from me because I know what I want from you but you have a boyfriend but I'm thinking it might not matter to you and I'm beginning to wonder if it matters to me.* Before I can verbalize a response, Pete sits back, the air instantly cooling around me as he withdraws. His body is relaxed but his gaze has an intensity that heats me from the inside. I raise my glass to my lips and tip it all the way back, disappointed to discover that it's empty.

"How did you end up in Detroit?" Ice clinks as Pete swirls his glass.

"Oh, you know, the usual." I eye Pete's drink and accept it when he holds it out to me. I suck in an ice cube and let it melt on my tongue. The realization that this same chunk of frozen water could have been in Pete's mouth makes me undo the top

two buttons of my shirt to increase ventilation even though the
ice almost gives me a brain freeze.

"What are the usual circumstances that leads someone to
uproot from a dairy farm in Iowa and transplant himself to the
rust belt?"

"I finished school and got an internship with the *Detroit
News*." That is a partial truth, the lie being one of omission.
Lying, or at least lying well, is not in my nature, so I add, "There
weren't a lot of options where I'm from." That statement just
adorns the mistruth. I accepted the *News*'s offer for an unpaid
internship instead of a paid position closer to home because I
was suffocating in all that fertile Iowa soil.

"Not a lot of options because you're gay?"

"I guess that's part of it." I nod, noticing I don't feel exposed
sharing this with Pete. I don't have much practice being out.

"Are you dating anyone?"

"Uh . . . no."

"Are you a virgin?"

Okay, now I feel exposed.

"How do you define being a virgin?" I ask. If the definition
is some physical barrier being breached, then no, I am not a
virgin. I have inserted all sorts of toys in my ass.

"Have you ever had a cock in your ass, a *real* cock?" Pete's
tone is curious, not accusatory. It lacks all of the implica-
tions that usually come with this discussion. *How can you be
a twenty-four-year-old gay man and still be a virgin? Is there
something wrong with you?*

"No." The alcohol makes it easy to let the truth slip out.

"Blowjob, given or received?"

"No."

Pete nods as if he has just confirmed that my birthday is in
June. "So I have found myself a unicorn," he murmurs, almost

to himself. He bends forward and places his elbows on his knees, bringing his face very close to mine. "How much longer do you feel the need to maintain your virginal status?"

"No need . . . I mean . . . I don't want to be . . . "

"You mean you would like to have sex."

"Y-yes."

"Would you like to have sex with me?"

This time I don't stutter.

"Yes."

Pete removes the empty glass from my hand and pulls me to my feet. We're almost the same height, but in this moment his presence feels like it outweighs mine by a hundred pounds. With a single movement he places a hand on the back of my neck and brings his mouth to mine. I have kissed before, tentative, asking type kisses. *Do you mind if my lips touch yours? Do you mind if I flick my tongue out to taste you?* There is no inquiry to Pete's kiss. His lips part and demand that mine open in response. He tastes like rum and his skin is gritty with end of the day stubble, but his mouth is sweet and accommodating. I feel breathless, but there is nothing wrong with my oxygen supply. I have plenty of opportunity to take gasping breaths as Pete works his lips across my jaw and down my throat, pulling the neck of my shirt to one side so he can kiss my collarbone. When he runs his tongue from the base of my neck to just behind my ear, I arch into him and make an indelicate sound.

"Come home with me," he says, when he finally pulls away.

"Why?" That question makes me sound more naïve than I really am. I know exactly what he wants. His fingers stroke my chin as he draws me in to brush his lips across mine.

"So we can have sex, silly. You have an amazing ass and"— he gives my erection pushing into his thigh a light squeeze—"I

know you want me." The full body flush I experience threatens
to melt off my lightweight shirt.

"What about . . . you have a boyfriend . . . "

"Nick. Come home with me, I want you to meet him." Pete
smiles and tugs at my hand. My mind is fuzzy from the rum and
the lingering taste of Pete on my tongue. I want this, so bad, so
I follow.

Pete and I make our way down the quiet street, storefronts
dark and streetlights buzzing. I can't stop touching him. I feel
defiant, and turned on, kissing him in public. It's just a small
part of the freedom I was craving when I uprooted my entire
existence and moved here.

There comes a time in a person's life when virginity becomes
a burden. Once a prize to be protected, it transforms into something that needs to be disposed of. The label feels like a neon
sign brashly declaring that you are un-fuckable. What's worse,
the longer you think other people see you that way, the more
you believe it yourself.

The way Pete kisses me when we reach the door to his
building makes me feel as if I am so hot and desirable I may
just spontaneously combust. He tempers my urgency with slow
gentle sweeps of his tongue along my lips as he kneads my
ass, grinding my erection against his. I have to hold onto him
for balance as he punches in the code on the keypad to his
building, then I trot behind him as he leads me to the door of
his apartment.

"Honey, we're home," Pete calls out as we enter, and a large
figure emerges from a doorway next to the foyer. The man is
several inches taller than Pete, and about a foot wider. Broad
shoulders stretch out a light blue T-shirt, and colorful tattoos
peek out from where the short sleeves strain over well-formed
biceps. He takes Pete into his arms, kissing him passionately.

When the embrace ends, the bear of a man turns to me with a smile that reveals both rows of perfect teeth.

"You must be Troy." He extends a hand, but I can't reach it because I am backing up with quick baby steps. My pre-first time jitters escalate to a heart-pounding fear that I have been tricked into something much more hardcore than I agreed to. I bump into the thick wooden entry door and freeze. *They will find me broken and bruised on a park bench tomorrow. The headlines will read "Gay Man Molested in Well-Appointed Brownstone. He should have known better. What kind of idiot goes home with someone he barely knows?"*

"Hey, hey . . ." Pete cajoles. "Don't worry, sweetheart. It's just Nick." Nick tucks him possessively under one arm and kisses him on the forehead and Pete runs fingers across the large man's broad chest. "It's okay, it's just Nick." Pete says again, which reassures me about as much as the statement *It's okay, it's just Gay Eating Godzilla.*

"Can I get you guys something to eat?" Nick starts toward another doorway off of the foyer. "I can heat up some vegetarian lasagna." Beyond his shoulders I can see a large stainless steel refrigerator with scraps of paper attached by magnets—photos, a grocery list, Pete's work schedule.

"You've got to be kidding me." Pete hooks his fingers into Nick's arm and draws him back, kissing his cheek lightly. My fears of making the morning paper begin to dissolve as I take in the vibe between these two. There is something real and intimate here, and it is extending out to include me. I want to be a part of it.

Pete untangles himself from Nick and comes to me, reaching for my hand and pulling me into another kiss. My dick makes it to half-mast again before he pulls away and holds my face in both of his hands.

"Nick is going to watch. He's only going to watch." I can't take my eyes off of Pete's mouth, his breath touching my lips just like his kiss. "He's not going to touch you, he's just going to watch. Okay?"

The tender connection between Pete and Nick must work some alchemy with the liquid courage of the rum because suddenly I have never wanted anything more than for Pete to deflower me under the heated gaze of his lover.

"Yes." I feel breathless again even though I'm standing still. Pete and Nick share a smile, followed by another kiss over Pete's shoulder. Then I follow the tug of Pete's hand as he leads me up the stairs.

Pete has his shirt off before he even reaches into the large shower to turn on the water. I start to lift my shirt over my head but Pete swats my hands away.

"May I?" he asks, and when I nod he draws my shirt up, tracing his thumbs along my ribs and making me shiver. Next goes my belt, then his, then his pants, then mine. Pete's skin is a golden olive tone and perfectly smooth, with a dusting of silky dark hair across his chest and a thicker line that widens at the waistband of tight boxer briefs. I reach out and run my palm along the ridge of Pete's erection, which presses the stretchy material into a peak. My fingers trace the waistband, then dip below the elastic, brushing through the thick hair that encircles the wide stalk of his cock. I grab at him, dying to wrap my hand around it.

"Ah-ah . . . no rush . . ." He angles away and catches my wrist. Just then Nick appears at the bathroom door, whiskeys in hand. He sets two glasses down on the vanity. Pete takes one and hands it to me, which I empty before he even turns back with his own. He takes a small sip, exchanging a glance with Nick over the rim as he does, then his fingers return to my waistband and my boxers slide to the floor.

With two hands on my shoulders, Pete guides me to the shower. When the warm spray hits my back I reach for him again, and this time he lets me make contact. I draw my fingers through his chest hair and trace his nipples, then follow the rivulets of water that run down his abs. I have never touched a dick besides my own, and I inhale sharply when I wrap my hand around the velvet hot skin of Pete's. He allows me a moment of play, letting me explore the texture of the veins on his shaft and the way his foreskin retracts completely as I circle my thumb over the slit, the water making it slick.

"Okay, sweetheart, that's enough for now. I have plans for that later." He lifts my arms to place them on a glass wall that separates the shower from the rest of the room, putting me on display. Pete runs soapy hands from my wrists down my arms then along my ribs, repositioning my hands on the glass when they start to slide as I squirm under his slippery fingers. He moves over the ridges of my abdominal muscles, and down between my legs, pumping my cock a few times and making me whimper. It's obvious that we are putting on a show, a soapy, sexy, citrus scented show. When I catch Nick's gaze, a momentary spear of shame, and a sudden need to cover myself, shoot through me and my whole body tenses. Pete whispers quiet reassurances and sucks gently on the skin behind my ear as he presses his slippery chest along my back. Soon I am melting into him, letting his body support me as my arms drop back around his neck.

"Beautiful." Nick breathes out. He has moved closer to the glass wall, and gives me a small nod when I lift my chin to meet his eyes at the sound of his voice. "Beautiful," he says again. Pete reloads with soap then turns me around and pushes my legs apart, angling my rear so that I am open and exposed for his lover to see.

"Look at this perfect ass, Nick." Pete's fingers spread me wide, stretching the sensitive skin of my hole.

"Mmmm," Nick responds. I can picture Nick's view, watching Pete splay my ass cheeks open, watching as he strokes circles with slippery fingers around the sensitive puckered skin, then down to my balls where he runs his fingernails over my sac.

"Your ass is perfect, Troy," Pete growls. "I can't wait to fuck your virgin asshole. Do you want me to do that? Do you want me to fuck you?" *Yes yes yes.* I arch and press back. A small noise escapes my lips in response to the tip of Pete's finger probing me.

"Fuck it's tight on my finger. I can't wait to feel my cock in that tight hole." I shudder at the image of the fat head of Pete's cock pressing into me. Nick licks his lips when Pete spins me around and presses his erection into my rear crease. I arch into Pete's hardness and both men groan in unison. The two lovers are sharing an experience, and that experience is my arousal.

Pete pushes me under the spray for an abrupt rinse, then wraps me in a thick robe and pulls me to the bedroom with Nick close behind.

When Pete tugs me down onto the bed a needling urgency starts to build as I kiss him—part arousal, part let's get this the hell over with. Pete ignores my increasingly desperate moans and my hard-on grinding into the fluffy robe covering his thigh. He soothes his hands down my back, over my backside, up my flanks. One pass slides the robe off of my shoulders and I sit back to shrug it off. Pete flares his own robe open and I stop to regard the view.

We were nude in the shower, but now that he is laid out in front of me, I can take in the beauty of his form in its entirety. Nothing in my hours of gawking at the Internet's collection of two-dimensional well-oiled man flesh holds a candle to the sensory experience of this moment—the scent of Pete's shower damp hair, the way his fingertips leave a sizzling trail across my skin, and the knowledge that his insistent cock will soon be inside me. I work my mouth down his body, hungry to taste every part of him. I lick the warm skin on his neck and swirl my tongue around the flat disks of his nipples that harden to tight peaks in my mouth. When my nose brushes his navel and then my open lips encounter the burning hot skin of his erection I hesitate.

"Can I . . ."

"It's your party, sweetheart. Help yourself." He arches his hips, bringing the swollen head closer to my mouth. When I flick my tongue across the slit, I get a taste of precome that makes my mouth water. I am embarrassed at my inexperience, but Pete's fingers come to the back of my head and gently bring me down to him. This time I open my mouth and take in as much of him as I can and I am rewarded with a rumbling "Oh, fuck" from Pete. When I feel the head of his cock at the back of my throat, I close my lips around the shaft, tracing it up then circling my tongue around the fat swollen head.

"Ohh, fuck, Troy . . ."

I salivate around his dick in my mouth as I move my head up and down, sweeping my tongue along the back with every upstroke, each time exploring a new contour. My own cock seeps and I fight off the urge to rut against Pete's thigh. I choke down a gag, my eyes water, and I worry that I might cut Pete with my teeth, but Pete gently fucking my mouth drives me to a near erotic insanity. I give my erection a firmer than comfortable squeeze to try to reset things a little, I'm afraid I'm going to jizz on the sheets like a man much younger.

"How does that feel, baby?" Nick's voice comes close. My eyes flick up to see that he has taken a position near Pete's head, cradling it with one arm. "How does his mouth feel sucking your cock?"

"Shit, it's good. Oh, shit. Troy . . . you have to stop, I'm going to come . . . " Pete tries to lift my head off of him, but I push his hands away. My last few strokes have drawn out more pre-come, and there is no way I'm giving up the chance to have the entire load.

"I want to finish." I take him back in, pulsing my lips and tongue as he thrusts. Pete's body tenses and his cock vibrates. I almost choke on the thick rope that hits the back of my throat, filling my senses with the salty hot flavor. I suck and swallow until he is shuddering underneath me, taking one last stroke with my tongue and then reluctantly releasing him. Pete breaks a kiss with Nick to raise his head to look at me with half-closed eyes.

"Fuck, Troy." He flops back down with arms outstretched and lets out a long exhale, then pops up on his elbows. "You're going to have to give me a few minutes to recover after that. Lie down." I take Pete's place on the pillow, and Nick returns to the chair in the corner, shedding his clothes as he goes. He resumes his seated position, cock in one hand, drink in the other, a dark and watchful gaze on his face.

Pete spreads my legs wide and positions me so that Nick can watch as he plays with me. He teases me at first, stroking spit-slicked fingers down my crease then dipping his fingertip into me and withdrawing when I try to press onto him, greedy for more. When he sweeps a finger in deep, my cock seeps with need and Pete runs his hot tongue across my slit, making me cry out, my desire so great I'm in pain. I start to pump in to his mouth but he pulls away.

"I want to make you come when I'm fucking you," he tells me. "Are you ready?"

"Yes."

"Do you want me to put my cock in your ass, Troy?"

"*Yesss . . . yessss.*" I flip over and press my face into the sheets, arching my back and presenting my ass in the air. "Please . . . yes . . ."

Cool lube drizzles onto my backside, and fingertips follow, first tracing around my hole then gliding in. One, then two fingers, then a burn with a third. Each new introduction is preceded by more lube and grunts of approval from Nick.

When Pete holds three fingers in my ass, pressing deep, I wobble forward.

"Whoa there, honey. You okay?" Nick's arm darts out to steady me.

"I may have had a few drinks tonight."

"You don't say?" Nick raises amused eyebrows. I hear the crinkle of a condom wrapper, then a firm pressure on my entrance. I push into it, resulting in a searing spear of heat in my ass that travels up my spine and makes me buck.

"Holy fuck." I lose my balance and pitch forward toward the edge of the bed. In my slow-motion whiskey brain I see the floor approaching and a headline that reads *"Gay Man Gets Concussion Trying Anal Sex For the First Time."* Nick catches me again, but this time I keep a hold of his thick forearm.

"His dick is bigger than my toys," I whisper, pressing my face into his palm.

He brushes his lips to my forehead with a chuckle. "Do you want me to go back to the chair?"

"No. I like you here." Nick settles himself on the bed next to me as the ass spear advances and I let out a sort of scream sigh.

"Relax, sweetheart. Slow breaths, bear down a little." Nick strokes my back lightly with one hand as he wraps the other around his massive erection. The heat of Nick's body and the scent of his arousal surround me, an intoxicating combination more powerful than the whiskey, and Pete slides in past my resistance. I moan, a low guttural sound, as I open to take him completely.

"You okay, baby? You want him to stop?" Nick asks.

"Don't stop, don't stop." The burning transforms into an exquisite heat that radiates from the base of my spine. I bring my hand to my erection, slick with precome, and this time my moan is pure pleasure as I begin to stroke.

"There you go," Nick says as Pete pushes in deep, his balls brushing mine. The thought of him being so far inside me makes me whimper.

"Are you still okay?" Pete asks me in a throaty voice.

"Fuck me, please fuck me," I beg, completely unashamed. The flare of sparks that Pete is creating with his entry is like a fuse burning on the stick of TNT that is my cock. I let my body rock with Pete's thrusts, one of my hands working my cock at a frantic pace and the other gripping Nick's thigh as if I might fall off this wild ride.

"I'm going to come. Oh, god, I'm coming." I cry out as if my body is a bomb about to detonate and everyone should take cover. A blinding white heat rushes through my entire body as hot jets of come explode from my cock. Nick holds me tight as Pete digs his fingers into my hips and pounds into me with his own release.

Nick eases me to my side and I lie there for a moment, trying to gather all the pieces of myself that shattered with that epic orgasm. Through heavy lidded eyes I watch as Pete and Nick come together, mouths seeking. Nick consumes Pete like he is starving, devouring him with a kiss that is both tender and possessive. Nick purrs deeply when Pete presses him back onto the bed and takes the big man's large cock into his mouth.

In the dim light I catch a glint of metal on Nick's chest. Curiosity overwhelms my postcoital haze and I move to Nick's side so I can flick my tongue across the ring adorning his nipple. He reacts with a sharp inhale and Pete pulls back, his eyes flashing to me. For a second I worry that I have violated some unspoken rule, but then Nick curls me under his massive arm and pulls me to him, which seems to translate into *more please*. When I pull the ring between my teeth and flick it with my tongue, Nick buries his face in my hair and crushes me to his chest.

"Oh, fuck, Troy."

His breath heats my scalp as he whimpers out my name, and something inside me sort of . . . breaks. Not in a destructive sense, but as if something has escaped from a confinement that was limiting. A molten heat flows through my body and infuses me in entirety, from behind my eyes to my toes. It is the ecstasy of a connection with a person, two people, anchored by the physical but extending to so much more.

Pete's head bobs in between Nick's legs and my fingers find Nick's other nipple ring so I can tug on it as I continue to work the one in my mouth. Nick's large body writhes and his exertions heat the whole room. Soon the three of us are slick with sweat.

"Pete, oh, baby, I'm going to come." I suck hard on the ring in my mouth and press my teeth into the point of Nick's nipple. "Fuck, fuck. Oh, *shitPetefuuuuckkkk.*" Nick's orgasm seems to last forever, his body rippling with waves of pleasure as he pumps into Pete's mouth. Finally, his straining is replaced with shudders as he whoops and chuckles in that sort of maniacal way one does when he has been both delighted and surprised.

"Oh . . . Pete . . . sweetheart . . . Troy . . . come here . . ." Nick pulls Pete on top of him as he crushes my lips with a kiss. When he pulls away, Pete replaces Nick's lips with his own. I work my tongue aggressively into Pete's mouth, trying to consume as much of Nick as I can. Then I melt against Nick's solid body with the realization that now I have the essence of both of these men inside me.

There is more kissing and then just as the awkward feeling of *what happens now?* starts to settle into my brain, Nick scoops me up and rearranges me in the bed, fluffing a pillow and pulling the sheets over me like it's where I belong. I drift off to sleep, sweaty, satisfied, and deflowered.

Bright light wakes me, and before I even open my eyes I'm confused. The light is at the wrong angle for my own bedroom and there is an unfamiliar scent of bed-warmed man that makes the skin on my morning wood pull tight. My eyes open and fall on Pete's face, gazing at me with a sleepy smile. The little gasp I emit results in Nick's head peeking over Pete's shoulder with a matching grin. A second later, the rest of the large naked man pops up and he makes his way to the bathroom. I try not to stare. Pete continues to grin at me.

"Good morning, gorgeous."

"Uh, morning . . ." *Oh, god, now what?* I have no concept of morning after protocol. *Should I offer to make breakfast? Do laundry? I can't believe I fell asleep. Should I have even stayed the night?* Fuck. So many questions. Before I can enter panic mode, Pete pulls back the sheet to reveal my erection.

"Nick says you have the most adorable O face." He brushes his fingers along my jaw. "He wants to give you a blow job so I can watch. Is that okay?"

I know the answer to that one.

TAKE ONE

Rose P. Lethe

"That's not waterproof, is it?"

Sheri didn't look away from the bathroom mirror, although she did wrinkle her nose as she batted her long lashes into the mascara wand. "Right, because I want to ruin my eyelash extensions before the expo's even started. What do you think I am, an amateur?"

First coat finished, she shoved the wand back into the tube and turned to Tori, who stood in the open doorway, the very picture of casual in her worn jeans and blue flannel overshirt. As Sheri watched, one side of the shirt slipped off Tori's shoulder, exposing the thin strap of the white tank top underneath, along with her smooth, tan skin.

"Don't worry," Sheri added with a smirk. "I'm not about to miss out on a shot of it running down my face when I'm all fucked out."

Tori didn't respond, other than to fish her phone from her

pocket and aim it at Sheri.

Knowing her partner well after two years of shooting together, and four months of living together, Sheri turned back to the mirror and applied her second coat of mascara with her ass shoved backward. Her black silk robe—already short enough to be obscene—slid even higher up her thighs.

Whenever Tori edited and posted the photo online, it would no doubt be in black and white with the contrast heavily adjusted. Whereas Sheri put as little effort as possible into her behind-the-scenes and promo pics, Tori went full artsy in everything she did.

Not that Sheri was complaining. Her sales had exploded when Tori had taken over the post-production. Just like Tori's had improved when Sheri had applied her own marketing and SEO know-how to the video descriptions.

They made a damn good team—part of why they were nearly booked solid for the next five days. Cons and expos were good for not just networking, but for trade shoots, and Tori and Sheri had no shortage of industry friends eager to benefit from their combined expertise.

Her mascara applied and the phone back in Tori's pocket, Sheri stood up straight again and eyed herself in the mirror. She looked made-up but classically so—smoky eyeshadow, winged liner, chiseled cheekbones—and her hair lay sleek against her scalp in a gelled high ponytail that fell down her neck like a dirty-blonde waterfall. Perfect.

The bathroom counter was a disaster, the glossy marble strewn with four separate makeup and hair kits. She and Tori had splurged on a spacious, high-end hotel room specifically for this shoot, ensuring they had the space—and the thick, sound-proof walls—they needed.

The bathroom still smelled strongly of hair spray, setting

mist, and perfume, although everyone else had finished getting ready a few minutes ago. From the other room, their voices rose and fell in surges, occasionally erupting into laughter or delighted shrieks.

As though summoned by Sheri's wandering mind, Amber appeared in the doorway. Dark-skinned, curvaceous, and in her early forties, she wore a black corset, black push-up bra, black panty harness, and black fishnets, and carried a bottle of toy cleaner and six dildos of varying colors, shapes, and sizes.

"Hey," she said, scooting past Tori. "We're ready whenever y'all are. No rush though, obviously."

Instead of claiming the first sink, she crowded beside Sheri in front of the second, playfully nipping Sheri's shoulder through her robe.

"Hey," Sheri said, just as playfully flicking Amber's elbow. "You can bite me when we film your stuff, not before."

Amber heaved a sigh like she was greatly inconvenienced. "Four long days from now. You're depriving me, Cherry-girl."

Amber knew Sheri's legal name, just as Sheri knew hers and everyone else's—thanks to the model release forms and STD results, if nothing else—but they used stage names exclusively. Today Sheri was Cherry Love, working with Goddess Amber Shia, Tori-X, Candy-Lynn Cruise, and Violet Payne.

Sheri let herself be shoved away from the sink, muttering about bossy and power-crazed dommes, and sidled up to Tori, who was watching with interest as Amber scrubbed and rinsed the toys one by one.

"You sure you don't want to be part of it?" Sheri asked. "We could set up a second tripod . . . or do the POV thing . . ."

Tori hesitated, clearly considering it, but shook her head. "Probably not. I'm not really feeling it today."

"Well, if you change your mind . . ."

"Not feeling the performance on camera?" Amber spoke up. "Or not feeling anything?"

Tori made as though to tuck a piece of hair behind her ear, a coy little tell she still hadn't lost even though she'd chopped her floppy pixie cut into an undercut months ago. Sheri grinned, loving when she got shy. It was such a difference from her on-screen persona, which could rival Amber's in brashness and self-assurance.

"The camera," Tori muttered, gazing down at her own feet.

When she didn't elaborate, Sheri offered, "I'm not the only one who's been on the blandest diet ever for the last week. Trust me: she's looking forward to later."

With Amber humming approvingly and Tori groaning, "*Cherry*," Sheri padded out of the bathroom, still grinning.

The lights had already been set up around the hotel room, although thankfully not turned on yet. The ring light especially put out as much heat as a space heater, Sheri's least favorite part of filming by far. A DSLR, which would serve as their stationary camera, had been mounted to a tripod and positioned to capture the full length of the neatly made bed, where the scene would take place.

The colors of the room were muted, mostly shades of gray, silver, and white, and the décor minimalist. Just outside the bathroom was a sitting area, where Candy-Lynn and Violet were sharing one side of a gray velvet sectional, leaning against each other as they pored over something on Candy-Lynn's phone.

"Drama?" Sheri asked.

Violet clicked her tongue. She wore a leopard-print halter bralette and black boyshorts, and her dark hair fell in voluminous curls just past her ears. "Always."

Candy-Lynn, dressed in a white graphic tee and underwear as rosy pink as her neck-length wavy hair, made a noise of agreement.

Whereas Violet marketed herself as a bratty switch, Candy-Lynn was as sweet and girl-next-door as her stage name implied. Sheri had worked with them both during last year's expo and kept in close touch on social media. They had good chemistry together, giving off a sort of flirty-twentysomethings-at-a-slumber-party vibe that customers just ate up.

"I don't miss camming," Amber said, coming out of the bathroom with her freshly cleaned dildos. "All that cattiness, whew."

"It's only because I love you," said Violet, "that I won't point out you can be just as bad."

"Worse," Candy-Lynn added cheerfully.

Amber snorted, but before she could deny it, Tori joined them and clapped her hands loudly, getting everyone's attention.

"All right," she said. "Are we about ready to get started?"

They were. The lights were flicked on, chasing away the shadows from the bed. Sheri removed her robe, leaving herself nude, her fresh spray tan giving her usually pale skin a sun-kissed glow.

As Tori adjusted the settings on the handheld camera—her baby, a 4K professional camcorder that she'd scrimped and saved for—she said, "Don't forget: I'm just the cameraperson today. As far as you're concerned, I'm not here."

Various noises of acknowledgment followed the reminder. Amber was securing the smallest of the clean toys, a ruby-colored dildo with a short, smooth shaft and a gentle upward slope, into her panty harness. Violet perused the other options before selecting a thick realistic dildo. Candy-Lynn, watching over her shoulder, oohed at the choice.

There was nothing more to say. Sheri had already outlined the scene she had in mind, and they knew her brand: casual and natural, sex that felt intimate and—most importantly—real to the viewer.

Sheri double-checked the bottle of lubricant, which had been placed within easy reach on the nightstand along with a few folded towels. A pack of water sat on the coffee table in front of the sectional, a few bottles cooling in the mini fridge.

When she turned back, satisfied, she gave Tori a nod, which Tori returned.

"Okay," Tori said. "Lesbian gangbang, take one."

Amber kissed like she did everything else: confidently, holding nothing back. She hauled Sheri's body against her own, crushing her large breasts to Sheri's smaller ones and grabbing one of Sheri's ass cheeks in each hand. Her teeth closed gently around Sheri's bottom lip, not quite biting—heeding Sheri's limits—and she sucked until it stung. Her perfume, something expensive and woodsy, enveloped Sheri, taking over her senses as surely as if someone had thrown a hood over her head.

It would've been hotter without the dildo poking Sheri in the pelvis, but it was plenty hot anyway. Amber manhandled and took charge like no one else Sheri had ever fucked. It drew out a submissiveness in her that rarely saw the light of day otherwise, like a flower waiting for the perfect sliver of sunlight to coax it from its soil.

That's what made her Goddess Amber, Sheri supposed.

Still sucking at Sheri's lips, Amber started to walk her backward. Toward the bed, Sheri thought, until she collided with something taller and more solid than a mattress. Something that wrapped its arms around her and placed a closed-mouth kiss behind her ear.

Violet, tall and sculpted with her dancer's body, her curls tickling Sheri's skin. She laid a palm across Sheri's throat, her thumb tracing Sheri's jawline, and said, mockingly, "Come on, *Goddess*. Don't hog her. Let someone else have a turn."

Amber broke away, grinning. "No need to get pissy, Vi. There's plenty to go around."

Twisting Sheri's chin to the side, Violet smeared their mouths together. Her lips were gentler, less demanding than Amber's, but now that Amber had nudged Sheri toward the proper head-space, she had no problem giving herself over to the kiss as if Violet had commanded it.

Amber dragged her fingertips over Sheri's ass, along her hips, and up her stomach until she was cupping Sheri's breasts, squeezing them together. Sheri arched into the touch, both for the benefit of the camera and in a request for more.

Obligingly, Amber flicked her thumbs over Sheri's nipples and rumbled in approval when Sheri moaned into Violet's mouth and arched even further.

"Come on," Amber said. "Don't be shy. There we go."

Sheri assumed the words were aimed at her until she felt a second, more hesitant touch on one breast. A tongue replaced Amber's thumb, licking tentatively at her nipple.

Candy-Lynn, shy and sweet, her body warm and pillowy against Sheri's side.

Sheri tore her lips from Violet's, sank her fingers into Candy-Lynn's silky-soft pink waves, and waited, not-so-patiently, until Candy-Lynn finally raised her head and claimed her kiss next.

Hers was the gentlest of the three, all closed mouths and barely there pressure, but because she wore a thick coat of sparkly pink lip gloss, it was also the slickest. Their lips met, again and again, with one wet smack after another. The sound, loud and obscene in the quiet room, added a spark to Sheri's already simmering arousal.

Amber resumed playing with Sheri's tits, rolling the nipples between her thumbs and forefingers. Every so often she pinched and tugged just how Sheri liked, in a way that made her clench and ache between her thighs.

Violet was still plastered against her back, stroking Sheri everywhere she could reach: neck and ribs, hips and outer thighs. She pressed sloppy kisses along Sheri's nape, the wet noises playing a perfect counter melody to Candy-Lynn's kisses.

The best part of filming with friends, Sheri thought, was they knew just how to touch her, how to get her where she needed to be to make the scene perfect.

"Those are some hip movements, Cherry-girl," Amber murmured. "I bet you wish there was something to rub against."

Violet hummed against Sheri's bare shoulder. "We've barely even started. What do you want to bet she's already wet?"

"Oh, I wouldn't take that bet. You know I don't like to lose."

Candy-Lynn drew back, their lips parting with one last smack, just as Amber slipped a hand between Sheri's thighs.

"Yep," Amber crowed. "Wet. She's so easy."

"Sorry," Sheri said, breathless as Amber traced a firm finger from her entrance to her clit and back again. "I'll try to be harder from now on."

"Is she supposed to talk back?" Candy-Lynn asked.

"Toys don't talk," said Violet.

"They sure don't," Amber agreed. "Let's put something in that mouth to shut her up. Get her on the bed."

Aside from a halfhearted "I'm not a toy," Sheri didn't struggle as Violet and Candy-Lynn worked together to drag her the short distance to the bed. She was shoved backward, landing on the plush white duvet with a *whoomph.*

"Of course you are." Candy-Lynn's tone dripped like syrup as she climbed onto the mattress beside Sheri. Her tee clung to her full curves, stretched so tight that Sheri could see the pink of her bra beneath it. "You're *our* toy."

Violet settled on her knees on Sheri's opposite side, her nude-painted lips stretched wide in a grin. "You are. You can't pretend you're not. You wouldn't be so wet for us if you weren't. Now, up. You can't suck Goddess Amber's cock like that."

Sheri allowed herself to be positioned on her hands and knees. Amber knelt on the bed in front of her, one hand wrapped around the base of the red dildo. With the other hand, she fisted Sheri's ponytail and tipped Sheri's head back.

The vulnerable line of her throat exposed, Sheri gazed up at Amber. Under the lights, her gold cheek highlight gleamed and her skin glowed with a youthful dewiness and radiance that belied her age. *She really does look like a goddess*, Sheri thought, a little dreamily.

Then Amber smiled and said, "Open up," and Sheri soon stopped thinking of anything that wasn't the rigid silicone pushing past her lips.

Paying no attention to Sheri's oversensitive gag reflex, Amber drove the full length into Sheri's mouth in one thrust, hitting the back of Sheri's tongue, and held her in place as she gagged around the intrusion.

"Shh," Candy-Lynn said, stroking between Sheri's shoulder blades. "You can take it."

"Take it," Violet echoed, "like a good toy."

Her voice came not from beside Sheri, as Candy-Lynn's did, but behind, and it was followed by a sure grip on Sheri's hips, tilting them up. When Sheri's ass was as high as it could go, Violet spanked her. Her palm struck Sheri's left cheek with a resounding slap and a force that rocked Sheri forward, shoving the dildo deeper.

Her throat convulsed, and she gagged harder. Tears welled up in her eyes, and after another spank—to her right cheek this time—they began to fall.

Amber tugged at her ponytail, jerking her head back, and then thrust forward again, fucking her mouth roughly.

Candy-Lynn made low, soothing noises while Violet petted Sheri's vulva, dipping her fingers into the slit to get them wet. Then, without pause, she slid two into Sheri's cunt and quickly fell into the same hard, punishing rhythm as Amber.

Together, they swung Sheri from cock to fingers, cock to fingers, while Candy-Lynn continued to murmur sweet nonsense that Sheri could barely hear over her own gagging.

Not that Sheri needed soothing any longer. She'd sunk fully into her role: a willing toy with enough holes to accommodate anything these lovely women could want, even if she had to choke and cry to do it.

"You're hogging her mouth again," said Violet, laughter in her voice. "Why don't you give Candy a turn, hm?"

Grunting, Amber withdrew. The dildo jerked free, taking a glob of saliva with it that dribbled down Sheri's chin to join the tears on her cheeks.

Tori stood behind Amber, camera poised to capture Sheri's face—probably getting a close-up of the mascara trails, Sheri thought. She just barely remembered not to acknowledge her or the camera.

"Fine, fine," Amber sighed. "She's all yours, sugar."

Sheri was jostled like a rag doll, Violet's wiry arms working to manhandle her around the bed until Candy-Lynn could comfortably lie on her back in front of her. Candy-Lynn had removed her panties and rucked her tee out of the way, baring the heavy curve of her lower belly and her pubic mound with its dusting of blonde hair.

Once she was settled, Candy-Lynn parted her thighs, filling Sheri's nostrils with her musky scent. Candy-Lynn was soaked. Sheri could see the wetness glistening on her labia.

Her mouth watered, and she licked her lips, lowering to her elbows to get closer. Giggling girlishly, Candy-Lynn ran her fingertips along Sheri's hairline.

"Just a sec," she said. "Vi's about to . . ."

Something blunt and cool prodded at Sheri's entrance, answering the question of what Violet was about to do. Sheri moaned as her pussy opened around the toy, which was stiffer and thicker than Violet's fingers. Longer, too—it sank deeper and deeper until the tip pressed against Sheri's cervix. She circled her hips with another moan, relishing the stretch and the fullness.

Violet swatted the side of her ass, but it was Amber, taking up Candy-Lynn's former position beside Sheri, who said, "None of that. You take what we give you. If you're good, we'll make it good for you. If not . . ."

Violet spanked her again as if to illustrate and withdrew the dildo inch by creeping inch until Sheri felt the ridge of its flared tip. She groaned, dropping her forehead to the mattress.

It felt good. It made her want more.

Candy-Lynn grabbed her ponytail. Where Amber's grip had been a command, Candy-Lynn's was a suggestion.

A suggestion that Sheri gladly accepted.

She lifted her head and let Candy-Lynn guide her open, eager mouth to where she was hot and slick and waiting. Candy-Lynn sighed when Sheri's lips closed around her clit, and her thighs fell shut, loosely trapping Sheri between them.

Candy-Lynn was as responsive as ever, her whole body trembling with every flick of Sheri's tongue. Her noises of pleasure were soft and breathy, barely audible over the sounds of Sheri's mouth or Sheri's cunt sucking at the toy Violet was thrusting in and out in a slow but steady pace.

"Hand me the lube," Violet said.

Sheri whimpered, everything inside her going hot and tight. She knew what was coming, and she was more than ready for it.

The mattress bounced—Amber stretching long toward the nightstand—and the quiet snick of the lube bottle followed, then a squelch.

"You'll probably have to take over, sugar," Amber said. "You know how she gets."

And damn if it didn't make Sheri hotter to be talked about like she wasn't even here. *A toy,* she thought, suddenly aware of the way her clit throbbed, begging for attention it wasn't going to get. *Nothing but a toy.*

Candy-Lynn tightened her grip on Sheri's hair, holding her still, and rocked against Sheri's face. She moved haltingly at first, searching for the right angle and rhythm, and then harder once she'd found it.

Candy-Lynn's breathy cries crescendoed to loud, blissful whines. She started pulsing under Sheri's tongue just as Violet wiggled a lubed finger into Sheri's ass.

Oh, Sheri thought, *yes. Please.*

Her ass had long been Sheri's top selling point. Not only was it wide and round like a peach, but she loved to have it played with. She'd been named Anal Queen of the Year three years running for a reason, after all.

She relaxed into the sensation, giving herself over to it as she'd given herself over to Amber's kiss, while Candy-Lynn rode out her aftershocks against Sheri's face.

Violet kept the dildo motionless, still buried all the way to Sheri's cervix. She felt full in a way that seemed almost too much. Almost. But it wasn't, of course. If anything, it was too little. She could take so much more.

And she would.

If she wanted to be good, she would take everything these three women doled out.

By the time Candy-Lynn backed away, letting Sheri drop her forehead into her folded arms, Violet had two fingers inside her ass, going so slowly and carefully that Sheri ground her teeth, biting back the urge to beg.

"How was she?" asked Amber. She scraped her nails along Sheri's nape, the pressure just shy of painful.

"*So* good," Candy-Lynn said with feeling. "My legs are all wobbly. You should give her a try, Vi."

Groaning, Sheri bucked against Violet's hand—just slightly, before she caught herself, but enough that everyone surely saw her. The camera surely saw her.

Violet laughed. "Yeah, she knows what's coming. Look how bad she wants her ass fucked."

"Such a slut," Amber agreed. Sheri shivered at her tone, which was husky with sly delight.

"And no one knows how to handle sluts better than Goddess Amber," Violet said.

Gently, Violet eased both the toy and her fingers free. Sheri protested the emptiness with a whimper, although she wasn't empty long.

She'd only just raised her head to take in the sight of Violet standing in front of the bed, shimmying her boyshorts down her long legs, before Amber was clasping Sheri's hips, angling them higher.

Once Sheri was in position, Amber didn't hesitate. She drove her harnessed dildo into Sheri's ass, sinking all the way to the hilt in one thrust.

The toy wasn't much thicker than Violet's fingers, but it burned all the same. Some part of Sheri recognized the burn shouldn't have felt good, but it did. It felt so good she clawed at the duvet and cried out, her clit throbbing more insistently.

Violet took Candy-Lynn's former position, lying on the bed with her thighs spread. Her pubic hair was a riot of dark curls, her musk so thick that Sheri could taste it even before Violet hauled her forward by the back of her head, practically crashing Sheri's mouth into her wet vulva.

Violet rode her face with none of Candy-Lynn's gentleness. Instead, she matched Amber's brutal pace like she had before, ushering Sheri violently between dick and clit, dick and clit. They grunted together, Amber in exertion and Violet in pleasure.

Pinned between them, Sheri could only suck in desperate breaths through her nose and exhale them on stuttered moans.

"Good girl," Candy-Lynn murmured. Her voice seemed to come from far away. "You like that, don't you? Imagine when Violet gets the other strap-on out. You'll get it in your ass and your pussy . . . and you know what? I'll even give it to you in your mouth too."

"Holy shit, Candy," Violet hissed. She wrenched Sheri's head away and replaced Sheri's tongue with her own fingers. As she touched herself, groaning, she put space between them, staring down at Sheri like she was the hottest thing Violet had ever seen.

Amber's next thrust shoved Sheri almost flat on her belly, planting her face into the mattress. With her mouth free but muffled, Sheri gasped and swore and cried to her heart's content. She felt so full, so dirty. So perfect.

Then Amber wrapped an arm around her and slipped two fingers into Sheri's cunt from the front, filling her even more and grinding the heel of her hand into Sheri's clit.

The pace slowed. From one of Sheri's keening *oh*s to the next, it went from rough and hard to leisurely, almost tender.

It felt more like a massage than a fucking, soothing away the lingering burn.

"She's so tight," Amber said, practically purring, "and getting tighter. I think she's going to come for me. Aren't you, sweetheart?"

Someone grabbed a handful of Sheri's ponytail. Violet, she thought at first, but when she looked up—squinting into the lights, which suddenly seemed so painfully, eye-wateringly bright—she discovered it was Tori, holding the camera in one hand and Sheri's hair in the other.

Her voice hoarse, Tori said, "Can someone undo my pants please?"

It was Violet who closed in on Tori from behind and unzipped her jeans. Then, clearly knowing where this was leading as well as Sheri did, Violet unbuttoned the boxers Tori wore beneath and threaded Tori's packer through the opening.

The caramel-colored silicone was squishy and hung in a flaccid state, but with her slender fingers curled around the base, Violet aimed it toward Sheri's mouth like it was fully erect.

Tori's grip on Sheri's hair guided her roughly forward until she had no choice but to suck the packer into her mouth. Bigger than Amber's dildo in both length and width, it tasted salty, like sweat, and stretched her so wide her jaw ached.

Another hand grabbed her neck—Candy-Lynn, Sheri realized after a moment—and took over for Tori, making Sheri bob back and forth. Sculpted veins along the shaft rasped over Sheri's tongue, and the tip nudged the back of her throat, making her gag and tear up anew.

With Candy-Lynn and Violet in control of fucking Sheri's face, Tori was free to cup Sheri's jaw. She swept her thumb affectionately along Sheri's bottom lip and then slipped it in alongside her dick, stretching Sheri's jaw that much more.

Sheri wanted to gaze up into Tori's eyes, to see them dark and hooded with greedy satisfaction. Instead, she stared into the black hole of the camera lens, letting the viewer see her in all her teary, mascara-streaked, fucked-out beauty.

She came like that, choking on Tori's cock and clenching around the dildo in her ass and Amber's fingers in her cunt.

As Sheri's orgasm wound down, she continued to suck Tori's dick lazily, whirling her tongue around Tori's thumb. The scene, which had gone hazy in Sheri's lust-drunk mind, gradually sharpened. Reality returned.

Sheri was never more aware of the hairline fissure between Cherry Love and Sheri Greeson than in moments like this. They were the same, yes—mirrored facets of one personality, one sexual being—yet they were different too. Cherry reveled in being reduced to a toy and used, passed from partner to partner or sandwiched between them.

Sheri looked past the camera now, saw the faint smirk on Tori's lips, and thought, *Enjoy it while you can, baby. Because when the cameras are off tonight, you'll be the needy slut spit-roasted between my cock and Amber's.*

Tori's smirk widened. Her cheeks flushed the same pale pink as Candy-Lynn's hair, as though she knew exactly what Sheri was thinking.

Sheri suspected if Tori had a free hand, she'd be trying to tuck that nonexistent hair behind her ear again.

But when Tori spoke, she only said, "I don't think you were supposed to come yet."

"Fuck off," Sheri answered, although with her mouth still full, the words were unintelligible.

Spanked and then *spit-roasted*, she amended.

Tori chuckled, lowering the camera. "Uh-huh. Want to pause?"

* * *

And just like that, the scene broke. Candy-Lynn let go of Sheri's neck, Violet of Tori's packer, and Tori set the handheld camera down on the bed and moved to tuck herself away again.

As Amber pulled out, Sheri swallowed a moan, feeling loose and slick and used in that way that she—that Cherry—loved most.

In answer to Tori's question, Violet exclaimed, "God, yes. Let's pause. I need to pee."

Candy-Lynn giggled and singsonged, "You should've gone before we got started."

"All right, *Mom*."

"I could use some water," Amber said. She swiped the back of her arm over her forehead. "And a towel. Fuck, those lights are hot."

Sheri concurred. With nothing to distract her now, the beads of sweat dripping down the slopes and creases of her skin surged to the forefront of her awareness.

She sat up with a grimace, her face hot and her knees and elbows protesting noisily. She would spend the next part of the shoot on her back, she decided, to give her joints a break.

"All right," Tori said. "We're breaking for pee and water and whatever else you need to do. Then we'll get ready for take two."

TECHNOSEXUAL

Ida J

Gabriel and I are getting ready to go out, to the club where we spend most of our Sunday nights. I am pondering which improbable ensemble of straps to wear tonight. The full body leather harness, with all those buckles, matching handcuffs, and choker seems appropriate. I'm in a naughty mood and neither of us has to work tomorrow. I just turned in a job, he sets his own hours. Seems I'm not the only one.

That's why he was in the bathroom so long. He rarely does this.

But I find it wildly sexy when he does. I bet my makeup bag is a mess.

He has clearly been rummaging in my underwear drawer. I recognize that high-waisted black thong, the one with the mesh and the beautiful pinprick holes in the black material. Trust him to pick my best underwear, princess that he is.

He's beautiful, albeit usually in a more traditionally masculine way. His jaw looks like it was chiseled from a cliffside. His shoulders are broad and his biceps ripple; he is skinny at the waist, with long legs and a small tight butt. A hint of muscle on his stomach, a hint of ribcage belies the fact that he should probably take advantage of the döner place round the corner a little more often. Despite the masculinity of his body, he also has something of the feminine to him, in his exaggerated movements, a certain flair or flamboyance in his expansive gestures. And at the moment, with his tight ass in my best thong, his wide sinewy shoulders crammed into a mesh bra, his eyes dark lined and lips painted, he is a vision, a perfect melding of qualities, high drama in his revealing outfit. He's trimmed his pubic hair, I see as I pull him in toward me by the front of the panties to kiss his neck, careful not to smudge his red lipstick, painted delicately onto his fine lips. Cheeky bugger, that's my favorite. Egregiously expensive, but I had to have it.

I am rather more masculine tonight, with my shaved head and tattoos. I've been lifting a lot lately and my biceps are really starting to show, both strange and intensely gratifying for someone who has always been skinny and a little jiggly. I want these hard-earned muscles, this proof of growing strength. I lock the big wood door behind us, and we clatter through the stairwell with its black and white tiles. The clear night smells of recent rain and promise as we walk past the local bars with their warm lit interiors, a few Sunday stragglers lurking within them.

We get on the U-bahn, two wastrels in tattered fur coats, on our way to church again, the concrete monolith of fantasies fulfilled, the ultimate temple of hedonism. We are on the guest list tonight, lucky us. Courtesy of a most strange and extraordinary person who we've known for a while now. Marlowe was absolutely insistent that we come out tonight.

Paid up and stamped, we take our coats off in the cavernous entrance, the thud of music sending shivers down my spine. The place is open for the whole weekend and it shows, with people emerging to the coat check who have clearly been here for days.

Marlowe blusters up to us purposefully with kisses and darlings and "How AARRE you both, it's so nice to see you again!" A sexy German-accented whirlwind of extravagance, Marlowe is a force of nature, nowhere more so than in this place, their homeland. They're a casual acquaintance of ours, someone we only really ever see in the club, but who we always have fun with. Their hair is short and mussed, they are wearing a headpiece made of leather that sends dramatic arrows around their cheekbones. Their concave clavicles are adorned with thick chains, torso bare but for these chains, which graze the musculature of their arms invitingly. They wear a black thong and black platform goth boots of the stompiest pedigree.

Marlowe ushers us over to the bar on the ground floor. Beers for them, maté for me, we sit in one of the padded booths catching up. Marlowe had been away. "Can't you tell? I have a tan!"

"No Marlowe, you have all the tan of a snowy day!" I observe, leaning my head toward the flirtatiously proffered leg that extends for my inspection. The thigh before me is lean and defined and hairy, with a fetching leather garter buckled around it, thin and dramatic-looking. I'm not sure if Marlowe is male or female or somewhere in between. It would be rather rude to ask; we don't know each other that well. Either way, they're hot and they know it. Our eyes meet as I run a finger over the garter, prompting a slight eyebrow raise from both of us. Gabriel smiles and looks at me inquisitively.

We decide to go and dance, up the stairs and into the fray, the cacophonous clash of the music in the colossal room where the wraiths wield their limbs like weapons, the crowd heaving and ecstatic. The atmosphere hits you instantly, like the light-headedness of standing abruptly after a deep sleep. It's another universe, where people come to shed their inhibitions and dance to the thundering beat of their heart's desire.

Taking a break from the frenetic dance floor, there is a frisson as we stand in the bathroom queue, the three of us leaning against the wall. A gaggle of acquaintances drifting by say hello, cackling as one of them points out that all three of us are wearing thongs, what a bunch of butt-bearing sluts. We laugh over our mutual shamelessness, not that it's unusual in this place, where it's commonplace to see people wandering about wearing nothing but a cock ring or the hoops in their nipples. I am standing a little to the side, they are opposite each other, shoulders on the wall. It's like there's electricity between them as the noise and chaos recede into the background with the tension. Their crimson lips meet in a kiss so tentative it seems slow motion, as red meets red and they seem suspended in this kiss for so long.

Marlowe takes us each by the hand, leading as we weave our way through the people at the side of the room, toward the front where the dark rooms are. They look back at us coquettishly. We follow them into the pitch-black space populated with moving bodies shifting around us.

Marlowe's body is hard and skinny, masculine, with nipples that bulge fatly on an otherwise almost entirely flat chest, just a shade of muscle around the pecs. As we run hands down their body and they part their thighs, I notice there is no penis. We kiss, the three of us, lips on lips, on necks, hands groping, exploring each other's bodies in the darkness.

I say to Gabriel, "Would you like to take Marlowe home?" His eyes light up as he smiles in response. Walking back to mine in the morning light, sunglasses on, we chat idly.

Thank fuck I washed the sheets, I think on entering the apartment, as the light streams through my flimsy curtains.

My apartment is rather bare, white walls with battered wooden floorboards, one of those tiled stoves in the corner so typical of Berlin. At least the ceilings are high, with molding. I insist on white net curtains, white sheets, which is probably folly given the life I lead, but I love that hotel look. They smell fresh, just like the nice hotels I've only ever stayed in on a handful of occasions.

Gabriel and Marlowe plonk themselves down on the battered old Chesterfield I made Gabriel drag in off the street with me. I forage in the fridge for mimosa ingredients, pour Rotkäppchen and orange juice into my flea market crystal glasses. As I go back into the other room, they are on the bed kissing. I sashay over to them, still in my rave underwear, the buckles of my harness clinking.

They part to receive me. I hand them glasses and then fetch mine, collapsing onto the bed with them. We lie back in silence for a moment. Gabriel and I lock eyes, exchanging a small smile. I look at Marlowe, they look at me, their blue eyes shining, deep set in that angular face.

The pristine sheets are a contrast to our grubby club-stained bodies. Their long limbs interlock as they kiss on my duvet, cotton crackling beneath them and the light soft on their stained skin. Marlowe lifts their hips and looks expectantly at Gabriel, who takes the prompt and hooks fingers into the sides of the thong, sliding it down over Marlowe's ass.

A downy tuft between the long, slim, hard thighs gives way to a moist vulva, flushed. Sitting atop its taupe lips is a long and engorged clitoris, long enough that its length makes me want to suck on it. I take the tip of my tongue and wind it around the end. Marlowe shivers slightly.

I love this, the element of mystery, the not being sure and the general wondering, whenever I have sex with anyone. What does it feel like to have sex with your body, I wonder. Because

I run into the classic philosophical quandary of feeling that I know only what happens to my body, what I myself experience. But actually, perhaps this is a misconception.

I certainly feel like I can feel the sensations of my beautiful companions. I suck on Marlowe's clit and their pelvis thrusts toward me, as they utter a moan of pleasure. Gabriel is behind them, kissing their neck. His hands run over the slim chest. He takes a nipple between two fingers and squeezes gently, Marlowe writhing at his touch. They gasp and moan, one hand on my head, one clasping his ass. My hands running over their tattooed body, Gabriel's too. He runs a hand up their thigh, slips a large finger into their pussy and moves it gently, then another one. We slow down for a moment.

My sex toys sit on a small table by the bed. A few dildos, a couple of butt plugs. No vibrators. Marlowe deposits their headdress on the sex stand and eyes up a gelatinous black silicone dildo, giving it a suggestive poke. "You have a harness?" I certainly do, a sleek black stretchy one that's easy to navigate, even when you've just spent nine hours dancing. Marlowe slips into it and pokes their member of choice through the hole. They reach for my pussy, wetter by the second, gentle but firm fingers exploring my clit and then probing my cunt. Both of them team up to flip me over. Strong arms lift my ass and my head, and I feel the dildo slipping into my pussy as the cock enters my mouth. They enter in unison, the sensation mirrored between mouth and pussy, sliding and slippery and satisfying. The dildo pushes in right to the hilt so I can feel Marlowe close to me, the warmth of their body, the stretch and give of penetration. Gabriel's cock slips down my throat, I gorge and gulp on it.

I'm filled from both directions, Marlowe's hand grabbing my ass, slapping it. Gabriel's cock twitches as I suck, Marlowe fucks me slowly so I can still move my head. He's rock hard as he watches them fuck me from behind. He loves to watch me get fucked; I can feel his enjoyment. I can't see their faces, but I can hear them breathing, both restraining their movements, though it feels like they want to go faster, to fuck me senseless. I want them to ruin me like the filthy slut I am, but they're not going to give me the satisfaction just yet.

They're communicating, I can tell, wordless directions coordinating the two of them. Slowly, in together, out together, deep like they were going to meet at my core. Hands land on my neck and my hips simultaneously and they hold me in place as they go hard, forceful thrusts with building speed. I am overwhelmed, and I love it, the intensity of sensation at both ends, at the mercy of these two hot creatures of the night.

Marlowe pulls the dildo out for a second to finger my pussy, discovering how wet it is. When they give my pulsating cunt a sharp slap, I gasp with arousal. Gabriel's cock pops out of my mouth. The three of us breathe hard, I wonder what they'll do with me next. Marlowe pulls me up by my arms, holding them behind me. They go slow again, Marlowe with the cock, Gabriel in front with fingers on my clit, sometimes pushing them inside me with the dildo. He holds them there for a second as Marlowe fucks me, their lips on my neck, holding my hips to steady us. Gabriel's eyes meet mine as his fingers are in me, love and lust and pleasure in his look. It feels like melting, enclosed between these two beauties, the liquid runs between my legs and that ticking pressure builds. I scream-moan and shake with an earth-shattering orgasm. I fall sideways on the bed, exhausted, and reach for my drink as Marlowe and Gabriel start to make out intensely. They're running hands over ribs and waists and thighs.

A pause, and Marlowe turns to me, all full of bravado. "Do you think he'd like me to fuck him?" Gabriel flips onto his front, raises his buttocks, and looks over his shoulder suggestively. I think so, if the look on his face is anything to go by. Marlowe slips a condom over the black silicone and gives him a playful slap on the ass, at which Gabriel smiles and looks at them devilishly. "Don't look at me like that, I'm going to ruin your ass!" They've already got a couple of fingers full of lube in Gabriel's asshole, drawing them out and pushing them back in while I pour more lube as they prepare to insert the toy. He wriggles onto his back, legs spread with his knees to his shoulders. His ass swallows the toy and he moans long as it sinks further in.

Marlowe seems to be getting incredible pleasure from this ass fucking. "You like it when I fuck your boyfriend, sweetheart?" I do. Very much so. I love to see him enjoy it so much, without having to put in the work of doing it myself. This way I can immerse myself in his pleasure more fully, kiss his lips, touch his body.

"I love it, almost as much as when you fuck me."

Marlowe pauses to give me a coquettish smile. "Good response," they say.

"Harder," begs Gabriel. His cock twitches slightly. I lube up my hand and stroke it as Marlowe fucks him, he makes delightful noises of pleasure, his head thrown back in bliss. I slide my slippery hand down to his balls, his taint, caressing gently. "Yes, more, please." Gabriel is writhing in desperation.

Marlowe goes slow, gently easing into it. "Feels good?" they ask.

"Yes!" he replies, breathlessly. I bend my head to their chest and take one of the enticingly plump nipples in my mouth, causing them to emit a groan. "Mmmm, right there, keep doing that." I raise my hand to the other nipple and roll it between my fingers.

Gabriel is flushed and he grimaces, looking from one to the other of us like he can't believe his luck. Marlowe rides him faster, but gently, not pulling in and out too much, keeping their hips close to his body, just pushing in quickly. They place their hands on the backs of his thighs for balance, breathing fast. I move my hand to his dick as his excitement crescendoes. His cock seems to inflate as the come pumps out onto his stomach, his ass straining toward Marlowe.

It glistens on his skin and Marlowe bends down to lick a shiny droplet. They appear delighted, like all their Christmases have come at once. Playing with the liquid Gabriel's created, they grab another dildo, a red one, and hand it to me wordlessly, falling onto me as they reach between my legs with their come-slicked fingers. We roll around in a lingering kiss, I squeeze their ass with my free hand, moving my mouth to their slender neck. With the strap-on still in place, Gabriel's fingers reach to lube Marlowe's wet cunt.

Marlowe stretches out of the bed like a cat with a big cock pointing in the air, and spreads their legs in invitation. Gabriel is kissing them, hands wandering over their chest. I climb between their long legs, biting their thighs gently, putting a hand up to press into their pussy. Fingers parted, I suck on their clit, gently. They spread their legs wider, moaning, "Put it in, please put it in." I ease the dildo inside them, enjoying the view of it stretching them open, the contrast of flesh and bright red silicone. Their long clit is pulsating now as their movements become more urgent, hips gyrating up at me, their breathing quicker. "Hard," they command. I push it again and again, putting my weight behind the thrusts as I plunge in, pull out. Marlowe clings to Gabriel as they shudder and shout, clit twitching and pussy contracting, pushing the toy out. It rests there between their legs as I rest my head on their thigh, their elegant hand on my head.

As we drift to sleep in the daylight with Marlowe between us, Gabriel puts his hand on mine. We lock eyes and smile.

There is lipstick smeared on the sheets. None of it is mine.

THIS FIRE

Fallen Kittie

Ashen fumes leave Nina with unshed tears. She isn't pained by the fumes, but she still isn't used to the odor. Eight months have passed since she found herself on the farm. Each day is a constant shift. Glimmers of her former life flash along the horizon. It stands above the plains like a ghost that steals through the harvest. Dementia grayed and thinned out her uncle, Mac. The burly rancher is now an unshaven husk who roams the fields, raving about the need to repent.

Nina isn't much of a farmer, but she likes to think of herself as a good niece. The sun mottles her skin. Mud thickens her coveralls. Her feet ache despite her specialty boots. She has yet to find what drew Mac to this place. Nina gleans staid melancholy in this rust-bucket town of steep boulevards, cargo trains, and quaint countryside.

Rhett is an exception. He towers above it all in crisp black jeans. Nina thinks he embodies a character from a *Lonesome Dove* book. He sports a holstered gun and wears a Stetson the way cowboys do in the movies. He runs a mill some miles off and always musters something to spare. Heat pools within Nina whenever she catches sight of him. Everything he brings isn't overstock; he just says it is to spare her pride.

Rhett knows she has pride to spare.

Unlike Carson.

Because Carson has more pride than Nina. He has to. Everyone knows who he is: the golden son of an urban conglomerate who ranches several estates. Mac's farm neighbors one of his. Once or twice, when the mares unravel the fence, he's been civil enough to help her nudge them into a canter. When Carson's lips curl, Nina's heart dives.

Nina recalls the whispers she's heard from the townsfolk.

Carson resides in a palatial ranch that edges the outskirts. Nina's only been there once, way back when she first moved here. When Mac turned up in his hayloft, Carson was kind enough to play host. His walls are covered in rosewood heirlooms. Once in a blue moon, folks see svelte women there. There's no one name or face, but the women usually sport a pair of Louboutins or Jimmy Choos. None are from the town.

Then, there's Rhett: the playboy who doesn't play nice. His charm seems to be offset by hard energy. He lives in a sprawling tract ranch some miles off. On clearer nights, it stares down the tavern. Nina overhears women revisit their stays whenever she ventures to the bar. Antique fixtures and salvaged trinkets lead to a quilted king-sized bed. Those who make it further enjoy the cowhide that straggles his hearth. He always eyes Nina assuredly, resolutely, like he seeks a reaction to his perusal. Imagine relenting to those wicked, russet eyes, getting seared by the twin flames.

The thought of the men inclines Nina to repurpose the smoldering bumper crop. The smoke rivulets into lassos, which thread around, then through her. A sudden gust of wind thickens the exhaust. It unravels the ponytail that crimps past her shoulders, veering like a pendulum in tandem with her furious pulse.

Two figures halve the smoke. Husky incredulity identifies them. Nina clenches her eyes shut.

Perfect, as if I could look any uglier . . .

"Nina, what the hell are you doing—?"

"—standing so close!"

Rhett and Carson retrieve pieces of sheet metal and brisk them until the smoke clears. Nina coughs, too cumbersome to be anything but pliant, as they trudge to her sides. They each take an arm and guide her to the woodshed.

While Rhett murmurs assurances into her scalp, Carson observes the rusted mowers and the hiss of a baler whose engine is tarred. In the woodshed, disparate planks of lumber jut and spill over. Eventually, Rhett notices too. They survey the expanse and beyond. Their heads turn like spires.

Carson shakes his head. He examines the carpet of straw and dead leaves that crunch under their feet.

Rhett drifts around the stakes, grasps along the trim to muse upon the peeling basswood. He prods a loose block, then whistles as it falls out of place. "Nina, what the fuck were you doing?"

"The same thing you did before you knew better, I imagine," Carson says, glaring.

Rhett's eyes are incisive. They train upon Nina's. She forgets everything she knew when Carson squeezes her shoulder. Her back stiffens. Nina wills away the nerves that threaten to overtake her.

She clears her throat. "I was burning the leftover straw."

"With charcoal?" Rhett snorts. "The charcoal *I* gave you last week? If I'd known you'd use it like this . . ."

Carson crosses his arms. "You can't stand that close to the fire. You're not supposed to do it alone either."

Rhett replaces his Stetson, fans away what remains of the fumes. "You're lucky we came by when we did. Any later and you would've choked from inhalation."

Overhead, the wind picks up as if to augment Nina's heartbeat. It creates a current that unnerves the horses. The men treat them in kind. Carson croons after his pacer. Rhett whistles for his saddlebred.

"There's water in the barn," she offers. "I've also got some carrots if they're hungry."

Rhett thumbs the pockets of his jeans. "Got any beer?"

"I could go for a cold one." Carson toes the path, wrinkles his nose as he observes the thinning pea gravel.

"Yeah, of course," Nina blinks. "I should have a few."

"We'll meet you at the main house," Carson nods. Rhett follows suit.

Nina scampers to the lodge as they trail off to harness their horses. The day isn't too hot, but sweat beads down her neck and temples. Although the smoke clears, the molten stench still permeates and dizzies her.

By the main house, Mac waves Nina down. He reclines on the porch. Each day, his face grows sharper. Crow's-feet furrow his brow. An incorrigible particularity constrains his intake to cultivate a lanky form and sunken cheeks. As he nibbles sunflower seeds, Nina's heart clenches. She musters a small smile and brushes past him to the kitchen. From the window, she sees Carson and Rhett lead their stallions down the worn trail through the pines that dot the range. They weave through the groves of tall trees, discerning what lays ahead in the stable, whatever hasn't fallen to disuse. Nina thinks of the silver birches that whiten some thousand acres well into the grass mountains.

As Nina kicks off her boots, the door closes behind her. The tears spill over. Few remain despite how fiercely she wants to avert their descent.

What am I doing here?

Nina plunges her head into her hands, desperate to imbibe any morsel of her infamous will—something she shares with Mac. Neither of them inherited the deference or wanderlust that defines their family. They endure and resist. They long for roots.

At least, they used to.

Mac stood for something. Nina can barely stand at all. With how things are going, it's only a matter of time before this place comes crashing down.

Mac was ushered into a ward after one of his initial episodes. Before he was too far gone, he declared her his executor during what felt like an indefinite hospital stay. No one cared to dispute that.

No one cares about Mac.

Except Nina.

These days, even she has to wonder. Care translates to something viable, for one's own good. Like having this place sold into capable hands instead of her ungainly ones, then using the profit to have him comfortably institutionalized, tended by caregivers who are qualified . . .

Nina remembers stealing away to this place as a kid, how the crisp winters and torrid summers sped along her car windows on the long drives up. Spruce, cedar, and sequoia. Fragrant ordure, organics, and fantastic beasts: the kind of idyll that exists beyond suburbia and lifestyle magazines. How many times has she dreamed of the harvest moon, whose glow quickens her breath and makes her breasts quiver in her coveralls?

Lifetimes ago, Nina thinks. The sky seems deeper now. Everything is quieter. She trudges to the bathroom, strips down for a rinse, retrieves a T-shirt and a fresh pair of dungarees. Laving what suds cling to her breasts, she eyes their dusky peaks and the shapely flesh of her stomach that swells to the waistband of her panties.

Nina thinks of Carson and Rhett. Way out of her league. Still, she cleans up well. Funny how no one ever notices her when she wants them to. Every one of her profiles collects dust on personals sites. No matter how meticulous the description. Or the tastefully angled selfies in fuck-me heels. People only pay attention when she's a mess. Like when she's getting farm supplies in a comfy albeit tattered cardigan, or the odd time she tosses back a cold one at the tavern in her ripped jeans.

Which is why Nina doesn't have any friends. She refuses to confide in anyone. She always manages to straddle the line between tractable and hot mess. No one gives a fuck when you're in the red. They only emerge from the woodwork when you black out. Nina has too much pride to concede.

Foolish pride.

Nina goes barefoot into the hall. She passes the living room, a mess of shavings and misshapen carvings, a monument to Mac's lucid moments when he resolves to whittle. She finds Rhett and Carson in the kitchen.

Forcing a smile, Nina opens the fridge and retrieves two bottles. "Sorry for the wait—and the trouble."

"No trouble at all." Carson shrugs. "I was headed out this way."

"So was I." Rhett smirks. "Thought you were sending smoke signals."

"I can't thank you enough," Nina says.

Carson clears his throat. "Exactly, *why* were you burning?"

"Nobody burns 'round here," Rhett adds. "You got leftover straw, you chop and spread it so it doesn't clog your equipment."

"Or you till it into the soil," Carson offers. "People only burn if it's a rainy season."

Nina appreciates the insight. "Honestly, I was just doing what I read on a newbie farmer website. Burning is supposed to be efficient . . ."

"Not for the average farmer," Carson turns. "Just less than five percent."

"Well, you know I'm far from average." Nina rubs her temples. "I'm sure everybody knows."

Rhett levels her gaze. "And what do *you* know, Nina?"

Nina wants to remain silent, if not cordial, but she finds herself curiously frank. "Obviously, I know nothing about anything that matters."

"And, what matters?" Carson scoffs. "Or, *who* matters?"

"You know what," Nina murmurs. "And you know who . . ."

With a small smile, Carson cocks an eyebrow. "What do I know?"

"I'm in on this too," Rhett muses. "Tons of stuff I know, right?"

Nina knows Rhett and Carson are close enough to touch, but far enough away to be respectful. She knows she wants to feel them, yet to do so would unmask her as someone warm. What she doesn't know is if she can be anything but cold. Nina can't remember the last time she was ever hot, let alone warm. In this way, neither Carson or Rhett are hers to desire. How could she dare? Yearning for heat, to fulfill a part of her she isn't sure exists . . .

It's just easier to avoid people or push them away. Be cordial, not intimate. When they leave, Nina is vindicated. Proven right. Justified.

Why haven't Rhett and Carson left?

They always find something to spare. Their crisp scents—

Rhett's oceanic, Carson's like teakwood—underscore the snug fit of their jeans. Between swigs of their beers, they exchange glances until their eyes snap toward hers. Except she pries hers away from theirs, then curses herself for caving into their rugged allure.

Nina cracks inside, but her face remains intact. "Well, I shouldn't keep you. I really can't thank you two enough."

Rhett flashes a smile that warms down to her toes. "I've got no place to go."

"But you just happened to be out this way?" Nina crosses her arms. "What, were you tailing Carson?"

"Unless he came from two towns over, he couldn't have. I was headed home from several business meetings." He rubs his eyes. "I'm talking meetings that never end. I'm not entirely convinced I'm not dreaming this very moment."

Rhett raises his bottle. "Sounds like you could use another one."

"Not if you're heading out," Nina quips. "I mean, if you plan on driving . . ."

"Tell you what," Rhett says. "How about we take a room after we take care of that straw?"

Nodding, Carson peels at the label on his bottle. "I'm fine with that." His lips curl. "Are you all right with that, Nina?"

She frowns. "I'm fine with it, but that's too much—"

"Then, that's settled," Rhett stands. "I'll get the trencher started. It shouldn't take more than an hour."

"I've got fuel," Carson stretches. "I've also got steaks."

"Steaks?"

"Gifts from my last meeting," he clears. "They're on ice."

Nina gulps. "Are you sure about this?"

"We wouldn't have offered if we weren't." Rhett chuckles. "Isn't that right?"

"*You* offered. Carson just went along with it."

"I'm fine, really," Carson adds. "But thanks for thinking of me, Nina."

Before Nina knows it, the men empty their bottles and replace their Stetsons. She discerns the thunderous sputter of an engine and threshers, which gnash in the distance. Soon, the azure haze of day will redden and lift to reveal the stars. Relief softens her eyes as heat flushes her cheeks.

The thought of Rhett and Carson unnerves her. Chaos courses through her when they're in the flesh. It's good they know what to do, where everything is. Nina stumbles over everything that needs to be said. Time runs torturously, slowly, but the men eventually find their way back to the table. Carson unloads the steaks. Rhett proffers a sack that bears potatoes. He retrieves a knife and begins to peel while Nina aids Carson in seasoning.

Mac scampers to his room, content to retreat once Nina readies a bowl of oats. Oats, he insists. Nothing else will do.

Nina turns to Carson. "Do you always get steaks from your meetings?"

"Often, but not always. It's more or less a formality."

"Wish people around here were as *formal*," Rhett says. "Folks would sure get along better."

"They wouldn't," Nina muses. "Not with bad boys like you."

"Are you talking to me?" Carson grins sardonically.

"Couldn't be me." Rhett smirks at them.

Nina bites back a giggle. "Both of you. Don't you know you're as bad as they come?"

Carson and Rhett exchange glances.

"I've heard about your death glares, Carson," she explains. "You run a tight ship. Any tighter and it'll burst—at least, that's what people swear anyway." Then, she nods at Rhett. "And everyone knows you deck anyone without thinking twice. The fact you're the only supplier is the only reason you're still in business. Well, according to—"

"The town?" Rhett shakes his head. "This place is so small, they make everything a big deal."

"Take it from him," Carson responds. "He's from here."

Nina counters: "So, you're saying *everyone's* lying?"

Rhett shrugs. "I'm saying I've never given anyone a five finger discount unless they asked for one."

"And I'm saying I couldn't give a fuck what people think here," Carson adds.

"Here?" Nina prods. "So you give a fuck what people think elsewhere?"

Carson turns. "Is this how you talk to all of your neighbors?"

"Just the ones with steaks."

"You never answered me earlier," he says. "What matters to you, Nina? And who?"

"And why?" Rhett teases. "What do you know about them?"

What. Who. Know. Nina considers the words. "I don't know."

"Nah." Rhett leans in. "You sound like you know something."

Carson stills. "Like you know a lot."

"I know I can't farm for shit," she musters. "I know I should've probably stayed in the 'prestigious' arts program I aced all through college, but I also know nobody's hiring in the arts, which is why I know this is all probably for the best . . ."

Nina tells them she knows what it's like being the black sheep and that Mac once knew too. Which is why this place makes sense to her. At least, memories of this place. Memories are what she knows best. She recalls brisk steps through vast wheat stalks, past the furrowed parkland, the green smell of black ash.

Carson says it reminds him of charred plains, the Texas Blacklands. Back when he was a kid, he says, on one of his few family vacations. Yearning for a semblance of home is something he's not remiss to admit. To date, his parents hole themselves up in suites. He sees the lure as of late: locking himself away, leading a life of frigid precision and distance, as if to lord over the world and those who scurry within it. One learns to exist alone, to face and resolve their own problems, and carry another if need be. Except one cannot reconcile with isolation. Only a lover can—with touch, closeness, warmth . . . All Carson can do is wait and trust that if it's meant to be, one will come.

Rhett says this makes him think of his late uncle: a vicious fundamentalist who belted each psalm into him. He recites the second part of Psalm 126: "Our mouths were filled with laughter, our tongues with songs of joy." Everyone talks of love and light, but Rhett has always been a devout believer in the world's malevolence. As a child, he prayed intently to prevail. Now, he just resolves to overcome what he can, when he can in due course. His templar farmstead enshrines self-love and free love. Those alone are not unruly, just soulless. The truth is, he says, you can't connect to anyone unless you connect to yourself.

Nina listens to them intently. She grows hot when they turn on her, asking again what—or who—she really knows. She tells them that she knows many stories: "I majored in English, but I enjoyed Victorian literature the most."

Carson takes a pull on his beer. "What's your favorite story, Nina?"

"I don't have one."

"*Favorites?*"

"Maybe the anonymous works from the nineteenth century. Vivid erotica. Hate it or love it, it's impossible not to feel something. It leaps out at you from the page."

"*Maybe?*" Rhett asks.

"*Definitely*," Nina admits. "Too bad they didn't have cowboys."

"Cowboys have been around forever," Rhett scoffs. "They ain't going anywhere either."

Nina flushes. "I meant in the stories."

"Now, that's a real shame," Carson purrs.

Nina tries not to stare at Rhett and Carson even though she finds herself engrossed in their profiles. She turns away, willing her sense of reason to overrule their charms.

Too late.

Carson's voice trails off despite the unequivocal allusion: "Best laid plans . . . "

"What?"

"It sounds like you planned everything. Even if you didn't end up in English, you had a plan to."

"Some plan," she mutters. "It didn't beat coming back here, but at least I've got a home . . ."

"Home is where your heart is. Which says a lot. Not many people have heart," Rhett says.

"But most people have a plan," Carson adds. "Except they leave what they need out of the equation."

Nina wants to laugh, but doesn't dare. She recovers a modest portion of steak and murmurs between her last bites, "What do I need?"

Things take a dangerous albeit delicious turn. Nina glances across to check on Mac, whose reflection snores in the bay window. He isn't likely to notice anything. In the glass, she meets Rhett's and Carson's eyes. She notices Rhett's lips are thinner than Carson's. Watching them curve, she feels a surge in her stomach.

Carson studies her intently. His arm grazes the side of her leg, almost accidentally.

Almost.

Nina knows it's intentional. From the way he watches her, appraises her, it can't be anything but. Carson seeks a reaction.

React.

Nina nods. Nearly imperceptible, but enough. Carson's eyes flicker. Composure fades as hunger flares anew. He reaches for her hand, threads their fingers and flattens her palm. On the other side of her, Rhett shifts. Not that this bothers Carson. No fuss will come from a placid man with hard breaths that emerge from a hard chest, whose callused hands follow suit.

Somewhere in the distance, Nina hears a hum from the barn. She pictures Rhett's and Carson's horses, crunching hay between their teeth and beneath their hooves, taking rough breaths like their riders, and the fulsome scent of rawhide mixed with the smell of hay.

She clears her throat. "Have you ever seen the rest of the house?"

Carson shakes his head. "No, but I'm sure I'd enjoy the full view."

"Seems like there's plenty of room to take in," Rhett observes.

Room for three.

Nina pulls in a breath. She doesn't look at them as she tours them down the hall. Her gaze sinks lower once they ascend the stairs. It lifts when they reach her bedroom. Rhett and Carson ponder the magnanimous farm bed. They brood over her, walk their hands along her sides. She would be content to remain like this forever, entranced, as their strong, skillful hands paw at her pulse.

Nina musters the resolve to stroke their skin. Her fingers muse upon their veins, cadent threads which interlace their bodies and recede within muscles that constrict. Their eyes are feverish. Torrid waves quiver within them, then rise to crash upon her with passion she's never seen before.

After Rhett undoes the buckles of her dungarees, Carson teases them down until they fall to her feet. He raises her shirt, unclasps her breasts. Rhett edges down her panties to uncover a luscious sex whose vulva blushes with excitement. He kneels, parts her thighs, and licks into the molten apex. Carson takes her breasts, strokes until their peaks tauten and swell between his lips. He resolves to make love to them, inclines Nina to the bed, and lays her down.

As Rhett bows to her knees and resumes his oral ministrations, Carson wields his cock against her cheek. Nina receives the sex between her lips. She laves at the tip, suckles, swallows the length to the back of her throat. He comes to rest its breadth amid her breasts, purposing them as an erotic enclosure, only to withdraw once a creamy bead steals out of the head. Rhett replaces them. His sex makes her think of hot iron. It's longer than Carson's, but not as thick. He takes hold of the peaks, coasts within the valley between them. Her tongue leaps to the glans, swirls over the foreskin.

Below, Carson ignites a spark. He takes her ass in his hands, urges upward, while he strokes into the mouth of her sex. His tongue roams aplomb into the curve until it feels the posterior orifice. The jolt of sensation makes Nina thrust. All the while, his finger swims within her sex. She moves to enclose the tongue. Carson pushes it in farther, as far as the aperture permits. When Nina rises, she feels the flick of his finger that delves to the second knuckle. When she sinks, her ass engrosses the lashing tongue. Nina feels the rhythm hasten with each motion.

Rhett continues to rub himself between her breasts, grazing her lips as he fondles the areolae. His sex is volcanic. White wisps mount and balm the expanse. Nina trembles as beads of semen emerge.

As Rhett sears her chest with temperate decadence, Carson strums below. "Come, Nina."

She does.

She feels the quiver of pleasure: once, twice, three times. When she floats back to her senses, Carson unfurls his tongue and rescinds his fingers. He stands to her left. Rhett eases off to her right.

Some blinks later, they stand over her. She returns, then holds their gaze. It draws her to kneel, touch them with her mouth and hands. She palms their cocks in succession, swallowing one after the other until her nose bristles in the pubis.

Rhett is hardly sated against the insides of her cheeks and moves to rub himself against her clit. Nina's eyes blur as she devotes her mouth entirely to Carson, and moans as Rhett delves within her. Rhett is sweaty and feverish. He bows over her, like a stallion tearing into a mare with livid thrusts.

Nina muffles her cries with Carson. She cushions his sex upon her breasts, swallows it whole as the peaks cradle its underside. The breasts reap moisture through their heaving cleavage. His cock is hot, firm, as it passes in and out of her lips.

Carson then eyes the mouth of her sex, stretched and transfixed around Rhett. Along the roof of her mouth, Nina feels Carson harden more, overcome with intent. She pulls back from Rhett until his thrusts recede, then she turns to Carson to proffer her pussy. He shifts to take her from behind. Rhett fists her hair, touches the tip of his cock to her tongue before pushing farther.

This is how they take her, over and over: one in her sex, the other in her mouth. Their callused hands touch every part of her. So do their mouths, which are bristled with stubble. The mouths bear as much as their cocks. Bites. Licks. Kisses. They thrust until she is pungent, engulfed with desirous odors. The scent incites them. It spurs Carson and Rhett onward and inward, although it doesn't eclipse Nina's other senses. She is acutely aware of the heavy breaths, the sweet suckling, and the penises that swim within.

But it goes beyond the cocks. Altogether, the men embody sex themselves. The shape of them, stolid and tapered, and the way they move, wreathing, to impale. Every motion is potent, rippling, with immediacy that spirals and floods.

Nina is posed to tantalize.

On her hands and feet, pulled to Carson's cock, grasped by her pelvis as she seizes Rhett's waist with her thighs.

Lain on her side as Carson kneels, straddles, and curls her legs around his side as Rhett strokes against her lips.

Then, laid back with her legs resting on Rhett's shoulders as Carson throbs between her hands.

Held upright by Carson who clasps her breasts as she rides him facing his feet, while Rhett fills her mouth.

Nina kneels on top, pushes off Rhett's chest as she slides up and down his thighs. His mouth opens to enclose her nipple and she feels him grasp her backside. The presence of his Stetson comes as a belated realization. It haloes her head in a tawny aureole.

Carson thumbs her chin as she sucks his crown. "You make quite the cowgirl, Nina," he rasps. "Doesn't she, Rhett?"

"She sure does," Rhett croons. "I knew she would."

Nina glows. Their appraisal unravels her inhibitions. She continues to thrust, gathering strength from depths she has never known, as if she were indisposed. She is consumed with a fever that cannot, will not break.

Carson discerns the malaise. He walks his fingers down the back of her neck to the dimples at the end of her spine and probes the nearest orifice. Rhett slackens, then stops.

She sees stars as Carson edges into her ass.

Nina is between two fires. Rhett's fervid thrusts in one hole are augmented by Carson's slick impetus in the other. Rhett and Carson alternate thrusting into her intimates. They dislodge and replace one another, creaming into either space only to spur her to mold their sexes within her mouth or breasts until they harden again. They thrust in rapid succession. She throws herself into the euphoric cadence, back and forth, luminescent with joy. They revel in an ocean of bliss, bathe themselves in libidinous sensations, as she perforates in front and behind their searing cocks. Carson and Rhett wane in rich, seminal languor.

Their movements subside once Nina is drenched.

When Nina awakens the next morning, she finds herself alone. The window tenders a square of daylight. Linen waves roll at her feet. In the shower, she is roused by lewd tides. She takes careful notice of the aches that tantalize her amidst the steamy rivulets.

Nina finds Mac in the kitchen. He clasps a sweaty mug and takes long, pensive swigs. His eyes are closed. Nina closes hers too. Neither move for a while. Both fall into a dream.

But Nina is the first to move. She sets off for the barn. She recalls how long and hard she used to venture here from her urban campus for grains of a quieter slice of life. Now, she hears grunts and heavy steps that overturn rusted locomotives.

The ploughmen who dig her earth are the same who kept her view. They steal into her heart and yet the sight of them moves deeper within. There's no going back, Nina resolves. To think if she were deprived of the prowess which indulged her . . .

Rhett grins. "Hey, Nina."

"I trust you slept well," Carson says with a smirk. "We figured your baler could use some fine-tuning. I hope you don't mind."

"Not at all," Nina murmurs. "You've already given me so much. This shouldn't make a difference."

Carson nods. "I'd say we're well past formalities."

"If you want to stay that way," Rhett offers. "The choice is yours."

Nina doesn't have to think twice. She nods, entranced by the memory and the prospect. Rhett and Carson take pause at her acquiesce. Each assumes a side. Her breasts are tender. Deep breaths make them swell and fall, nostalgic of the nightly waves that pitched them to and fro.

Carson and Rhett delve into what ocean unfolds before them. Nina is afraid that she will fall, but they don't let that happen. Their strong arms suspend her between them.

MOVIE NIGHT

Jerica Taylor

D evon absolutely should not have agreed to join Rui at his boyfriend's house for movie night. He's sure it's going to end up with Rui and Jesse making out in the dark halfway through, and him trying to pretend it wasn't happening. But Devon is trying to be a good and supportive friend, and Jesse is the first guy Rui has been interested in since the awful breakup with Jon last summer. Devon can't help but be relieved at Jon's departure, despite how hard it was watching his friend struggle. He always suspected Jon was transphobic, though it wasn't something he ever wanted to say to Rui, like, hey, I think your boyfriend's kind of an asshole and also he implied that I'm not a real guy.

Jesse was sweet under a bristly exterior of awkwardness, and he was absolutely spoiling Rui with his attention. Movie night was Jesse's idea specifically, an attempt to include Devon, to get to know him. Devon didn't feel like he had a real reason to refuse the gesture.

When he gets to Jesse's place, he's introduced to Jesse's roommate, Kit, who's pulling out soda from the fridge. Rui doesn't drink and Devon's glad not to see the beer that had been omnipresent with Jon. Kit's quiet with a sharp jawline and smiles kindly at Devon and shows him around the kitchen to get more snacks.

"You don't have to hang out if you have things to do," Devon says once his arms are full of bags of pretzels, chips, trail mix, and something that might be a container of dried apricots. "I'm used to them being all coupley. Honestly it's not that bad. Jesse asked you so I wouldn't be the third wheel, right?"

"That's not why I'm staying," Kit says. Oh, this is flirting; he's such an idiot. He's falling all over himself not to be jealous of Rui and Jesse, and he's going to miss his chance to find out what flirting back feels like.

"I'm glad," Devon says and Kit's eyes are bright. Devon can't help grinning back, and he feels some of his insecurity start to fade in the glow of Kit's attention.

Jesse and Kit's couch is one of those sectionals with a long chair part that looks like it was meant for laying down. Jesse and Rui cuddle on that, and there's plenty of space for Devon and Kit to get comfortable, though Devon is secretly pleased that Kit chooses to sit a little closer to him, the kind of close that makes it easy to accidentally touch on purpose.

The movie is a little more erotic than any of them were expecting. Devon watches Kit's eyes go wide when the camera gets surprisingly close to where the couple is coming together intimately, and Jesse splutters and apologizes and says this was not what he thought this was going to be about. They all kind of awkwardly agree to leave it on, because they want to know what happens with the plot, not because they're horny and the sex is really hot, especially when a third person joins the couple on screen.

Devon's mind offers up all the times he had fantasized what

would happen if he wandered into Rui's bedroom when he knew Jesse was in there and pretended that he didn't. If he'd catch them fucking, if he'd get to see what Rui looked like in the throes of pleasure and if it matched up to the moaning he could hear through the walls when Jesse visited. Or before that, late at night when Rui was alone, and—

He pushes the thoughts away. Devon's just lonely. And horny. Very horny. Of course he's going to focus on all the sex his best friend is having, especially when his bedroom adjoins Rui's.

And Jesse is hot, with big hands and dark eyes and really nice arms. He and Rui are cute together, in a way that's perfectly okay to think your best friend is cute, especially when they stumble into the apartment after they've clearly been making out in Jesse's car and Rui's lips are all bitten red and swollen.

Kit's fingers keep brushing where their thighs are almost but not quite pressed together, and every pass ricochets through Devon, the newness and anticipation making each touch in the dark exponentially intense. He wonders what it would be like if Kit pressed him up against the wall in the hallway, asked if he wanted to make out a little bit, or maybe Kit would just make the decision for Devon and pin him down, wrap their hands around Devon's wrists, dig their nails with the sparkly blue nail polish into his skin.

Fuck. Devon closes his eyes, takes a deep breath, tries to cool the flush on his face. He doesn't notice until it's too late that he's gotten wet. So wet, in fact, that he's soaked through his jeans a little. When he shifts, he can see—oh, fuck, there's a mark on the couch.

He misses most of the end of the movie, wrapped up with worry, wondering how much is going to be visible on the microfiber of the light tan cushions. When Kit's hand brushes his, he lets out a sharp inhale.

"You okay?" Kit whispers, but their voice low and close to his ear just messes Devon up more.

"Yeah," he says, swallowing a few times. "Yeah."

Jesse turns off the movie as the credits roll, then flicks on the light. Jesse and Rui stretch as they stand. Kit offers their hand to Devon. He knows the mark is gonna be visible.

He takes Kit's hand, and gets up.

Rui sees it first. "Oh," he says, with a quiet gasp. He looks Devon up and down.

"What?" Kit says, and looks at Devon, who looks down at the mark for the first time. It's bigger than he'd thought. Unmistakably shaped. A diamond the shape of—

"What?" Jesse asks but then he just stutters to a stop when he figures it out.

Rui presses his fingers to the spot on the cushion and then brings them to his nose.

"Rui, what the fuck," Jesse swears. Rui freezes like he wasn't even aware of what he was doing. Rui tucks his hand into his back pocket.

"Okay, yes, I get super wet, I can't help it. That movie was hot, we all thought so."

"I sure did," Kit says. Devon's heart flutters wildly.

"Sorry about the couch," he says, embarrassed.

Jesse laughs, too loud. "Who cares about the couch?" He knows it's supposed to be kind, but it just makes him feel more exposed.

"Here, I'll show you the bathroom," Kit says.

Devon does not ask Kit to come in with him, but only just. The embarrassment isn't doing anything to lessen the ache between his legs, the desire to have someone touch him, make the way his underwear is sticking to him be good for something.

He thinks about Rui touching the wet spot on the couch.

He takes longer in the bathroom than necessary, just standing there, not looking at himself in the mirror. Wishing himself some kind of control, or relief.

Rui crowds Devon back into the bathroom the moment he opens the door. "I'm sorry if I was super weird, I wasn't trying to be gender essentialist or like fetishizing."

"Fetishizing," Devon scoffs.

"You know what I mean. I wasn't trying to be weird, I just." Rui runs his hand through his hair. "It just really turned me on," he says, his voice gone very quiet, "to see how turned on you were."

"Oh," Devon says. "You've never said—"

"What, that I think you're hot?"

"You tell me I'm hot all the time, you're an extremely supportive friend."

"Yeah, but I'm a liar, too," Rui says and Devon's stomach swoops. "Because I actually think you're hot like, so hot that sometimes I have to go jerk off after we work out together," Rui says all in a rush.

"Rui," Devon scolds even as he feels himself flush. "We're at your boyfriend's house."

"We've fucked about it," Rui says. "About you."

"Fucking Christ," Devon says. His pulse is so loud he can barely hear anything else.

Abruptly, there's another person in the doorway. Devon feels faint as he starts to panic.

"Are you telling him?" Jesse says.

"I'm sorry," Devon squeaks out. There has to be something he can say that can explain anything he overheard, that's not going to ruin Rui's relationship.

"Don't—don't freak out," Rui says though honestly he looks like the one who's going to freak out first.

"This wasn't how we talked about telling him," Jesse scolds. "You've cornered him in the bathroom, it's not really conducive to open conversation."

"I'm not-I'm not cornered," Devon stutters. "I'm just . . . Wait, telling me what?"

"Telling you that Rui wants you. And I want that, too," Jesse says, like that's a normal sentiment, like that's something you can just say to someone with a straight face.

"Are you fucking with me?" Devon asks.

"I'd like to be," Rui says, but there's no bravado in it. "Ah," Kit says, as they approach the three of them. "So I guess I missed my chance to tell Devon I thought he was super cute and did he want to get a coffee sometime."

"I would," Devon says. Kit's smile is gorgeous, making the corners of their eyes crinkle.

"So are we gonna—" Rui says and then looks at Jesse. "I mean, we should—"

"If you say go watch another filthy movie after all of this I am going to scream," Jesse murmurs and that's what breaks the tension finally.

Devon laughs until tears stream down his face, until he's coughing and Kit hands him a soda and Rui says, "Hey, they gave you a drink, does that make this a first date?"

"Not all of us put out on the first date," Kit teases.

"That's too bad," Devon risks saying and Kit's eyes snap to him, their mouth dropping open.

"Just kiss him," Jesse says.

"No way, I'm kissing him first," Rui says.

"Wait," Devon says. "Wait, since when does everyone want to kiss me?"

Jesse scoffs. "He really is like this, you weren't kidding," he says to Rui.

"Like what?"

"Completely unaware of how devastating your smile is," Rui says.

"Ah," Devon says, hands trembling and heart racing. Kit and Rui do an awkward "you first" dance with one another.

"Oh, my god," Jesse groans, and pushes between the two of them. "I'm gonna kiss him first, but unlike either of you, I am actually going to ask him if he wants to."

And then Devon has Jesse's thumb at the corner of his mouth, his fingers very, very gently touching his jaw.

"Do you want me to kiss you?" Jesse whispers like they're all alone. This is Rui's boyfriend but the way he's looking at Devon—the way Rui is looking at the two of them when Devon's gaze snaps up to him . . .

He nods at Jesse and then he's leaning in and Devon is being very sweetly kissed. He thinks of how sweet Jesse is to Rui, the treats and the attention and the presents and he wonders if this is how he kisses Rui, too. He wonders if this is how Rui kisses.

He groans into Jesse's mouth and the kiss deepens until they break away, both gasping for breath.

"Holy fuck," Rui says.

"There we go," Jesse says and he all but shoves Rui at Devon.

"Is this—you're okay with this?" Rui asks, tilting his head forward, so their foreheads are almost touching.

"I don't know how I am about this," Devon says. "It's a lot, but I . . . I don't want it to stop. I don't want to miss my chance to feel what it's like to kiss you," Devon says, all of the truth falling out, a whispered confession.

"I promise, it's not your only chance," Rui says, before he kisses Devon.

It's so good. It's warm and familiar even though they've never done this.

"Yeah?" Rui says, pressing a fleeting kiss to Devon's mouth again. "What are you thinking?"

"I want—"

"Yeah?" Rui says and of course Devon doesn't have to say it all. Rui's eyes are bright. When they both look over to Jesse and Kit, they're on the couch, Jesse practically in Kit's lap.

"Oh, yeah, so we've done this before," Kit says, and trails off in a gasp as Jesse scrapes his teeth down their throat.

"You have?" Rui asks indignantly.

"Oh, come on, of course we have," Jesse turns over his shoulder to say. "Why did you think I was so agreeable to you wanting to fuck your friend, too?"

Rui is struck silent and Devon can't help but laugh, so hard and loud that Rui grabs him around the middle in offense and takes him down to the couch. He ends up with his head tucked against Kit's arm, and Rui straddling him, and when Jesse leans down to suck a mark on Kit's throat, his braid falls over his shoulder and tickles Devon's cheek.

"You want to fuck me?" Devon whispers into Rui's ear. He feels Rui's hard shudder against him. "You want to see how wet I can get?"

"Jesus, Devon," Rui curses, breath hot against Devon's neck. "I had no idea you were so dirty."

"But you wanted me to be, didn't you?"

"I just wanted to know," Rui says. "What it was like, to touch you like this."

"So find out," Devon says, guiding Rui's hand between his legs. Rui's fingers curl, and he cups him, tentatively, then in a more exploratory way.

"Can I put my hand inside your pants?"

"Take them off," Devon says. "It'll be easier."

"Oh, fuck," Rui says and Devon has to help Rui with the

zipper. When he slips them down his thighs and onto the floor, they're both distracted by Kit doing the same and Jesse's cock springing free from his briefs. Kit immediately takes it into their mouth and Jesse arches back and moans.

"Fuck," Devon says, and then Rui's kneeling on the floor between his legs, hands on his thighs. He strokes at the seam of him, the wetness, spreading him open and stroking up over his clit.

"Oh, you're so silky, it's so slippery," Rui says and he strokes Devon experimentally, returning to any place where Devon gasps.

"Fuck, Rui, come on, put your fingers inside of me, please," Devon pleads and beside him Jesse gasps.

"Do it, Rui, give him your fingers, show him what you can do." Devon wants to ask Rui to tell him about how he's fingered his boyfriend, to show him, but then his words are lost as Rui slips his index finger inside Devon's cunt and starts to rock it inside, not quite thrusting.

"Yes, yes," Devon gasps and beside him he hears Kit choke, splutter.

Jesse starts to say, "You don't have to—" then shouts as Kit obviously does not listen.

"God, you're so hot," Rui says. "Can I put another finger in?"

"Yes," Devon pleads and then Rui is pumping two fingers into him.

"Kit, I'm gonna come," Jesse says. "Fuck, I'm gonna—Kit, I can't. Ahh, I'm gonna—"

Jesse's moan is high and sweet as he climaxes in Kit's mouth.

Rui moans as he moves his fingers inside Devon. Devon reaches down to circle his clit. "Yes," Rui says. "Show me, help me get you off."

"Don't stop," Devon whimpers, pressing fast circles to his clit as Rui thrusts in and out of him.

"Can I?" Rui asks but then Devon feels the stretch of Rui adding a third finger, filling him up, and it doesn't make more than a few thrusts before he comes, clenching hard around Rui's fingers. He distantly hears Rui curse as he shakes apart.

"Oh, fuck," Kit says. "That was gorgeous. Jesse, open your eyes and look how wrecked Devon is."

But when Devon looks at Jesse, he's actually watching Rui, who is rubbing his thumb over the dampness of his hand.

When Rui notices Jesse watching him, he grinds the heel of his hand against his dick.

"He really wants you to sit on his face," Jesse says and Rui actually hides his face in his arm. "How about you do it while I fuck him?"

"Yeah," Devon says and Rui whines, face still in his arm. Remembering there are four of them, Devon looks over to Kit.

"Oh, I like watching," Kit says. Their lips are red and puffy. "This is gonna be beautiful, I bet you'll make me come untouched."

"Fuck," Devon says. "Can you do that?"

"Oh, yeah," Kit says. "It's pretty great."

When Devon kisses Rui as Jesse spreads him open, it's intensely intimate to watch, the way Jesse knows his body, how obvious it is that they've done this before. Watching his best friend get fingered by his boyfriend is the sort of thing that's supposed to be relegated to middle-of-the-night fantasies.

The way Rui gasps against Devon's mouth when Jesse shifts the angle of Rui's legs, holding his knee up a little, makes Devon run hot.

He looks over at Kit, needing reassurance, someone else to witness this, to prove he's not as much of a pervert as he feels like.

"Do you know what I like about watching?" Kit brushes their fingers across the inside of Devon's wrist and his breath hitches and Kit's smile goes just the slightest bit sly. "I like watching because you get to see the moments you're usually too wrapped up in to really witness. You don't get to see the expression on your partner's face when your face is between their legs, and you don't get to see the way your hand disappears inside of them. I'm gonna get to see all of that," Kit murmurs. "I'm gonna get to see the way your hips roll when you ride Rui's face, what you do with your hands, whether you drop your head forward or arch your neck back. And I get to see Rui underneath you, trying to give you what you need while he's being speared open by Jesse's dick, trying not to bear down so hard against Jesse that he loses the rhythm he has on your clit."

"Fuck," Devon gasps.

"And I get to watch Jesse just melt. He's so prickly, he likes to be so in control, and it looks like he is, right, when he's moving Rui where he wants him, getting his hands full of his ass cheeks and spreading them. But if you watch closely, he gives himself away, goes all melty, so much of that tension easing away. Rui makes him so happy that he's desperate to give Rui what he needs no matter what."

"You mean . . . me," Devon says at Kit's raised eyebrows driving home their point. "I thought this was just—"

"Fucking? Sure," Kit says. "Sure, this can just be fucking, but you know Rui pretty well. Does he sleep around?"

"Rui," Devon asks, trying to stop his voice from shaking with the mix of nervousness and euphoria coursing through him. "Do you want to do this more than once?"

Rui groans and laughs. "Yeah, Devon, I wanna do this as many times as you can. I mean, as many times as I can, but I've never gotten past three and even then I ached for like a week."

"I don't just mean tonight. I mean—do you want us all to be boyfriends?"

Rui moans and grabs his cock. "Don't dirty talk me right now, I'm gonna come before you even sit on my face."

"Rui, I mean it," Devon laughs.

"I mean it," Rui says and then Devon watches as Jesse smacks Rui's hand away from where he is stroking his cock. Rui whines.

"Tell your boyfriend to stop distracting your other boyfriend and come over and help me wreck you."

"Come and wreck me," Rui pleads in a porn voice and Devon is still laughing as they arrange their bodies.

Sitting on Rui's face on the couch is awkward and unbalanced and it doesn't matter the second Rui's tongue is underneath him. "Oh, my god," Devon exclaims as Rui gasps under him.

"That's right," Kit says. "Take what you need from him, Jesse told me he can take it."

"Oh, he's gonna take it," Jesse says. Rui grabs Devon's hips and anchors him, pulling him flush to his face in a way Devon was trying not to do so he didn't suffocate him.

He feels the moment when Jesse starts to work Rui open, the way the rock of his hips brings his mouth closer, giving Devon pressure and stimulation everywhere at once.

"Grab the back of the couch," Kit says, at his ear. "Give yourself some leverage."

"What if I held onto you?" Devon asks, shocked at his own boldness. Kit's mouth drops open.

"Okay," Kit says. "Okay, let me make that happen."

It requires even more rearrangement of bodies but in the end, Rui ends up in Kit's lap, head against their chest, and Kit braces Devon's arms like they're doing tandem pushups.

Rui goes taut underneath him as Jesse gets his cock inside him. It's Rui's moan as Jesse starts to fuck him that brings Devon suddenly extremely close to coming.

"Look at your face, god, you're gorgeous," Kit says. "He's gorgeous, Rui, you should see what riding your mouth is doing to him."

"Oh, fuck, I'm—I'm so close, Rui, please," Devon gasps out.

"Take what you need from him," Kit urges again and underneath him Rui makes a desperate, needy sound. So Devon does. He rocks himself against Rui's face, fingers tangled with Kit's, clutching tight, leaning his weight forward, fucking himself down against Rui's mouth until he tips over, his whole body tingling.

He knows Kit helps him down, settles him at their side as Jesse starts to fuck into Rui harder.

"That's my good boy," Jesse praises. As Rui whimpers, Devon turns his head into Kit's shoulder, bites down hard against the material of their shirt, overwhelmed.

"Oh, fuck yes," Kit says. "Bite me again, do it hard. I'm gonna come with Rui in my lap just like this, fuck, I can feel Jesse fucking him, pushing him up against me—"

Rui moans, throws a hand up over his face. Devon bites Kit through their shirt and Kit gasps, so Devon scrapes his teeth across the skin of their throat.

"Yes, yes," Kit says and Rui makes a cut-off sound as Jesse starts to stroke his cock. "Oh, fuck, I'm gonna make a mess of my pants, I want to, I want to," Kit is telling them. Devon bites them hard and Kit gasps and starts to tremble.

"Come on," Jesse says. "Come on, Rui, Kit, both of you had better come before I do, you'd better hurry up, I'm close, Rui's so hot and tight, I'm gonna—"

Devon bites down hard at the juncture of Kit's neck and throat and they go tense, a high little noise in their throat, and then they go limp against Devon.

"I could feel it, Kit, I could feel you." Rui's words cut

off with a guttural groan and Devon watches as Rui comes, splashing up over his stomach and chest, some of it on Jesse's shirt.

"Good boy, good," Jesse says and with several quick, hard thrusts, he buries himself in Rui's ass and comes.

Devon is still breathing hard, still not quite sure he's in control of all of his limbs.

"RIP your couch," Rui says dreamily and then they're all laughing, clutching at one another weakly.

"Good thing I got it free off Craigslist," Kit says, and they press a soft kiss to Devon's temple. Devon leans into it. "You want the shower first?"

"Hey, I'm the messiest," Rui protests.

"Are you?" Jesse asks in a low voice. Devon feels himself flush.

"You said you, um, you made a mess of your pants," Devon says shyly.

"Yeah but I live here, I can go second."

"Okay, Devon can be the guest of honor, this one time," Rui says.

"Don't talk to your boyfriends that way," Devon replies, and Rui's eyes flash open, bright and hopeful. Yeah, this is right, this is what Devon wants. For Rui to always look at him like this, to get to see Jesse get all growly after sex, and for Kit to be tender and let him borrow their clothes.

"Sorry," Rui says. "I'll be better. I've got three of you to keep me in check now."

"Not gonna be enough," Kit says against Devon's ear as they walk to the bathroom, Kit's hand on Devon's back.

"I think I might have a crush on you, too," Devon says and Kit's peal of laughter delights him.

"Good," Kit says, hanging him a fluffy towel and switching

on the light to the bathroom. "You know, I think we could share the shower. What do you think?"

This is more than he thought he'd ever get. This night. This new thing unfolding before him, between the four of them. "Yeah, I think we can share."

ABOUT THE AUTHORS

NIKKI ALI is a black woman writer and activist based in Newark, New Jersey.

ADRIAN AMATO is a graduate of the University of Toronto, where he studied math and teaching, and took courses in creative writing. He is transgender and likes to explore the concept of gender in his writing. He works full time at a job completely unrelated to writing, but strives to make time for creative pursuits.

C.C. BRIDGES (ccbridges.net) is a librarian by day and author by night. She writes about amazing worlds with honorable characters and plenty of romance.

SIENNA CRANE is the author of the Hot Boss series. She loves painting pictures with words that titillate and challenge, shock and delight. She hopes her vivid ménage encounters stay with you even once the words have faded.

MICHELLE CRISTIANI (heart-pages.com) teaches at Portland Community College. She won the Calyx Press Margarita Donnelly Prose Prize for her memoir on stroke and brain surgeries (calyxpress.org/md-prize-2018/). She's published in *Awakenings Review* and *Verseweavers*. Michelle has recent stories in *Sad Girls Club* and *Apple in the Dark*.

Born in Brooklyn and raised in the New South, **ALEXA J. DAY** (alexajday.com) loves stories with just a touch of the inappropriate and heroines who are anything but innocent. Her literary mission is to stimulate the intellect and libido of her readers. She lives in upstate South Carolina.

LIN DEVON is an established artist with degrees in Fine Arts and Library Science reflecting a life-long polyamory for art and for books. She is of African-American and European descent and identifies as pansexual. Her stories span a wide spectrum.

LUCY EDEN (lucyeden.com) is the nom de plume of a romance-obsessed author who writes the kind of romance she loves to read. When Lucy isn't writing, she's busy reading every book she can get her hands on. She lives in New York with her husband, children, a turtle, and a Yorkshire Terrier.

IDA J writes real-life-inspired polysexual erotica set in Europe's techno clubs, from a female perspective. She has a particular interest in conveying the sensation, the experience of sex, always looking to give the reader the feeling of experiencing the story themselves. She writes for Berlinable and lives in Amsterdam.

KATRINA JACKSON is a history professor by day who writes diverse queer erotica and romance by night. She likes makeup and documentaries. She also spends more time than she should watching her cats fight or cuddle.

FALLEN KITTIE is a queer Afro-L'nu woman and interdisciplinary doctorate candidate with a concentration in cinema and media studies. She infrequently blogs at fallenkittie.com and her story is titled after her favorite Paula Cole album. Her erotica has appeared in various collections including *Best Lesbian Erotica of the Year Vol. 4*, *Sinister Wisdom Vol. 115*, and *Twisted Sheets: Tales of Sizzling Ménage*.

ROSE P. LETHE is a queer writer, editor, and sex worker. After completing an MFA in creative writing, she found she could no longer stomach "serious literature" and has since turned to more enjoyable pursuits. Her stories have been published in several erotica anthologies.

C.E. MCLEAN (@CanadianErotica) is a bisexual Canadian writer and erotica enthusiast. This is the author's first collaborative work.

SHAY MITCHEL (one L, not the actress) is a romance and erotica writer who lives in the Metro Detroit area. Shay writes early in the morning and late at night, and either time they will most likely be trying to type around a cat. They are currently working on the second book in their EastSide series and can be found on Instagram @shaym5512.

ANGORA SHADE (angorashade.blogspot.com) is an American erotic romance author, avid gardener, and tortoise mother.

Find her work in *Best Women's Erotica of the Year Volume 5*, *Best Lesbian Erotica of the Year Volume 4*, and *Best Bondage Erotica of the Year Volume 2*.

MISTY STEWART (mistywriter.com) is an Australian writer of erotic romance with a kink. Her debut novel, *Games: Truth or Dare*, was released in 2021 and she's currently working on the sequel. You can find her on her website, or on Twitter as @ misty_writer.

JERICA TAYLOR (jericataylor.com) is a nonbinary, neurodivergent queer cook, birder, and chicken herder. She has an MFA from Emerson College. Their work has appeared in *Postscript, Schuylkill Valley Journal,* and *Feral Poetry,* and they have a prose chapbook forthcoming from GASHER Press. She lives with her wife and young daughter in Western Massachusetts. Twitter @jericatruly.

ANUJA VARGHESE (anujavarghese.com) is a queer Canadian writer whose work has appeared in several literary magazines, as well as in the *Best Women's Erotica of the Year, Volume 6* anthology.

LILITH YOUNG is an autistic writer from Pennsylvania. Growing up in the Deep South she hopes to write the stories she wished she could have read when she was coming out in college. She identifies as a cisgender lesbian and uses pronouns she/her.

ABOUT
THE EDITOR

RACHEL KRAMER BUSSEL (rachelkramerbussel.com) is a New Jersey–based author, editor, blogger, and writing instructor. She has edited over seventy books of erotica, including *Coming Soon: Women's Orgasm Erotica; Dirty Dates: Erotic Fantasies for Couples; Come Again: Sex Toy Erotica; The Big Book of Orgasms, Volumes 1* and *2; The Big Book of Submission, Volumes 1* and *2; Lust in Latex; Anything for You; Baby Got Back: Anal Erotica; Suite Encounters; Gotta Have It; Women in Lust; Surrender; Orgasmic; Fast Girls; Going Down; Tasting Him; Tasting Her; Crossdressing; Cheeky Spanking Stories; Bottoms Up; Spanked: Red-Cheeked Erotica; Please, Sir; Please, Ma'am; He's on Top; She's on Top; Best Bondage Erotica of the Year, Volumes 1* and *2;* and *Best Women's Erotica of the Year, Volumes 1–7.* Her anthologies have won eight IPPY (Independent Publisher) Awards, and *The Big Book of Submission, Volume 2, Dirty Dates,* and *Surrender* won the National Leather Association Samois Anthology Award. Her short story

"Necessary Roughness" from *Best Bondage Erotica of the Year, Volume 1* won the 2021 National Leather Association-International John Preston Short Fiction Award.

Rachel has written for *AVN, Bust, Cosmopolitan, Curve,* The Daily Beast, Elle.com, Forbes.com, Fortune.com, *Glamour,* The Goods, Gothamist, *Harper's Bazaar,* Huffington Post, *Inked, InStyle, Marie Claire, MEL, Men's Health, Newsday, New York Post, New York Observer, The New York Times, O: The Oprah Magazine, Penthouse, The Philadelphia Inquirer,* Refinery29, *Rolling Stone,* The Root, Salon, *San Francisco Chronicle, Self,* Slate, Time.com, *Time Out New York,* and *Zink,* among others. She has appeared on "The Gayle King Show," "The Martha Stewart Show," "The Berman and Berman Show," NY1, and Showtime's "Family Business." She hosted the popular In the Flesh Erotic Reading Series, featuring readers from Susie Bright to Zane, speaks at conferences, and does readings and teaches erotic writing workshops around the world and online. She blogs at lustylady.blogspot.com and consults about erotica and sex-related nonfiction at eroticawriting101.com. Follow her @raquelita on Twitter.